Two little girls, holding hands and singing in the back seat of a car. There for each other, unafraid. Life for the Stone girls is a life lived on the edge. Singing for a living, Marley and Andi find their way through a childhood of upheaval marked by their mother Donna's dark, unpredictable flights. Today, Marley writes the songs her twin, country diva Andi Stone, makes famous, and the girls' connection struggles to survive the cuts and devastations of fame. "You girls," laments their manager. "One of you marries indiscriminately, the other not at all." When without warning Donna Stone takes her own life, alone at the family cabin, danger stalks Marley back to Lost Prince Lake, back into the loves and betrayals of the past. Hidden truths threaten to take the Stone sisters down, singly and together. A powerful, intimate portrait of love, ambition, and survival, *So Long As We're Together* takes the reader into the lives of three women who give song to broken hearts, and for whom music is the language of family.

Critical Praise for *So Long As We're Together*

"Music scores the lives of two sisters together from girlhood to adulthood in Burgess's sublime novel *So Long As We're Together*. About ambition and the price of fame and the ties that bind (and sometimes strangle us), it's also a fierce, frank portrayal of the ways we love one another—how we succeed and sometimes, how we fail. Piercingly honest and gorgeously written, and as indelible as a song you love." — Caroline Leavitt, *New York Times* bestselling author of *Is This Tomorrow*

"In Burgess's hand, the women of the Stone family are rendered as bright, as fractured, and as *real* as any characters I have ever read—and all with clean, direct prose that evokes the work of Jess Walter, Anthony Doerr, and Rebecca Makkai. This is a propulsive, moving book." — Christian Kiefer, author of *Phantoms*

"Glenda Burgess has written a deeply felt novel about families, particularly those made up of strong women. She beautifully explores both the sticky nature of sisterly love—the kind of love that persists even (or perhaps especially) when we're not even sure we like each other—and the mystery of maternal love, which is almost too big, even when imperfect, to comprehend. Her sentences ring with the music her characters make." — Peternelle van Arsdale, author of *The Cold is in Her Bones*

"*So Long As We're Together* broke my heart and stitched it back together with endlessly sweet music. Tender, tough, and dazzling as an early snow. I loved this book." — Laura Benedict, author of *The Stranger Inside*

Also by the Author

Loose Threads

Exposures

The Geography of Love

So Long As We're Together

Glenda Burgess

A Black Opal Books Publication

GENRE: LITERARY FICTION

This is a work of fiction. Names, places, characters and incidents are either the product of the author's imagination or are used fictitiously, and any resemblance to any actual persons, living or dead, businesses, organizations, events or locales is entirely coincidental. All trademarks, service marks, registered trademarks, and registered service marks are the property of their respective owners and are used herein for identification purposes only. The publisher does not have any control over or assume any responsibility for author or third-party websites or their contents.

For my father, Thomas, who loved Hank Williams

And my mother, Louise, who was anything but ordinary

I hope and pray this wish you grant
From one man's heart to a falling star
We always remember who we are

Robert Hunter, The Grateful Dead

Act One

Lyrics

"Everybody Wants to Go to Heaven,"

Loretta Lynn

Prologue

The past asks only to be remembered.

How difficult it is to remember. To let one's self fall back, disarmed, vulnerable. When I place my fingertips on the cool resin piano keys and let them rest there, becoming not my hands but a vast waiting universe of notes and chords and arpeggios that speak to me as sentences, let them rest there, still silent, no sound, no strike against the strings made, only then do I stand in the doorway of things past.

The language of keys. Notes that form themselves on the black and white keyboard. Here is where memory lies. A melody loose, unexpectedly free. Shaped not by image or event but a deconstructed splinter of feeling. I become the conductor of histories, dramas at my command. I hesitate at the precipice, overwhelmed by the colors of known things.

It has taken most of my life to open to music. To play the sentiments as my fingers give them up. Generous, layered, dark tones. And light-filled notes so bright my heart hurts. I never know which they will be, the dark or the light. This corridor of the past commands surrender.

Trust. What happens between my hands and the keys feels raw. Honest. Composed entirely of me and nothing of me. The tempo is time. Time paints the keyboard.

The past asks only to be remembered. It does not ask to be understood. My work, the reason for this dark and light, is to arrive at story. A song tells a story and I am a songwriter.

My fingertips register the smoothness of the keys and test the strike, sense the immediacy of sound. I breathe deep and play one clear note: the plain, openhearted middle C. Middle C, modest pitch note of the major keys, untainted by the complexities of sharps or flats. A beginning note. No accidentals. No accumulations of story fragments cling to middle C. Not yet. Middle C might be my narrative—a beginning I've endeavored my whole life to coax forward to its given high note. Not my sister's narrative, or my mother's, but mine. Middle C, the invisible note I find myself to be.

Family. History. Memory. Yes, there is a beginning. There was an end. And the middle resonates still—that unreasonable reasonable middle, pivot point between lower and upper registers, past and future chord, root and arpeggio, center of my keyboard and somehow my life. My impasse. The past deep in the bass clef, tomorrow in the treble.

My hands hover above the keys. I will tell you my story.

I woke to the grind of a bus shifting gears away from the curb somewhere beyond where I lay half-covered in a tangled sheet. I ran my tongue against the coating on the backside of my front teeth. Good God, I'd kill for a toothbrush.

Disoriented, I looked around. A runny yellow spill of sunlight fell between the curtains drawn across the window above my head, striping my body in darks and brights. One side of the curtain rod appeared broken, held in place with a twist of wire hanger. The hem of the curtain, knotted up off the floor, had a wide stain that might either be from a tipped bong, or possibly pancake syrup. The memory of the night came rushing back and I cursed silently.

My contacts were shellacked to my eyeballs and they hurt like a mother. I pried one eyelid up gently with my thumb and index finger, then the other. Sticking a finger into the water glass on the bedside stand, I dropped one bead of water into each eye. The liquid stung but the lenses released their dehydrated suction, allowing me to crimp each lens by its edge and lift the thin film. I rolled it between my thumb and index finger and flicked it to the floor.

Damn. At a hundred bucks a box, I couldn't go around wasting contacts on yet another Saturday night cowboy.

Cowboy. Aw, God no.

I turned slowly to not disturb the man lying beside me. Face turned to the wall, soft drunken snores rolled in and out beneath the crook of his arm. Every naked inch of him splayed splendidly in the morning light. The body was good. On the floor, a cap embroidered with a bold purple university logo. Cowboy? Definitely not. College maybe. Baseball player. I wracked my brain for a memory of the guy's face, his name. Something more than whiskey shots and a hot band and somewhere in there, a hand up my shirt and not saying no.

I slid out sideways from under the sheet, my bottom hitting the cold floor with a thud. Holding my breath, I rolled onto all fours and crawled across the room, collecting my jeans, bra, and shirt along the way. My boots stood at the door. Shivering in the unheated room, I riffled through khakis tossed over a backpack. Gently I extracted a wallet, taking a ten for the bus and a Starbucks. I slid the baseball player's wallet back where I'd found it and folded the pants. I'd have rather stuffed a couple of hundreds in. And would have, if I hadn't left my money and ID with the night bartender for safekeeping.

Billy was decent that way. He kept your wallet behind the counter when the tequila ran strong. Not the first time I'd dressed in a hallway or ridden the bus home at some ungodly hour with the all-night drunks and nurses coming off shift.

I twisted the doorknob silently and slipped out of the bedroom, clothes and boots under one arm. I winced in the glare bounced from the fluorescent overheads off the well-waxed dormitory floor. A door creaked on its hinges a few rooms down and a tousled blonde tiptoed out, adjusting her sweatshirt down over her hips and gathering her hair up into a ponytail with a rubber band slipped from her wrist. She stopped, and stared. The mascara smudges under her lashes mirrored my own. She sized me up, a naked, disheveled woman tugging on jeans.

I buttoned my shirt and felt for my phone, still safely tucked in the back pocket of my pants. I pulled on my boots, and ran a hand through my hair, wishing for a hair tie. If only I were half as prepared as this coed.

I picked my jacket off the floor outside the door and flashed a friendly smile as I passed by the blonde. Girl's gotta do what a girl's gotta do, I said.

Girl? Who are you calling a girl? she said. You're as old as my mother.

ɞɷɛɷ

I stood at the campus bus stop in the pearl predawn gray, my free hand tucked under my armpit for warmth. My sister's face wavered across the small screen of my phone.

She killed herself because we left, Marley.

Don't be ridiculous, Andi. My tone was sharp.

I examined my sister closely, alarmed. Her familiar Ruby Slipper red hair hung loose, barely combed for a woman who considered "combed" hot rollers followed by a generous tease and a concrete setting of spray. Her water-stone eyes, a deep lake green. That generous mouth—usually quick with a wide smile, something halfway between a horse laugh and the polished flash of a pageant queen—drawn tight in restrained emotion. Her image broke apart, and I waited impatiently for the connection to synch back up.

We're living the dream, remember? I said, softening. Her dream. Our dream. Donna knew what that meant, Andi. She's the reason for the road. We both know that.

You're wrong, Marley. It's our fault. I know it. Andi's voice crumbled, and she turned away from me.

Andi, Andi… Helpless, I touched my fingers to the image of her cheek. Willing myself through the cool, hard surface of the glass screen.

When we were small and one of us woke from a bad dream, the other would find her sister's hand. Fold it in against her chest. Against a steady heart. Holding tight, no words, until once more sleep came. That last summer, the hard, final year of high school when I woke often in the night, unable to breathe, crushed and feverish and afraid, Andi, knowing only I was in trouble, in battle against some darkness that chased through my dreams, would slip from her twin bed across from mine and lay down beside me on the cool floor in her cotton nightgown. Her arm a pale branch in the dim moonlight rising to mine, twining fingers, until the thrashing stopped, the silence deepened, and sleep came again.

This was our way. Reaching across the stage, a bus, the back seat of a car. Hand upon hand. Some part of ourselves against or around the other, locked, as if we were two seedlings twisted by a common root to make one tree. A single unbroken trunk, a living heart reaching upward.

Even now, separated by a continent of geography.

Andi, I said. Please, don't.

She turned to me and touched her own hand to mine, covering her screen. I closed my eyes, reaching, reaching.

Well, she said finally, steadying her breath. She faked me that famous smile, turning on the high-beam diva we both knew she could deploy under the worst of circumstances, for any photographer, any fan shouting,

Andi Stone! Give us some love, girl! She wiped a slow finger under her lashes, neatening the tear-smeared layers of mascara.

Gotta go, Mar, she said. Schedule meeting at nine. Always a meeting. Her voice crisp, wry.

We smiled. It was a big job, being the queen of big band country.

Be good to you, I said. I could hear the approach of the downtown bus, my ride. Talk soon.

Talk soon, Andi replied.

She hung up, and I pocketed my phone. So far apart, I thought. Too far apart.

꽃꽃꽃

I palmed open the black door to The Corral and poked my head inside, scanning the dim interior for Billy, the bartender. I called out his name.

Back here, answered a voice from behind the bar.

I came for my wallet, I said.

Thought you might, he said. Opened early.

I slipped inside, assaulted instantly by a staled mash of odors. Piss, sweat, leather, and an eye-burning residue from some fancy e-cig—clove oil, maybe. In the main room the chairs had been upturned on the tables. A wheeled mop bucket blocked the back hallway to the washrooms, the red doors to Heifers and Bulls propped open for cleaning.

Billy tossed the rag he was using to wipe down the bar into the stainless-steel sink behind him. Hang on, Marley, he said. It's in the safe.

I nodded. I sat on a stool, resting my elbows on the mahogany bar. I felt the lack of sleep and an urgent need for a shower, hating the taste of cheap weed in my mouth. Billy returned and handed me my wallet. I pocketed it silently. Billy was part Aleut, his flat cheekbones and coffee-colored skin a contrast to a population of pale Seattleites rarely exposed to the sun. He had an uneven scar over one eyebrow, his dark hair tied back with a twist of leather. Considering the denim shirt and black cords, the mid-sized ear gauges—his of a dark stripey wood—Billy could be any easygoing downtown Seattle guy.

He looked fifty although I knew him to be thirty-five.

He stared straight at me and I looked frankly back. The midnight lives of bartenders and travelling bands. Fellow creatures of the night.

Billy broke the silence. You look like hell, he said. What can I get you?

I craved coffee. But then I recalled little miss raccoon-eyes in the hallway, telling me I looked as old as her mother.

Virgin Mary, I said. Double the tequila.

Billy set the drink down in front of me. He looked about to say something—wavering between sympathetic friendliness and a darker pity—apparently thought better of it and turned his attention back to his shelves of well liquor, consolidating the half-empties. Preparing for the afternoon crowd.

I doused the tequila Mary with sriracha and then stirred it slowly with a straw. I sat there with my cheek in my palm, thinking about baseball, the unsettling call from Andi, and the unread messages that flashed on my phone. I spun my drink. A party for breakfast. What was I doing with my life?

Dude came in here last week looking for you, Billy said, talking over his shoulder. He was methodically restocking his cash drawer with a pack of new bills in low denominations, counting under his breath. Five, ten, twenty, forty, fifty, fifty-five…

Me? I said, surprised.

Pretty sure the picture was you.

Billy had my full attention now and I stopped sucking tequila up the straw long enough to stare at him, puzzled. Say what he want?

Billy placed the twenties in the drawer last, careful to separate the crisp bills between his thumb and index finger. He slipped the bigger denominations under his receipts. Not that I recall, he said. Mentioned your name. Said he knew you from school or something, heard you hung with the bands downtown. He slammed the cash drawer shut. I was too busy to deal, you know? Sorry.

I yawned. Another creeper fan, hunting a signature. Guy must have mixed me up with Andi, I thought. What'd he look like? I asked, off-hand.

Billy turned to face me, folding his arms. I dunno. Didn't really notice the guy. Like I said, The KillJoys were on stage—couldn't pull beers fast enough. Fuckin' blew a keg. He sighed then, taking pity on me. Biker jacket. Tall kinda, he offered at last. Beard, I think. Any of that ring a bell?

I shook my head. You sure it was me in that photo? Not a celeb shot of Andi?

Billy retucked his shirt into the back of his jeans. Naw, not sure of nothin'. But this was old school, unnatural-like. Like a yearbook picture or those outdated passport shots. Teeny, right? Real weird if you ask me. He shrugged a shoulder. Anyway.

I took a long suck on the straw, eyes watering as the tequila Mary bit. I frowned. None of it made sense. Nor honestly, did I truthfully care.

What'd you do, Billy asked. Forget to pay your cable bill?

He topped off my drink.

Must've forgot to pay something, I said. I mean, heavy leathers?

America's Most Wanted, Billed cracked.

From high school.

The eighties want you back, girl.

I turned away with a laugh.

If you asked me, high school photos were crime enough. You got zero cred as any kind of band groupie if you hoped to get something that uncool signed.

I picked up the drink, and headed across the dance floor, shadowy in the dim light. I circled the tables to reach the low stage, stepped up on the platform, and pulled a chair over to the upright piano at the back. The Corral kept a real piano, though most bands preferred their own electronic keyboards. Story was, the owner of The Corral before Billy, a grouse named Captain Mel, brought the piano south to the mainland from Anchorage. Deep scratches scarred the length of the upright. Captain Mel claimed he'd faced down a Grizzly from the backside of that piano. Claimed they were claw marks. I wondered what would tempt a bear to break into a bar.

I drained a third of the not-so-virgin Mary in one gulp and pushed up my shirtsleeves. My brain buzzed with fatigue and booze and the heat of the sriracha. I rested my fingers on the keys and looked down. Always piano keys appear alien to me. Strange pale bones. And above them, the black icicles of night.

My fingers sprawled easily from one end of the octave to the other—a knuckled starfish anchored to the old ivory. Blues hands, Donna had said. Not tiny like hers, so they must have been like my father's. And ivory it was. Maybe walrus tusk. Each key covered by a thick cap yellowed with age. A piano built perhaps a hundred years earlier. A world before 1972, before the ivory trade was at last outlawed.

I closed my eyes.

The pads of my fingertips felt for the hollows worn into the keys by the players before me. This. The way in. Inviting the music in. Or maybe it was out. I don't know, really. Shutting down the brain. Opening to something else, a thing deeper.

I'd thought to fiddle with the arrangement I had to finish for Andi and the band—a "beer, my girl, and my truck" kind of tune—but could not begin. I opened my eyes and glanced up. Blue colors floated visible in the light, caught by the dust.

I ran a few scales and chord progressions, letting my hands wander until I settled down in a major key. No sunny-side-up plate of notes this, but the tonal mirror of a long ago beauty gone to seed. I worked the chord triads and ran through the familiar pentatonic of country music—the major scale minus the fourth and seventh notes, making a shift to the minor, muted and layered. Something stark at its core. My hands drifted. My fingertips, imaginary cherry blossoms falling on the black and white keys. Petals blown into the street, crushed underfoot, flattened by passersby. A melody inhabited by the voice of blossoms. The delicate, stenciled perfection.

Abruptly, I stopped. Dug the plastic straw around several times in my drink, mixing tomato juice and tequila into the melted ice.

That new? Something for Andi? Billy asked from across the room.

No, I said. But I felt a quiver inside. This small something was the first original anything I'd composed at the keyboard in months. Andi would hate this, my second thought. Andi Stone, glam country diva, front woman for the Grammy-hit band The Andi Stone Tour, would not be interested in any sad little piano riff. I should know. I am the band's songwriter. Have been for more than twenty years.

Lyrics and beats, that's me.

Too bad, Billy said. He jabbed the mop to the floor, scrubbing away barbecue sauce and beer stains. Like it, he said. Made pictures in my head.

I played another thirty minutes or so, laying the bricks of the new theme to memory. Theme and chorus. I could flip this straight to honky-tonk cliché, but what I liked about it, felt for it, was the music's crushed, almost beauty. A hookup and no last names. The stark pink light of a dormitory hall. Dignity, crushed in the sheets.

Tucking the imagery of street blossoms in my back pocket, I dropped the lid down over the keyboard and walked my empty glass behind the bar. I pulled a fifty out of my wallet and left it by the register for Billy, for thanks and the drink.

See ya around, Billy.

He nodded. Touched his brow with a forefinger.

I remembered my manners and pulled another bill out. I folded it and stuck it under an empty shot glass. You know that baseball player? I asked. The one I was with last night? He a regular?

Billy rolled the mop bucket back toward the storage closet. Yeah, he said over his shoulder. Kid comes in every Friday after a game. Real slugger.

He returned and leaned against the bar, eyeing me. Take it he lived up to the reputation?

A lady doesn't tell, I said lightly. I hooked a thumb toward the folded twenty. See he gets that? I owe him.

Sure, Billy said. He stared at the wet gray street through the blinds. Still fuckin' raining, he said.

I followed his gaze. On the street, a dented white pickup idled at the curb. A girl in a green sweater climbed out and leaned in to say something to the driver before closing the door. The pickup jammed gears and drove off, picking up speed, leaving the girl standing unprotected in the elements. Rain hit her face, drenching her hair, but she didn't seem to care. Something about her fixed expression stirred an old feeling in me. I knew that look. This was a girl saying goodbye. Making up a story to explain an ending.

That look was about wanting reasons for endings when endings never seemed to have one.

I zipped up my jacket. A relic of my own college days. Years of northwest damp had faded the leather to the texture and color of barn siding.

I should go, I said, thinking of Nathan.

Nathan, whom I'd stood up yet again. Left to go it alone at a Seahawks recruits party, all to sample a little spring training of my own. Nathan, my boyfriend of six years. Nathan the Good, Andi sometimes mocked. Only he was good. Too decent for me, that was for sure.

Rain's okay, Billy. I kind of like it, I said. I twisted my hair up, securing the knot with a swizzle stick from the bar. I slid a glance his direction. You know, I'm too damn old to be explaining myself anymore.

He grunted, his expression a shell of some memory he'd evidently crawled deep inside. If it's all the same to you, he said, let the dude end it.

How did he know I'd meant Nathan? Why? I asked, curious.

He spit neatly in the sink. Give the dude his pride.

I rode the bus from Pine Street through wet streets toward the Queen Anne neighborhood I lived in. Early Saturday. Everywhere a busy world sliding into motion.

I thought about Billy's remark. Whatever else he might be, Nathan was no softie. A sports talent agent, the Nathan Pepperell I knew was all about the win. But decent in his way, I'd give him that. He'd been good to

me and for me—we'd racked up some years. Grown
comfortable with the grind of our edges. But if I couldn't
show up, and I never did—I consistently failed to hold up
my end at Nathan's work events—there was no win in
Team Marley-Nathan. Nathan would end things soon
enough if I did not.

A young bearded dad, a Baby Bjorn snugged to his
chest under his flapping rain jacket, climbed onto the bus,
his dark-haired wife coming up the steps behind him
holding the hand of their young daughter. The mother
waited as the little girl approached the driver and
carefully swiped their bus pass, her expression watchful
and amused. Billy was right, I thought observing the dad
pat the lump in the Bjorn protectively.

Nathan had cut me a great deal of slack. I'd give him
that. Let him break it off.

I slipped on sunglasses, protection from the glare of
too much world, and stood up for my stop, humming the
crushed blossom theme.

2

There was a note written on the back of a receipt and taped to the front of the voice recorder when I let myself into the condo.

"Out. xo NP."

Maybe for the better. I was tired.

I headed down a short, carpeted hallway to the back of the apartment and our bedroom of muted grays and silver. It had once been decorated in cool ocean greens but Nathan preferred a hard modern palette—his office was also in shades of gray, silver, and black. I tilted the blinds closed and tossed my clothes on the chair at the foot of the bed. In the tiled bathroom, a pair of Nathan's glasses sat to the side of the sink. I set my phone down beside them. Pulling my hair out of its topknot, I turned the double shower on, full and hot. The bathroom billowed in steam.

As I sudsed my hair, I thought about the song I was being paid to write, the one I couldn't seem to focus on. One of three I owed the band. A light, soda pop tune, Andi had instructed. Something to anchor the album. You know, she said. Upbeat, breezy. A catchy pre-release cut.

Country had evolved, in our years alone, from the golden age voices of the 60s through the 80s, from the soulful ballads of Charlie Pride, Waylon, Loretta, and Dolly, to bands like Rascal Flatts, Florida Georgia Line, the Zac Brown Band, and Sugarland, belting out rhythms with the rawness of a rock band and lyrics that seemed to pair better with margaritas than beer. I'd gone with the flow before, why not now?

I heard my cell phone ring from the counter by the sink. That had to be Andi, checking in from Miami, doing whatever she and her new boyfriend, Marco, did on a Saturday afternoon by their pool. I let the call roll over to voicemail, wondering if Marco would be husband number four. If Stephan, number three, was even fully out of the picture.

Andi was like Donna in that way, I thought. Impulsive and unpredictable.

I let the hot water pound my shoulders, thinking about the comings and goings of men throughout our childhood—men that came and departed too quickly for names, men that had names but left after a few months. The imaginary men I made up with Andi as someday dads.

In the end it was always just the three of us. The Stone girls. Why so glum, sweethearts? Donna would ask, hugging us close. A missed note in a solo, a poorly attended show, even a spat between Andi and me, and Donna would tease us into giggles, our woes become a thing of the past, everything fixing with my mother's smile.

Donna could pitch a ladder to the moon to hang party lights, but her lows...her lows became silences that stretched into weeks. Dinners of boxed macaroni and fried spam. Road trips under moonless skies.

Night Train, I thought, thinking of the old Pontiac.

Donna called the unexplained and unplanned car trips of our childhood "catching the night train." Jumping a ride to someplace new cloaked in the invisibility of night. Traveling the empty miles from wherever we were living month-to-month to destinations unknown. Road trips that sometimes led to our grandparents' farm in southeastern Washington, other times just the three of us moving on, our belongings crammed in the yaw of the trunk and beside Donna in the front, stuffed under our feet, and under the blankets in the back. Part hobo, part scofflaw.

Sometimes the Night Train was just a trip around the state, the FM radio on low, Donna chain-smoking without saying a word. The tip of her cigarette glowed red in the dark as clouds of exhale drifted out a crack in the window, the stars streaming by as Andi and I slept through the miles.

Moving from place to place colored the landscape of those years. I could hear my mother's voice in my head when one of us complained or dragged our feet climbing into the back seat. Baby, she said, the future is forward. Rolling Stones gather no moss, girls! Her laughter rang out.

I wondered what she meant then. And I still do. The past was the past, so yes, the future was forward by definition. I guessed by "rolling Stones" she meant us, not the rock band. But what, exactly, was the problem with moss? It felt like a clue, this small thing she would say. That if I could understand her words I would know something important, something concrete about why our lives differed from that of other kids, other families.

Wherever we ended the night, my last image of my mother before falling asleep would be her silhouette at the wheel, her eyes staring distantly down a tunnel of light. I pushed the lever in and shut the shower off. Water dripped down my back and shoulders to swirl down the drain.

Donna was the beat to all our songs, Andi and me. We were each half the heart of our mother—Andi, the lamplighter of highs, and I, the guardian of lows. One twin given to men swinging in as fast as they swung out. In love with the show, the bright lights and loud music, the costumes and the drama. The other awake in the night alone, with or without men. Navigating a private constellation of secrets. In search of a melody to harbor in.

A trio. A subset. Sisters. I toweled off and couldn't help but wonder, Would we survive our shared history?

じじじ

A slash of rain hit the wide windows of the apartment and water droplets blurred to a smear across the panes. Fishies, we'd called them as children. Playing racing games, tracing raindrops down the car windows. Andi liked the skinny fast dragon-tails, but I preferred the fat ones—the bulging drops pushed by the streaming air until they gave way and jostled down the glass.

Nathan was a dragon tail. He had finally shaken loose and raced away.

He faced me across the table in the candlelight. Our table. The wobbly English antique we'd found at the import warehouse on Lake Union the first week we moved in together. Dinner had been quiet.

Nathan threaded his fingers through his short brown hair, hair the color of the varnish on old pine floors. The gesture was distracted and hinted of a mix of surrender and frustration.

All right, he said. Cards on the table. I ran into Renee

and Mark at Trader Joe's. He paused. They said they never saw you last night.

How handsome he is, I thought for the thousandth time, admiring his classic almost superhero features. Composed. A fiercely successful negotiator because of that unflappable cool. But six years together is a good deal of time. I knew his tells: the weighted brow, the compressed mouth. Nathan was not happy.

If I recall, he said, choosing his words, you texted you were going to miss the new recruits' dinner because you were going to Renee's. Because—and I quote—she needed you. His eyes drilled into mine from behind his bold black glasses. He drummed the fingers of his right hand on the table.

However, he continued, Renee said she and Mark were at softball practice all night. So, he asked, where were you?

This wasn't about a cowboy or a missed steak dinner. What I did with my free time was my business. There had been an understanding, what with his constant travel, my studio sessions. Sometimes the thought of another meal in a bar alone was just too grim. Or what you did when you drank too much. None of that mattered, we'd agreed. A lapse in passing. We'd been good that way. There had never been a need to lie.

I'm sorry, Nathan, I said. I owed him more explanation than that and I knew it. You know the schmoozing thing kills me, I said. I went downtown, to The Corral. Granger and the Hot Spurs were in town.

He wasn't buying it.

Last night was a big deal, Marley, Nathan stated. The 'Hawks signed Damien Prower from the Bears practice squad as a new tight end. That was my doing. My deal. He folded his arms. The disappointment on his face clear. It meant something, he said. You should have been there.

It was a major coup to sign a player. Recruit dinners were lavish, crowded affairs. Between the team staff, the players' wives and girlfriends, their families, the interviews, and the media, it was a big happening.

Nathan said nothing more for several moments.

I don't like that you lied to me, he said finally. I know we've kept it loose, cut each other a lot of slack. But I have to trust you. I have to believe you'll keep your word. I love you, Marley. But I don't think you love me. Not enough anyway to make this—us—work.

He opened his hands and dropped them on the table, defeated.

My perfect Nathan. Seated at our table, a glass of good wine at his elbow. The immaculate hair, the strong even teeth, brows straight as trusses over his narrow English nose. The ridiculous schoolboy glasses he thought made him look so *GQ*.

The breath leaked from my chest. Are you angry because I—I stayed out late? I asked.

All night is not late, he snapped.

He calmed before speaking again.

You're an adult, he said. So am I. But we are supposed to be a couple and that's not possible if you're always gone, Marley. Not just last night—all the time.

He reached for his wine glass and gripped the stem. You go out. You come back…I'm not an idiot. I doubt you've been alone.

He held up his hand. No, don't tell me.

You promised you'd be there—and you weren't, he said. His mouth tightened. Everyone was expecting you. You're one half of a big deal in music, you know. People want to, whatever, have you sign their cocktail napkins. You let me down. You humiliated me.

I'm sorry, I repeated, my words choked, hating who I had become in his eyes.

You promised, Marley, he said quietly. You promised me you would be there. When I finally reached you at the bar, you handed me that bullshit story about Renee and her big fight with Mark. How she needed you. He paused. I needed you.

Puzzled, he asked, Is there someone else? I mean someone serious? Is this why?

No. There isn't, I said.

He shook his head. You don't know how I wish there was. You're just fucking broken. You know that, right?

Only then did I notice the duffle bag propped against the door.

You're leaving, I said slowly. Where? Where are you going?

Bradley's. He has a spare room.

Nathan wiped the corners of his mouth on his napkin and folded the cloth in even squares before laying it beside his plate.

I'll come for the rest of my things later, he said.

He stood, hesitated, and then dropped a kiss on the top of my head. A gentle gesture.

He collected his phone charger off the kitchen counter, lifted his trench coat from its closet hook, grabbed his bag, and opened the front door. His expression was unreadable but I recognized the attitude, the unshakeable decisiveness. Nathan had made up his mind, and there was no going back.

How strong the urge to cling to the known world in the face of chaos, I thought, holding back all the irrational words that would beg him to stay.

Billy was right. Nathan had to be the one to go. He deserved that.

The expenses are paid through December, Nathan

stated. Need anything, you know where to find me. He turned and was gone.

I folded my hands together, resting them on the table.

For two hundred years, this plank of pine had been carted about England before it had been left for sale among the trunks and cabinets of a Pacific Northwest antiques dealer. Celebrations, bankruptcies, dark betrayals, reunions, and goodbyes. All said in the presence of this table.

And now another.

I leaned over and blew out the candles, locked the front door, and switched off the kitchen lights. I stood in the semi-dark of the living room, the half empty bottle of Bordeaux from dinner in my hand.

I stared into the dark. A vast field of empty heart. My heart.

Seattle was mine. That had not changed. The aroma of the bread bakeries down in Pioneer Square on Saturdays would forever remind me of my grandmother's baking. The morning sun against brick walls slowed me down. Gave me reason to linger. Melodies rose from the delivery trucks, the clang of refuse bins, the swoosh of the light rail.

And always there were the long low songs of the ferries.

Nathan was gone but the city remained.

3

I keep a close watch on this heart of mine
I keep my eyes wide open all the time…
Because you're mine, I walk the line

Boom-chicka-boom. The freight train rhythm of
Johnny Cash's song pounded through my head. "I Walk
the Line." The song mocked me. Not just because Cash
had written a song that was purely and simply a hard-core
pledge of devotion, a devotion he felt, but because he had
done so in twenty minutes. In 1956, a man writes a hit
song on the back of an envelope balanced on his knee.
Backstage, Gladewater, Texas, waiting to perform—the
lyrics coming as fast as he can write them down—and
here I was, with all my recording gear, my tapes, and
nothing to say for myself.

I tidied the kitchen, placing my portion of uneaten
salad in the refrigerator. I shut the door, face to face with
the crinkled photograph of the lake cabin. The
photograph, anchored by magnets, was the only personal
memento tacked to the appliance. Dapplewood. A
snapshot of a small cabin at the edge of a sandy beach,

tranquil in the shadows of a late summer twilight. The photograph traveled as I did: taped to a rental fridge in Bozeman, to the freezer door of a meat-locker in Anchorage, the front of a one-door saffron relic of the seventies in Nashville, and to here, the modern stainless-steel side-by-side of my first home.

The thought of the family cabin, sitting empty and unused, clunked about in my head like a brick. It couldn't be put off forever. A decision had to be made.

I turned from the photograph and a square package on the counter caught my eye.

I tugged the package out from under a stack of unopened household bills and Nathan's sports journals. The front was addressed to M. Stone, the return address illegible.

One corner of the packaging had torn open in handling and an edge of red leather binding revealed—leather the same deep burgundy as the 1969 200th Anniversary Edition of Encyclopedia Britannica that had sat on the shelf in Grandpa Kurt and Grandma Leila's TV room on the farm.

I hefted the package, thinking how much such an awkward heavy thing would have cost to mail. I guessed it a book of some kind. Had I ordered something online and forgotten about it?

I peeled off the brown wrapping paper—an inside-out QFC grocery paper bag as it turned out, cut and taped. Not just a book, but a yearbook. I ran a finger across the gold lettering emblazoned on the front of the red cover. Paulette High School. The school Andi and I had attended in northern Idaho. The yearbook wasn't from our graduation year of 1989 however, but the year before.

I cracked the book open on the counter, noticing the pages were dog-eared, as if frequently perused, but unsigned. So not a student's book, I thought.

I thumbed straight back to the junior class pictures, to the tail of the alphabet.

I smiled. Heavens, but we were homely and freckled and four-eyed and awkward. There was Ralph Reacher, Sandy Ritter, Davey Roach. Our buddy Tom Shultz. Sam Stinson, Liz Stockman, even Ricky Strongbow from music class. In every case our first names abbreviated to a single initial and grouped in the margin to the right of the photographs to save space.

There, A. Stone. Andi, grinning from her junior year photo, flashing her big-toothed smile, her straw rodeo hat perched at a flirtatious angle over a dandelion of teased and sprayed hair.

Next to her, a blank windowpane.

I stared. My picture was gone. Neatly cut from the page.

I slapped the book shut. What the hell was this? A bad joke? Some prank modeled on a trashy slasher movie? I remembered Billy suddenly, and the man who had come into his bar. Billy saying how the man showed him a photo...*old school, unnatural-like. Like a yearbook picture*. But Billy hadn't said whether the man asked for an M. Stone or a Marley Stone.

Did I have a stalker? Some fool who didn't yet realize I wasn't the face of The Andi Stone Tour, my sister was?

I pushed the album away from me, noticing then the small 3x5 notecard that had fallen from the folds of wrapping. I picked the card off the floor and turned it over. Hand-printed on the face was a single sentence. *If this is the M Stone from PHS Class of 1989, please call 311-555-2371.* The note was unsigned.

Okay, not a stalker, I thought, relaxing a little. No stalker left that kind of traceable digital fingerprint. I half wanted to dial the number, tease out what I was dealing with. But I also knew it would be foolish to do so. Andi and I had learned any form of encouragement or contact with an over-zealous fan was to triple their determination.

Who mails a yearbook? I wondered aloud. Most people would make a copy of the photo page and stick it in an envelope, save the postage. And why a yearbook from before our actual class year? Was that by accident or intent?

Perhaps the yearbook had traveled around and around, returned from more than a few Mandys or Margarets or Marys who had no connection with Paulette High before coming here, finally, to me.

How many M. Stones in any one place could there be? I shook my head, amazed. And how was someone to return the book if they weren't the right M. Stone?

They wouldn't, I realized. Someone had searched M. Stone online, attempting to match a photo to an address, and took a gamble I might be the same girl as the photo shopped from bar to bar. They kept the photo, mailed the yearbook, hoping M. Stone would make the match.

I placed the card back in the yearbook. In all probability my sleuth was no more than some dude in a Barcalounger with a laptop and an IRS lien who would be crushed to learn he'd tracked down the wrong Stone girl. Best hand the book over to Ben, I decided. He'd know what to do.

I left the kitchen and turned on the low lamp over the sofa, gazing out the rain-streaked glass at the dark pointillism of Seattle night. The rain had ended, and beyond the rooftops, white fog blurred the maritime lights of the ferries on the Sound into streaks of blue and gold and red.

Seurat, I thought. Night by Seurat these unsettled watercolors, thinking of the paintings in the art books at the library. Someday, I would stand before one of Seurat's works in person. Stand in a wash of color and form that lost all shape up close and fell together again at a perfect distance.

At what exact measure should one stand to reflect upon one's life, I'd have asked the painter. He seemed to know.

I crossed to the piano and lifted the lid on the keyboard and plunked a random note. Clear high E rippled the silence. I touched another key and cocked an ear as the two tones faded into an echo of one another. I sat down, and fingered the keys experimentally, lyrics offering themselves up to the dark.

In the candlelight tonight I saw in your eyes, such beautiful eyes

as would not look into mine, something unsaid, said in your eyes tonight.

A five-four syllable repeat, maybe. A standard measure, with a layup at the beginning and at the end. *Tonight I saw…*

Dear God. I was writing my own breakup song. I closed the lid, leaning my forehead against the ebony wood. When would it stop, when would it stop?

Every night, endings waited at the piano for me.

Time for the Night Train, Donna said as she scooped us out of our beds and into the Pontiac. Let's catch the Night Train.

You afraid? I ask my sister.

No, she whispers. You?

Not so long as we're together.

My mother smiles as she slips in behind the wheel.

4

Open any door on any corner coffee shop, order a coffee, and watch the faces. The tense, focused expressions? Those belong to the software engineers and lawyers. The cryptic glances, to the lonely and would-be sweethearts. I make up stories for them—the bored daydreamers, the reunited friends, the dazed insomniacs. Sometimes the song is right there.

But today my notebook was blank. There was a damp coffee ring to one side of the page, and the crumbs of a particularly satisfying blackberry scone on the paper, the table, and my lap. I couldn't seem to round up a cheery phrase or a note to save myself, although I'd camped out every day this week at my usual inspiring haunts. I'd drunk a bucket of coffee, a cup at a time, and one more scone and my jeans wouldn't fit.

The coffee shop was in that lazy lull between the breakfast rush and lunch, and I felt invisible and unbothered at my corner table. The painted table wobbled, so I'd wedged a folded corner of napkin under one chipped-white leg, and that seemed to work. Both arms crossed comfortably in front of me, I stared out the window. It was a blue sky day, crisp with an autumn chill, and people on the street walked that much faster, clutching their jackets close. At the back of the shop pumpkin bread was baking, and the aromatic spices floated light in the air. All this lead to a particularly sweet memory and I found myself sketching on the page where a picket line of notes, a new melody should be. Drawing a farmhouse, a few tall cottonwood trees, and a night full of stars.

As I filled in the trees, I remembered me and Andi sprawled across the rear seat of the car. We were leaving our apartment in Longview to spend Thanksgiving at the farm. We were young, perhaps kindergarten age, and drowsy with the smell of warm pumpkin, the aromas of cinnamon and nutmeg from pies packed in the trunk.

I blackened the lines of the lane up to the farmhouse in my sketch, shading in the weight of the heavy dark. Remembering the empty quiet of the highway.

The cold had settled in the wide valley. A cow lowed from the barn. Uncle Ben and Aunt Charlotte were already there with their boys, Kurt and Joe. I remembered the familiar smells of cedar and oil cloth, of the musty quilts Grandma Leila pulled from the chest to make beds for us girls on the living room floor, felt the radiating heat of the potbelly stove, the old German cuckoo clock counting the dark hours. Home. We have traveled home.

Abode, asylum, grave, habitat, infirmary, native land.

Home is where one starts. The words not, as I'd thought, the red-checkered logo of a canned pea manufacturer, but the words of T. S. Eliot, that melancholy London wordsmith with the soul of a sober Hank Williams and the landscape of his native St. Louis. Did I care that the professor who introduced me to Eliot claimed him as his own—an elite, Oxford intellectual? Not in the least. I felt the ache in the poet's words.

However prettied in language, Eliot's was the same cracked sky sung from the farm radio at night.

It was the music, not the poetry, that grounded me. A sense of home was to be located, placed, habituated. And by consequence, homesick was the expression of its opposite—to be vulnerable, dislocated, dislodged. My mother had died and I was dislodged from home. Home, the locus of the heart. The farm was a constellation in my night, and in the days after Donna's death, I found myself constantly searching that sky.

One song is like another song, but not so you'd notice.

One love is like another love, but not absolutely.

One heart breaks like any other heart breaks, but not altogether. And only of late have I known this to be true.

Before the kid talent competitions, and the state fairs, before radio became the focus of Donna's life, my earliest memories begin knowing home, the place where one starts, was my mother.

We're a team, Donna says to us.

We're a team, we answer.

I glanced down at my sketch and then ripped it from the notebook and balled it up in my hand. I tapped the end of my pencil against a fresh page, unsettled. There was literally no point to all this moody memory business. Facts were facts and Donna was dead, and I'd better get a song down in hard ink or I'd be in a world of hurt.

I wrote a word on the page. The word "ordinary." I stared at it. What sort of song could you make for a world you didn't understand?

Ordinary. Ordinal. Precept and decree.

My mother, I understood, had been anything but ordinary. She had little to no interest in laying her hand to plain living; turning hours into days in a steady, socially productive way. Donna had been devoted to living life forward. Upstream, downslope, across the horizon. Never mind the measured days, the setting of the sun to the moon, the companionable march of seasons. Clock strokes counted things that might be, even as the black filigreed hands marked the seconds and hours and moved away and around the moonface of day. My mother had been devoted to possibilities. Uninterested, incompetent perhaps to be otherwise. Hers was the push, the breakaway. The freefall and the flight. What more, she might ask. What more might there be to it all?

We were not quite ten when the three of us left Longview and the rainy coast to settle in the summer burnt hills of Boise. The map of our sky expanded and new constellations took their place. Donna rented a two-bedroom cottage within walking distance of a pink concrete middle school. No more homeschooling, Donna announced.

Andi started studies with a real voice teacher. No more singing along with Loretta and Dolly and Patsy on the farm radio to learn our way around a song. No more fairs with fold-away stages and Radio Shack mics, or the sweet smells of lamb's wool and fresh straw that masked a kettle of other odors, from manure to burnt caramel.

We became citizens of the city and the ordinary.

You know, girls, I'm good with scraps and a needle, Donna said to us one November night. We had just sat down to dinner in the new cottage over plates of spaghetti with plain tomato sauce, done the way we liked it. I make your fancy show costumes, she said, right? I think I could teach people how to make things. All sorts of things. Things people actually need.

Late near the end of the school year she came home wearing her best dress and of all things, lipstick.

Girls! she called excitedly, coming into the house and letting the screen door bang behind her. I got it! I got a gig on the radio!

We squealed—not at all sure what a gig on the radio meant.

She laughed, twirling us around her.

You're looking at the newest Stone girl to get herself a show, she said and kissed us both.

That night we gathered at the table doing our homework as Donna prepared dinner. She turned from the stove.

Look at me, girls, she said, adopting an expression of mock seriousness. I say look at me!

She gripped a newly-peeled carrot intended for the stew in front of her mouth like a microphone. Her flyaway hair made a halo of the kitchen light behind her as she began to carefully and clearly explain to the carrot how to sieve homemade yogurt with cheesecloth. Andi and I rolled off our chairs onto the floor in a paroxysm of giggles, not daring to break Donna's stern "radio silence."

The Donna Stone Show became an instant half-hour hit. In six months, a full-hour broadcast, Saturday mornings at ten. The show was a variety show of sorts. A ragout of recipes and crafts, from candle-making to laying in a weave of straw and sheep's wool to insulate walls. Donna was a natural performer. She was friendly and practical and her ideas for ways to live off the grid dovetailed with the popularity of the homestead lifestyle in the intermountain west.

Donna wrote a craft book, sold it, and the station syndicated her radio show. We had TV and ice cream in the freezer like other families, and shoes that fit every fall.

Bright new stars shimmered in our sky.

I flipped the pencil and erased the word off the page. I finished my coffee and the barista, a thin blonde girl with heavy turquoise glasses and a knit cap pulled low over her dreadlocks, picked up my mug and set it on her tray.

Get you another? she asked, her tone pleasant, bored.

I nodded.

Latte, right? Hey, that's pretty good, she said.

I looked down at my notebook. As I'd drunk the last of my coffee I had also half-sketched something new, a drawing of a cabin, a lake shore abutting a stony ridge of pine forests, a line of smoke drifting from a hidden chimney.

Where is that? the barista asked, curious.

Northern Idaho, I replied. One of the lakes.

You grow up there?

Just summers, I said.

Wow, lucky you, the girl said. She sighed. I grew up over a laundromat. My summers were hot. And smelled like lint.

I smiled slightly and she moved away, back behind the coffee bar, drawing me another latte.

I added a loon to the drawing, a slash of black against the shoreline. Not just one of the lakes, I thought. Our lake.

The years we were little we spent one summer week of each year with our grandparents on the farm. At times the sun blistered so hot over the fields the dirt caked under our bare feet and we stripped to our underwear and splashed around in the farm pond. We waded only in the shallows, the small fish Grampa Kurt stocked in the pond whisking about our toes. We would scramble up and down the banks of slippery grass until muddied and cool. Then Grandma Leila hosed us off in the yard and made peanut butter and jelly sandwiches from homemade raspberry jam. The year we moved too far away for our summer week on the farm, Donna saved enough money that first year in Boise to rent a nearby cabin on a real lake for one long August weekend. We went back there the following year. And the year after that.

The year we turned fourteen, after the move north to Paulette, Donna found a small cabin for sale on a lake a hundred miles nearer to Canada and secretly laid down cash.

Two weeks later, a Friday after school, we raced in the house, dropped our jackets on the pegs by the door, and hit the kitchen for snacks.

Another sticky note.

The house was, as a rule, papered in them. Donna messaged us in a banner of multi-colored notes Monday through Sunday. Groceries, reminders, ideas for her show, school dates, and deadlines. Pack up, said the note on the refrigerator. Weekend at the lake. Andi and I looked at each other.

Hurry up, girls! Donna called from the driveway. She stood by the Pontiac, holding groceries, the smile on her face huge. Let's go make s'mores!

We grabbed our pillows and jumped in the car, headed north beneath a panorama of stars to the steady vibration of the big V-8 engine.

Night Train.

The flick of a deer tail caught in the headlights.

Night Train.

Straight to the locus of the heart.

Dark forests in silent canyons towered over the slim ribbon of road, the rickrack of their low branches closing rank behind us as the car rumbled through. The night sky trembled above our heads. A revolving planetarium of strange shapes. The cabin lay low in the trees, illuminated by moonlight. A plain and magical shack protected by tree giants and horned owls and waves upon waves of white-capped soldiers stumbling to the shore.

Night Train.

Lost Prince Lake.

We're here, Donna said, her eyes sparkling.

Never the ordinary. Forward. Upstream, downslope, across the horizon. I looked one last time at my simple drawing, closed the notebook, and took my latte to go.

Fourteen months had passed since Donna's death. A year and two months.

5

We stood at the end of the dock, our toes curled over the edge. Donna waited in the deep water in front of us. She treaded water easily, the back and forth of her legs stirring the languorous waterweeds. A fish darted out from the shadows beneath the sunbaked boards and disappeared into the faraway blue, into the water over our heads and over the heads of the mermaids, and where we knew cold watery caves hid sea dragons and biting sprites.

Andi and I shivered, gripping each other's elbows tightly.

Come in, girls! Donna called. You can do it! You've got to try sometime. The water's fine!

We locked glances, giggling and petrified. Skinny, shaped like kidney beans, our yellow swimsuits from the Kmart drooped below our fannies, wet and sandy from building sandcastles on the shore.

You first, I hissed to Andi. No, you, she whispered back. You go first.

Donna's gaze fixed on us, urging us in. I'll be here the whole time, she called. I won't let anything happen to you, I promise. Now one at a time, jump in and start paddling like I showed you. Her smile widened. I'm not coming out of the water until you do!

I looked at Andi. Would Donna just stay out there? Until her legs fell asleep and she sank?

You first! Andi begged, her eyes round and frightened. She ducked behind me.

I glared fiercely at Donna, took a giant breath, and leapt off the end of the dock straight at my mother. Down, down, down. I sank below the surface, the waves from my plunge thundering in my ear drums. My hands thrashed against the underwater gloom. Rocketing down. Sunlight a wavering spangle above me.

Beneath the water a face closed near mine curtained in bubbles rising like mermaid hair. Donna grinned and blew me a slow-motion kiss. Then she grabbed me by the waist with both hands and propelled my body upward like a shot. I broke the surface, arms flailing, water flying, smiling as I flew from my mother's arms.

ලාලා

I hit the floor hard with an Oof! and lay there, confused, staring at the ceiling. I realized I had fallen asleep on my notebooks again, had rolled off the sofa in my jump from the dock in my dream. I had to stop doing this, I thought. If only for the sake of my back. And my face.

The phone rang from the crevice of the sofa cushion and I reached one hand up and dug for it, still flat on the floor. Hello? I said.

Still not sleeping?

Andi.

I can't even remember what sleep is, I admitted.

In the circle of light beneath the brass floor lamp lay

sheets of scored music. I so often worked late my sister had grown accustomed to calling at the oddest hours. Not that I wanted it this way, but work found me in the quiet. I learned to attend each moment of possibility, regardless of the hour, or else lose the idea in its winged and shimmering form.

You're writing? Andi asked. The clink of something in a glass.

I crawled up into a corner of the gray sofa. Nathan's sofa. He'd be coming for this soon. Some college babe said I looked as old as her mother, I said.

That's harsh, Andi said.

I thought so.

Then again, you're nearly forty-four.

We're both nearly forty-four.

Don't remind me, Andi said. There was a waltz to her vowels now, Nashville honeyed her voice. But traces of Idaho remained. Growing up in the backseat of a car might be as country as country could get, but loving the road, any road, was to truly own it. And Andi loved the road. My sister collaged her dressing rooms and road coaches with colorful maps of all the places she had been or dreamed she might go. Andi gathered no moss, the true rolling stone.

I, on the other hand, was the hermit crab.

Since you called, I have something, I said.

About damn time, Andi replied. The television in the background clicked off. Sing it to me, she said. I'll record you on my phone.

I left the sofa and took a seat at the piano, switched the phone over to speaker, and set the device on the stack of music near the keyboard.

"I Could Be So Good for You." October 10, 2014. Piano opening. Key of A, I noted aloud.

I played the opening piano bars and launched into the

lyrics, projecting my voice so Andi could record me clearly. *I could be so good for you,* I sang, *if baby you only knew, knew what to do. Say hello, buy me coffee, tell me a thing that's true...* I played another set of stanzas and then stopped. That bit at the beginning would make a decent refrain, I said, pushing back loose strands of hair.

Andi grunted as she clicked off her recording. Marley, Marley. You're killing me. Killing me. She took a dramatic breath. I mean, it's not awful. But honey buns, this is country. Where's the happy?

Where's the happy? I echoed. It was if her phone call just days before declaring we'd killed our mother had never occurred. You mean the bruised hearts and bad luck? I said. The dreamers and cheaters and last-dime losers? That country, Andi?

Dig deep, Texan Billy Joe Shaver used to say—shovel straight to the heart of the thing. And then tell someone about it. Like penning a letter to someone you love.

Don't get your britches in a knot, Andi said, a slight chill edging her voice. It's a job, not a studio jam. If you can't or won't deliver what this album needs, we can ask that new duo Ben raves about to take over. Let them finish the last three songs. They're hungry. I bet they'd jump at the chance.

Bart Owens and Amelia Parleur? I asked. I was stunned, not least by the discovery my sister and my uncle had backup waiting in the wings. But they're a West Coast sound, I protested. How would that play in Oklahoma? Or Texas? What about your Nashville fans?

All I'm saying, Marley, is I know what I need and it isn't this, Andi repeated, her tone even.

There it was. The twins in hair ribbons and matching dresses, singing standards arm-in-arm across a small stage, had vanished. In their place a million-dollar diva and her team. I did not care about the gap in our earnings.

Andi was no sparkle pony trotted out to perform, given champagne and foot rubs when she was done. She worked for it. Hard. From the earliest days knocking on the doors of storefront studios with her recorded single in her bag, to just last month, forced to cancel a vacation to chase down a bassist to replace the Memphis stringer who'd dropped out and into rehab. She spent months on tour and hours on stage.

I was beats and lyrics. And because I was family, lucky, that in addition to commission I made a percentage. I had enough. It was just that Andi had more. Much more. And money makes decisions.

Do it or don't, Andi said. But I need to know now. We're on a tight schedule and the dollometer's ticking.

The dollometer. Something Grandpa Kurt had made up. An imaginary meter that spun wildly as dollars flew out the door. I kind of loved it, as ticked off as I was, that Andi would still use such a silly word, and had just done so without a bit of embarrassment.

She was right, I realized. Practically speaking, I was no longer splitting expenses around the condo. My personal dollometer was about to become a matter of some importance. I'd placed my songwriting eggs in The Andi Stone Tour basket a long time ago and it wasn't exactly a seller's market.

Yes. I'll do it, I said. I felt like a sellout, but writing for the band was a job. My only job. You're right, I said. I'm just tired.

But Andi was elsewhere, whispering off line. Waiting, I observed my reflection in the wide window, a rain-streaked cross-legged shadow. Beyond, the city sky glowed. The belly of the clouds lit from below by the coral-colored fluorescents of high-rise buildings. Rain waxed the pavement.

Andi came back, laughing lightly. You were saying?

The song, I said. Can we save anything here?

Let me think about it, baby sis. She was gentle now, softening, having won.

Baby sis. By three minutes. We're fraternal twins, Andi and me, yet in matters of everything but looks and shoe size, as distinct from one another as planetary moons. She never grasped how hard songwriting was for me, without collaborators. There were hundreds of ways to work the jigsaw of potential harmonies and melody lines. To her, tunes and notations, bridges and the like, were cereal box jingles. She paid no attention to music theory, and didn't need to. She had a natural ear and unfailing pitch.

One more time, I said.

Andi sighed. Sure, peach. Sure.

With the phone back on speaker again, I ran through the melody line, beginning to end. I gave the lyrics upbeat nuances and repeated a phrase I believed had strong possibilities as a chorus—where the guys on strings could bring in the bass and counterpoint Andi's treble.

Andi tapped off the recorder at her end with the click of a manicured nail and then played it back. Twice. She hummed the melody under her breath. I toyed with a broken pencil stub as I awaited her final verdict. The Tascam Portastudio 424, my compact mixer, blinked silently from its resting place on the piano lid. On the floor the cassette deck hummed next to the studio mic. Sheet music and shreds of pencil erasure littered the carpet.

I like the idea of it, Andi offered. You do have a way with the words, sugar. But this album's about love gone away. Vamoosed. That tune sounds like love never even came to town.

I heard her lean back in her chaise. She sighed. I gotta

say it, Marley. The fans want happy. Andi emphasized the word happy. Somewhere in there, you gotta bring the happy.

I closed the lid on the keyboard.

The song is about falling in love, Andi. Standing on the brink. Knowing deep in your gut this new thing could be good, but the next step lies in the other person's hands—and they won't, or maybe can't, make the magic happen. About taking a leap. Love is freefall. Happy? Happy is for Sesame Street.

Lord. She laughed. You have been up all night, haven't you?

The grind of a blender mashing ice and a man's voice with a strong Latin accent interrupted, asking about lime.

Margaritas? I glanced at my watch, calculating the time difference. It was closing on nine in the morning Miami-time. Near enough brunch, I supposed.

Thank you, sugar, Andi murmured to the male voice I assumed to be the new guy, Marco. The album is supposed to be sweet, Marley, she said. A tease. Like a summer picnic! Try up-tempo. Maybe another key? She hummed a riff somewhere between pop Taylor Swift and vintage Belinda Carlisle. Happy, she repeated. Like that, okay?

Happy. Like that. Someone should distill the essence of my sister and bottle the miracle. Live stream the whole happy thing. Then there would be no need for multi-city tours and recording studios—not to mention the snowdrifts of crumpled paper at my feet. I burrowed the eraser end of the pencil between my brows. I had lost the battle for my song. *Baby Look Away* would be just another album in a string of achy-breaky, kickass, danceable hits. I wanted Patsy Cline. I wanted Hank Williams. I wanted…

The silver slant of light. I gazed out at the slender

sheen on the horizon gradually, so slowly, separating sea from sky. Whiskey weather, I said abruptly. It's October and already whiskey weather.

A blue and green Seahawks banner snapped in the wind from an upper apartment balcony across the street. The guy lines clanged against the steel railing with that peculiar rhythm—the ring of metal on metal—that reminded me of the lake, the metallic clink of the boat tie-downs as offshore waves pushed against the piers and bumped the boats about on their tethers.

Tequila. Please, Andi said. Keep your fog.

I fingered the cuff of my cabled Irish cardigan. The sweater had been a gift from Donna, worried I would freeze to death over my first Bozeman winter at Montana State. I'd worn the sweater to class. Then in Alaska. And now here. Aren't you on tour soon? I asked.

Not till February, Andi answered. England and Europe. She ticked off the stops on the band's thirty-city tour and described her list of themed costume changes, jumping thought to thought as she ran down the band's all-platinum playlist.

I jotted a shopping list as she talked. I couldn't write songs as fast as my sister was axing them. I needed more coffee, and a fresh pack of blank recording cassettes, harder to find now than ever before. Old school sure, but as any studio hand would tell you, if you worked on large format cassette it was an easy conversion from master tape to digital. And time was of the essence.

You know that bastard Stephan is suing me for alimony. Me! Andi said, meaning Stephan Brandt, her soon-to-be third ex, *Sports Illustrated* all-around fun guy and four-time cover. He claims, she said with heavy sarcasm, that he's lost soccer matches and major endorsements because he's—and I quote—emotionally compromised. That asshat thinks I'll give him money for his marital stress! The balls!

I laughed. What, did you break his…you know…his dudeness?

His precious Austrian prick? Andi scoffed. I wish. There were women, Marley. Lots of them. Models, princesses, bar girls, poodles, whatever.

None of the others got alimony though. Did they? I thought back. I couldn't honestly keep up with the drama and the details. Uncle Ben hired you a good lawyer?

Andi snorted. Yes. Same firm as the last two. Those lawyers own vacation homes courtesy of me.

Thank God for prenups, I thought.

We'd begged Andi not to marry the big Austrian. Derek Cauley, Andi's second husband, and a former Nashville weightlifter on the pro-wrestling circuit, who for a time rather badly managed the band, even went as far as to send a fax of a soccer ball slashed by an X. But something about Stephan's Schwarzenegger jawline and his rock-hard quads had done her in, and with typical bone-headedness she tied the knot anyway. Castle wedding on the Rhine—the whole tapestries-and-antlers glazed strudel. If it had sequins and pizazz and a strong hit of sexy, Andi was in, rolling in the swash.

I bussed my mug to the sink.

I'm thinking of getting a little something done, Andi announced. An unflattering close-up had surfaced from last year's Country Music Awards. Liposuction? she asked. A breast lift? Anyway, something perky. The Red Carpet's gone totally braless. Practically see-through, she complained.

But you're perfect, I protested.

Forty-four is fucking ancient in this business, her flat reply.

Forty-three, I corrected gently. Still forty-three. And

your boobs are perfection. Like the alps. Everything points up. And there's not one gray hair on your head.

We were born blondes but Andi had adopted a shimmering Reba red in Nashville and never looked back. You're beautiful, I said, and I meant it. You're an icon. Like Dolly.

The drizzle outside had doubled-down to a steady drumming, distant lamps in the windows of houses and apartments pinprick lighthouses on a sea of northern dark. I carried the phone into the bedroom and crawled into bed beneath the thick comforter. Television resumed in the background again. Sports. Lacrosse? Ah, Marco. Same quads, different sport. I sank into the featherbed, eyes heavy.

Thanks, peach, Andi said. And how are you and sports boy?

Sports boy? It occurred to me then that Andi and I had a type. I pulled the comforter over my head.

Good. We're good, I said, muffled.

I can hardly hear you, M. Oh, and I'm worried about the cabin. We can't let it sit another winter.

I know. I was thinking I'd drive over after I see Uncle Ben in LA, I said. Clean the place out. Finish the album. I can do both.

And why not I thought. Lost Prince might be good for me. The original Canadian trappers who had centuries ago mapped the lake and hunted its shores had named the blue water, *Le Lac du Prince Perdu*. That suited me. As lost as a prince could be.

It's gonna be weird up there, Andi said and drained her drink.

Weird we knew. Weird was the Stone sisters in spades.

She unexpectedly laughed. You know what I was

thinking about last week? That appearance on national TV when we were kids. Dressed as cows! Remember that?

That the year you set the tulle skirts on fire?

Mar, it was The Grand Ole Opry! And a real hotel. Those little scented soaps and everything. Mom stuffed like six in her suitcase.

I grunted. If you recall, Beth Sinclare got her hands on the promo still for that show—and published it in the yearbook.

Yearbook, I thought. Mustn't forget to tell Andi about the yearbook.

It's a miracle that thing hasn't shown up in People magazine, Andi said.

Yet, I warned humorously.

I hadn't thought about that show in perhaps forever. We turned nine the summer we won the Washington State Fair, held every year in Puyallup, Washington. We competed in the Family Vocals competition, all "Hee-Haw" adorable in gingham and braids. And then by invitation of Miss Dolly Parton herself, travelled east that fall to Nashville, Tennessee, for a nationally televised show saluting the fifty states.

Grandpa Kurt paid our way and we sang our state duet on that famous stage in a brand-new costume sketch. Andi was "Belle," after a famous yodeling cartoon cow, and I was "Moo," the sidekick. Moo and Belle—all Donna's idea. We could see her laughing as we sang, peeking out at us from behind the stage curtains of The Grand Ole Opry as we four-squared under the spotlights, big blue bows flopping about our necks.

Miss Parton had gone on to open Dollywood in Pigeon Forge, and we guested with her twice more. And then just Andi. Seventeen, with a debut single.

That sketch sure did get us noticed, Andi said. Her

laugh was rich with appreciation. And didn't Mom make all three of us Guernsey cow costumes after that? For Halloween?

She had indeed. There were pink udders constructed from latex dishwashing gloves—each costume complete with a clanging bell. All hand sewn on Donna's traveling Singer sewing machine. You could take the girl off the farm, but the farm, apparently, traveled with the girl. Weird? Weird we knew.

Crazy, Andi said. But I still feel like that kid. One foot at the fair, the other at the Grammy's...

She hung up and I closed my eyes, listening for the rhythm in the rain, willing sleep. In six hours, I would be on a southbound jet to LA and I hadn't told Andi about Nathan, I realized. Or the yearbook.

Why? Why not? Why? Why not?

The rain tapped the words over and over. Lyrics and beats.

6

Whipping sharply away from the curb, a Mariachi station cranked loud on the radio, the Uber car headed north to Studio City. I glanced at the driver, a paunchy young Latino with aviator sunglasses. Too beat to complain about the pounding volume of the music, I uncapped a water bottle. Noon glare angled off the passenger window, giving back not only my own gaze, but the cumulus heap of everything Marley. Tight ponytail, dark glasses, leather jacket. Pulled together enough, I hoped, for lunch with an uncle.

Bull, I thought. Ben would know. Like Grandpa Kurt, Ben was the kind of man you couldn't fool. Or if you did, rarely. And with consequences.

The driver glanced at me in his rearview mirror. Miss?

I'd apparently spoken aloud. But for the rosaries, soccer flags, and Mardi Gras beads hanging off the mirror, I doubted the driver could see me.

Nothing, I said.

In town for business? He rolled an unlit cigarillo

between his teeth. You look kinda familiar. You make movies?

Nope.

You famous?

Nope.

I stared out the window at the passing storefronts, the splashy billboards for late night chat lines and personal injury attorneys. "Famous" would be Andi and The Andi Stone Tour, I thought. Hard to argue with seventeen Country Music Awards and nine Grammys; eight albums currently on the country charts. The fabulous Miss Stone was one hundred percent sensation, possessed of a voice Rolling Stone Magazine called "Janis Joplin, twice-rolled in Southern Comfort." Never seen in public without a scion of industry at her elbow, my sister effortlessly adorned herself in the sparkle of the moment. Only I knew how much of that sparkle was the direct result of her innate gift for staging and the hard cost of the road. She traveled in shoes of satin and dust. It was no surprise Andi was weeks from the end of her third marriage. Or that coffee was delivered mornings by the same admiring stringer from TMZ outside the gates of her home in Nashville, or for the moment, Marco's estate. Fame was strategic, but at a cost.

The car hit a curb with considerable force, and I gripped the door handle.

Go ahead and hit it next time, why don't you? I said. The driver shrugged.

Los Angeles would work for The Andi Stone Tour, just as Nashville had, I understood. The band's success lay entirely in my sister's hands. She had an instinct, like Donna, for roughness and honesty. The will to create the future from the past. I was backup. Had been from the first—Andi belting out Barbara Mandrell on a pawnshop mic, me on harmony in light alto slightly behind her so she could cue me if I forgot the words. What began as a sister act evolved in due time to The Andi Stone Tour. Andi Stone, billboard superstar. Marley Stone, songwriter.

I recapped the water bottle and stashed it in my satchel.

The driver braked hard in front of 1182 Cienga Avenue, a squat stucco building with a red tile roof. I stepped out and the man peeled off in a spool of dust. I stood in a shadowy canyon of buildings entirely alike apart from a pair of cylindrical high-rises. My first visit to the new office. My uncle hadn't so much invited me down as commanded it.

Inside, I pushed the elevator button for the fourth floor and straightened my wrinkled Sugarland 2012 Tour T-shirt. I brushed my teeth with my finger as I rode the elevator up.

My uncle met the elevator and wrapped me in a strong hug.

There you are! Come in, come in.

A tall man, he stepped back and swept me into his office with a flourish. What do you think? Nice digs, am I right? You can spit on Universal Studios from here. He steered me to the window. See it? There.

I shrugged off my leather jacket. The bank drive-thru across the street displayed a temperature of ninety-seven degrees and an eggplant-colored O-ring of smog hovered above the San Fernando Valley. Palm fronds along the avenues hung limp in the absence of the coastal breeze that would come later, with sunset. A metallic glitter in the distance could be either sunlight on the ocean or the reflection of light off the hoods of cars snaked on the 405. It was hard to tell.

I turned from the view and, rummaging in my satchel, handed over a pound of Seattle's Best Coffee. Roasted

Hazelnut, Ben's favorite. Ben was Donna's older brother—and our manager—going on forever now after the failure of Andi's number two, Derek.

Tears prickled and I looked away. It was good to see him.

How are you and Aunt Charlotte? I said. The boys? Families well?

Never better, Ben said. He grinned broadly, his face a curtain of wrinkles gathered at the jaw. Land of opportunity, LA. What's not to like about twenty-four-hour sunshine? Thanks for the beans, kiddo, he said. That's one thing LA doesn't do. Coffee here tastes like cat piss.

He walked to his desk and lifted an already brewed pot of coffee from the hot plate on the credenza. He poured us two cups in stained Dollywood mugs.

It's the water. Or so they say, he added, and shrugged. Cream or sugar? he asked. His hand hovered in the air, holding packets of raw sugar. I recommend both.

Just black, I said.

He eased his frame into a chair. In the last year Ben had moved himself and Aunt Charlotte out of Nashville, where they'd lived a ten-minute drive from Donna and Andi's old apartment, west to Los Angeles. They'd settled into a sixties Spanish style house near Toluca Lake. The leafy trees there reminded him of home.

The move was a calculated gamble. The country music scene had shifted, Ben declared. Dominated now by a younger, pop-country trend. Eager to rub elbows with the Big Dogs—schmooze the Hollywood agents and producers with the best of his good ol' boy country charm—Ben was wily and determined. The plan was to stake out the entertainment business. Andi would find better traction for her aging career here in LA, in the emerging market of celebrity judge gigs. Dance offs, music competitions, television talent searches, bookings as a talk show regular. If he could place her in films as well, so much the better. He would have successfully moved The Andi Stone music sensation into multi-media stardom.

Career longevity and steady residuals? Andi was fully on board. All she needed, she said, was a stage and her name in lights. Big lights.

I studied my uncle over the rim of my coffee cup. He looked comfortable in his new environment. He'd shucked his bell-bottomed western suits and much-loved Stetson for a trendy, cream-linen jacket and slim designer jeans. Embossed, I noted, trying not to smile, with a flare of rhinestones across the butt. Like Donna. You could take the boy out of Nashville…

Caffeine up, girl, Ben barked. Your head's a bobbin'. We need to talk hits and hard dates.

He powered up his computer and the TV-sized monitor sprang to life papered in a thousand app icons. My eye caught Nashville Top 40 and Solitaire. ICM. NASDAQ. Gold Coast Real Estate.

As I drank my coffee, I absorbed the concrete prospect of declining residuals. Andi was going in new directions. Should I?

Marley, Ben said. The album?

Sorry. Just taking in the new digs, I said. Pretty snazzy, compared to Nashville.

Hell, yes! No more remodeled barbecue joint for Team Andi, he said. Smelled mesquite in those walls for years. He double-thumped his chest. This city is like those things they slap on flat-lined patients in the hospital shows. You know, what jolts 'em alive? Let me tell you, LA is two big-ass shocking Hellos. His tan face cracked into a smile. His once sandy hair was now white and cut in a trendy brush-cut like Harrison Ford's. A horse-faced Harrison Ford.

I leaned in. Are you wearing an earring, Uncle Ben? I asked.

He reddened. Yeah. Gift from the boys. It's the thing now. Even Morgan Freeman has one. Not half sure they aren't messing with me. But back to business. How're the songs coming along?

Um, fine, I said. It's all fine.

I missed Ben's Stetson. And I was close to sure no dude wore earrings anymore. At least not in their ears. The trend was ink. But better a tiny diamond than an uncle in eye-of-the-tiger sleeves. I twisted my left arm slightly inward, hiding my own ink.

Good, he said. The recording studio is booked for November. He drummed the tip of his pencil on his desk and swiveled around to consult his computer screen. His scheduler was open and he flipped back and forth between the final three months of the year as he hummed.

Was that "Bayou Baby"? I wondered. Of course it was.

The plan is to record all the tracks of *Baby Look Away* in one pass, he said, staring at the screen. Andi's gotta get in and get out real quick. She's got that Mel Gibson film shooting the end of December in Australia and the tour in February. Gotta wrap before that. We've got the musicians and what-all lined up for five full-day studio sessions. 'Course we need you here for rewrites.

Mel Gibson? That fit. A box office star just passé enough to take on a music newcomer as a costar. Cross your fingers Andi didn't marry the guy. Then again, it would be something different. Premiers instead of playoffs. Australian accent, not Austrian.

Ben twisted back around and peered over the top of his bifocals. You'll have the final songs mid-October? he

asked. I need your word, Marley. No bull. Things cost a
helluva lot more out here in LA. We can't afford a delay.
He added then, not unkindly, There's always Owens and
Parleur, you know. If you need an assist.

The color of his eyes reminded me of Donna's. That
not blue, not green color of mountain lakes. My hands
felt sweaty. Was I being fired? I took a bracing slug of
coffee.

You have my word, I said.

He turned and typed a note in his scheduler. I added
quietly, We've decided it's time to take care of business
with the cabin.

He swung back around. The look in his eyes softened.
You girls certain you want to sell the place?

Totally certain, I said. No point hanging onto it. It's
not like either of us have kids who might use it. But we
can't sell the place with Mom's stuff in it. Even dead,
she'd be pissed.

He laughed. That she would. Andi's not going to Lost
Prince with you, I hope?

I shook my head. Andi was to stay out of the public
eye as she waited out her divorce to Stephan. The
Austrian soccer star was equally desperate to avoid
negative publicity. There were mega-commercials on the
line. Nike. Under Armour. Gatorade.

Ben tented his fingers and considered me. He made
note of the scrunchy, my rumpled hair, the tour T-shirt
shrunk a few sizes too small. Boots in ninety-degree heat.

Still, he said, his tone concerned. Take someone with
you. Call Kurt—or maybe Joey. Joey could get away
from the boat shop for a week. That's a big job, clearing
things out. Not to mention unsettling. I'd go if Charlotte
didn't—

I nodded. No worries, Ben.

My Aunt Charlotte, a few years older than Ben in her

early seventies, was sliding sideways through Alzheimer's. Moving from Nashville had exacerbated her wanderings. More than once Ben had ducked out of a meeting and hunted the streets for Charlotte alongside her caregiver, Rosaria. The last time they found Charlotte drifting toward Walgreen's in her bathrobe. Before that, swinging on the playground at the elementary school, singing tunes from *The Pirates of Penzance*. She had once played Mabel the Major-General's daughter in a high school play. Ben, forever in her mind, her Frederic.

Call the boys, Ben urged. Don't take that on alone.

Beneath the upbeat smile, spray tan, and fashionable clothes, Ben abruptly seemed sad and aged to me. I felt the pang of a future when even Ben would be gone. I tugged my ponytail tight, tucking the stray strands behind my ears.

I got this, Uncle Ben, I said. I'll wrap things up at the lake by the end of next week. The last three songs will be delivered on time, promise.

I didn't mention my disagreement with Andi over what constituted an acceptable song. That would have to work itself out in studio. I might only be an employee, but I knew my way around my sister and a country song better than most.

His relief was palpable.

Let me buy you lunch, he said. Or is it early dinner? He checked his watch. He hesitated. But first I must tell you something. And I'm not sure how to begin, frankly.

He closed his computer. It's about your mom, he said.

I tensed.

Donna called me from the cabin. Before, before— He stumbled to a stop. Pain crossed my uncle's face. The two had been close.

I'm sorry, Ben, I said. I didn't know what else to say. I hadn't a clue where this was going. Conversations between Ben and Donna had been commonplace. But the timing of this one felt significant. I waited.

After a moment he stated simply, Your mom received a letter, Marley. From your father.

Fred? I gaped. Our Fred?

One and the same, Ben said.

I couldn't believe it. I set my coffee on Ben's desk and let the news sink in. Mythical missing Fred. This was the first, and only, communication I knew of between my parents. Although in truth there was so much left unsaid about their relationship I could be wrong about even that.

Only once had Donna talked in any detail about that college summer and the boy with the big grin who'd danced her off her feet under the hazy stars. We knew the barest facts, Andi and me. An eastern seaboard college romance—if you could call three dates a romance. A Grateful Dead concert. Soon after Donna discovered she was pregnant. According to the story, Fred—no known last name, although what are the odds you wouldn't know a last name after three dates—never knew about the pregnancy. Donna quit St. John's the fall term of her second year. Back to Washington, and the isolation of the farm.

Fred and Donna never spoke again.

I know, Ben said. It was a surprise to me too.

It was impossible to interpret the expression on his face. A letter, I repeated.

Yes. Sometime the year before she died, Ben confirmed, meaning sometime in 2012. Your mom refused to tell me any real details. I couldn't tell if it was a big deal or just—unusual.

But that's more than two years ago! I burst out. I stood, then fell back into the chair. Why didn't you say something before now?

He removed his glasses and rubbed a hand across his eyes.

Your mom made me promise not to tell a soul, he said. Particularly you girls. I'm only breaking that promise now as you're headed to the lake. You—you might keep an eye out for it up there. If you—if you wanted to follow up.

He seemed unsure and uncomfortable as hell.

So Fred's alive, I said, releasing my breath.

I leaned back and focused blankly on the tiled ceiling. I had not expected this. Fred was myth, history, the all-but-forgotten. One of the closed doors in my mother's secret house of crazy. I was faced with an irreconcilable difference between acknowledging and examining. Andi and I had always accepted the fact of Fred, but now I felt forced into contemplating the why when I least wanted to. What was the point? Donna was gone. And with her all the unspoken distinctions between truth and story. There was nothing left to examine but melancholy and loss.

I collected myself and met Ben's gaze. My fury evaporated. Ben had possessed no more sway over my mother and her choices than we had. Donna had unwittingly given him a burden no more his to bear than it was ours.

Fred knew where to find her? It was all I could think of to say.

Apparently, Ben said.

Do you think he knows about us? About Andi and me?

That I do not know. Ben sighed.

But why call you? And why wouldn't she tell Andi and me?

He hesitated. I think the letter genuinely upset your mom. I worry... He trailed off.

What, Ben?

She talked about buying a ticket to meet with him. I gather he wanted to connect. Ben paused. I—I urged her to think about it. He plunged into an expression of deep guilt, his thumbs tapping against each other.

She decided not to, I said, a guess.

He nodded.

I nodded too.

I would have supposed Donna would not meet Fred, but not because of Ben. Of that I was certain. Donna had been too headstrong to do anything but exactly the thing she wanted, and what she wanted could change in a flash. Another thought floated up. Perhaps Donna received other letters, or even telephone calls from Fred none of us knew about. Only for some reason, this one letter had upset her enough to want to talk to her brother. Perhaps there been more to the college romance story than three dates. Maybe an entire summer. Perhaps nothing was as we understood it to be.

It was a slim line between a secret, an omission, and a lie, and I wasn't entirely sure Donna Stone hadn't skated back and forth between them her entire life. What do you do when the who of what you are is a subject of such deep ambiguity? But Donna wouldn't lie to Andi and me about something as monumental as Fred. I felt sure of this. She might have been unwise. Unpredictable, yes. But she was never cruel. No, Donna must have been as surprised to hear from her long ago beau as I was now.

I reached across the desk and touched my uncle's hand.

Ben, I said. It's okay. You were right to warn her. That was the smart thing. But I do wish you'd mentioned this before—now.

He met my eyes, thinking the very thing I was. July 2013. The summer my mother drowned herself at the lake. That Fred had reached out to her before was tremendously unsettling.

Does Andi know? I asked.

She does not, he said. You're the first person I've shared this with. I didn't want you to be, you know, ambushed, if you found something at the cabin.

I'll keep an eye out, I said, voice calm. I fought an intense craving for a piano and a tequila. In any order. Really, it doesn't matter, Ben. Water under the bridge, I said. In my heart the beating wings of an angel of desolation.

ೲೲ

We took seats beneath a shade parasol at a table set with hand-blown glassware in bold fiesta colors discreetly separated by large pots of geranium and ornamental grasses, a convenient screen for business over drinks and tapas.

I was quiet, still trying to process that Fred, who for our entire lives had been a mystery date from Donna's past, was in fact a real person. Out there someplace with a life, very much alive.

Over sole amandine, although I was sure both of us would have preferred beer and food-truck tacos, Ben brought me up to date on the business ledgers of the band and The Andi Stone Tour's latest record deal. He laid out our investments and informed me I would see a nice bump in royalties from the new Andi Stone commercials for Clairol and Cover Girl.

They're using one of your songs as the theme, Marley, he said with a wink. Andi makes money…so do you.

Andi taking on other media and doing new things was good, but if she stopped singing, I'd be out of work. My work had such an Andi Stone signature, it was doubtful any newcomer to the music scene would invite me to write. Even if they did, how would I handle the uncertainty and nerves of actual auditions?

You have nothing to fret about, Ben said, reading my thoughts. Don't forget, "Bayou Baby" made bank. All of us got very rich.

He grinned, aware even the mention of that spectacularly bad hit made my teeth ache. In what world was it fair the good stuff slipped under the table unnoticed and my one regret—this terrible, awful, sappy cliché of a country ballad about a boy and his first love— would hit platinum one month out? I'd written the tune on a cocktail napkin at a dive outside of El Paso— scribbling and shelling peanuts between boilermakers, two-stepping around with rednecks from the oil fields. "Bayou Baby" was everything a good song wasn't, but Andi had spun it, like Rumpelstiltskin, into pure gold. "Bayou Baby" was everywhere: piped into elevators, looped endlessly on the Starbucks playlist, streamed on Pandora, Apple music. You name it. There was a candy bar and a whiskey shooter and a restaurant chain franchised from the song. It was beyond horrible.

Maybe I would always feel poor, would never forget the days we lived in the back of the Pontiac, sleeping with our heads pillowed on the spare wheel mount and everything we owned in the station wagon packed around us. Boxes of music, guitars, camping gear, bags of food, shoes, costumes and booking schedules, craft supplies. We knew poor. It was half the reason Andi spent so extravagantly.

That was a lot to take in about your father, Ben said. He placed his big hand over mine, squeezing my fingers. You okay?

I've wondered my whole life if they loved each other, I said. Uncle Ben, do you believe in lasting love?

He leaned back from his salad. He set his fork down, arranging it across the rim of his plate. I met your Aunt Charlotte the summer I joined the Navy, he said. She was selling taffy on the pier. Had on this ruffly, blue gingham apron, and had the prettiest blonde curls I'd ever seen. I was nineteen, she was twenty-two. I've never loved another woman, so yes. I suppose I do.

He looked straight at me. I don't know if your mother loved your father, but she sure as hell loved you two. He pursed his mouth. You and that Nathan got problems?

Nathan left last week, Ben.

He shook his head. You okay?

I can't sleep, I said.

Paxil helps Charlotte.

I laughed. Noted.

We weren't in love, I said. Not like you and Aunt Charlotte. I considered the hazy sky. Nathan and I were stuck. Caught in some kind of zero gravity, I said. And then—boom—someone threw the switch and it all fell apart.

I threw the switch. It was all me. But I wasn't going to tell my uncle that.

Ben pulled a notepad out of his pocket and clicked his pen. The gesture reminded me of Donna. Ready to start a list, make a note, begin planning, make sense of the chaos life presented.

Do you share bank accounts? he asked. No? Good. He made a quick note. You'll have to divvy up stuff like sofas and silverware but nothing else is community property. He scratched his upper lip. Thank Jesus, the condo is yours. Wouldn't do to be scrambling for a down payment at your age—or defusing a scandal. Career-enders. He shook his head.

Ben had seen a lot of celebrity disasters, not to

mention pushing the wheelbarrow and broom after Andi's never-ending parade. A songwriter rarely merited bad press. No press at all, in fact. None of the tabloid headlines my sister's romantic fiascos seemed to bring.

Ben sighed. You girls, he said. One of you marries indiscriminately, the other not at all.

Blame it on the maternal role model, I said.

Your mother would hate to see either of you heartbroken, Ben corrected gently.

I lifted my chardonnay. Buffer, buffer, buffer, I thought.

Why not move here, Marley? Ben said. He helped himself to a slice of sourdough, cutting deeply into the butter before he stopped himself and laid the knife, the bread and butter, back on his plate. Nope, no butter, he said. Charlotte would kill me. My cholesterol's terrible.

Didn't Grandma always say, What's good bread without real butter? I asked.

I thought of the farm and the fresh eggs from the barn coop, washed and dried on a tea towel, still warm as Grandma Leila churned butter as her grandmother had. Don't like the store-bought stuff, she pronounced. She pumped the butter churn vigorously. Tastes like colored wax. Might be wax, for all you know.

LA is for the young and beautiful, Ben. Seattle suits me.

He laughed and wiped his hands on his napkin. That means you, sweetheart. You know, I'd always thought you'd be singing, not writing music. But after high school you just up and quit. Ever think about starting again?

I stared down the rabbit hole. A cappella choir, the State competition, stage lights. No, I said.

Lucky for you, you're a damn good songwriter. Ben cocked an eyebrow. You want, though, I can explore some screenwriting gigs—maybe you'd like to try that?

Have you thought about writing primetime drama? Pays huge.

Speaking of high school, he said. Some guy has been pestering me all year for your direct contact info. Says he was a teacher of yours in Paulette. Name of Carville. Want I should give him your email? I haven't as yet.

I froze. The man in the bar. The yearbook I had forgotten to bring for Ben.

Robby Carville? I asked.

That's the one.

No. Please don't. I mean no thanks, I said. My hand shook as I set down my wine glass. Just the PHS reunion committee trying to rope Andi and me into their big twenty-fifth—and who has time for that?

Ben looked at me oddly but said nothing.

We stood and I kissed my uncle on the cheek. I'll come down and see you and Charlotte for Christmas?

Counting on it, he said. He pocketed the lunch receipt, meticulous as ever with expenses. Can't miss the traditional Stone family chili. Joey sent spices from Austin!

He walked me across the parking lot and opened the passenger door on his late model BMW for me. Navigating Century Boulevard and the 405 as if he'd lived his entire life on LA roads, Ben swung the car to the curb at LAX near the Alaska Airlines departure gates.

Lifting his sunglasses, he hugged me. See you in studio. Good luck with the cabin, honey.

I stepped out and shut the car door.

That Nathan guy's a schmuck! Ben yelled as he pulled away.

7

The apartment was dark when I let myself in the door. I dropped my bag and reached for the wall light, hitting my shin on something sharp. Six moving cartons jutted into the space between the door and the hall. I had banged my leg on the edge of a carton—Nathan's name with Bradley's address neatly labeled on each box.

I lifted the note taped to the top box.

Moving service will pick these up tomorrow. Key's in the mailbox. NP

I made my way past the cartons to the kitchen, turning on all the lights, and glanced at the answering machine. One voicemail. I punched the play button.

Nathan's voice. *Hey. Hi. Tried your cell but you weren't answering. The movers will be there around nine. Seeing how things are and all, hope you don't mind I gave the second in our set of Seahawks tickets to Bradley. That's all...Oh, it's Nathan.*

The machine beeped off.

The Seahawks. That burned. My team. My tickets.

Or they had been, before Nathan convinced me to

cancel my seats and upgrade to his corporate box.

I poured a drink. Tequila in hand, I opened the slider and stepped into the breezy twilight, leaning against the balcony railing. Nathan's efficiency was stunning. He'd boxed his things in the ten hours he knew I would be in LA, scheduled movers, and given my game seat away. I should learn from this. Clearly this was how it was done, the breakup thing.

I sipped my drink, staring at the lights of the city. Today had not gone as planned. The album, it turned out, was the least of it. And the west coast business move? No big deal.

I swirled the ice in the tequila. I had not expected news of Fred to rise out of Donna's death. The experience had left me shaken. Ben had somehow pried apart a fresh set of family secrets. Our hidden lives tucked inside one another like Matryoshka nesting dolls.

There was the apparent, and beyond the apparent.

The fact of a letter, a letter without illusory cause but undoubted effect, cast a troubling pall over my mother's already dramatic and shocking suicide. Fred, last name unknown. I couldn't begin to fathom what a letter between them might signify. But it meant something. Worry, like a foundered craft, settled beneath the ice of my drink.

At the edge of this lightless domain lay more watery palaces. My breakup with Nathan floated near the surface, a water skipper sliding away into the murky reeds. His departure foreshadowed a more ominous event.

Robby Carville had emerged from the forgotten years. What did that man want from me after two and a half decades of silence?

It couldn't be good. I knew that.

The trouble with secrets is the secrecy required to keep

them. A sequence of cause and consequence.

The crushed blossom theme from Billy's bar rose in my thoughts and I listened within, wistful. There, that song. That was the closest to originality I had ever come, and there was no place for it in my life. What was music now, in the amplitude of time? No longer salvation but exposure. The notes of every song I had ever written, these splinters of light, dimmed.

Fred reaching out to Donna. My mother drowning herself, alone. Her secrets like stones. The breaking of hearts. They uncurl, like too cold birds and kite away.

And now, Robby Carville.

I drained the tequila and set the glass on the patio table. One of a matched set. A Christmas gift from Nathan.

I picked the glass back up and hurled it over the railing. The pitch was impressive. The tumbler arced through the air, spinning ten flights down before hitting the street. The sound of the crash was sharp, violent. Almost musical.

Shards of glass winked in the glow of the streetlight. *Shining from shook foil*, I thought, remembering the words on the old postcard I'd found in a library book. I'd looked them up. Gerard Manley Hopkins, another of the poets of desolation.

Tunneling through the night, the headlights of the Number 18 bus to Ballard swung around the corner and roared down the street.

Run, I thought. Follow that bus to wherever it's going. Escape what you can't bear or fix or see across to the other side. Drive into the night. But there was no comfort on the road for me. My life lay heaped and cracked on the asphalt, spangled alongside the glass.

I glanced down at the nearly invisible script tattooed on my inner arm. *Don't Look Back.*

It was time to let the secrets go. There was no imaginable circumstance in which Fred could change our lives now or bring Donna back from the dead. No unraveled truth might save Andi from another devastating divorce or rescue me from the bone desert songwriting had become. And if twenty-six years later I had to face Robby Carville—a ghost memory, a black and sharp and broken Giacometti—it would be to vanquish the ghost forever or myself trying.

The terrible terrifying truth could give me all it had. I was a Stone girl. And Stone girls can hold back hell. We did it all the time.

I went to bed.

Act Two

Beats

"When You're Tired of Breaking Other Hearts,"
Hank Williams

8

Nathan had done a haphazard job collecting and boxing his things. I moved efficiently about the apartment, gathering up his shampoos, his shaving lotion, nail clippers, the whitening strips for his teeth. I hunted down the gifts, including the candlesticks from his parents, and tossed everything in an open box, along with the work shoes left under the bed, and taped the box shut. I bagged his spare glasses from the living room, his UW Foster School of Business alumni mug, and the stack of back issues of *GQ* and *Sports Illustrated* and placed the bag and his Nordic skis against the wall by the door. A purple and gold UW basketball and set of free weights were the last of it.

I dusted my hands. If you say goodbye, say it like you mean it.

I tucked the line in the back of my mind. Might make a song. A Nathan song.

I glanced at the yearbook on the counter. There was no point forwarding it to Ben. I had a good idea now who had sent it. I picked the book up and marched down the hallway of the building to the trash room. I tossed it in the chute and listened with satisfaction as it banged its way sixteen floors down to the trash bin and returned to the apartment. In jeans and a Brooks and Dunn concert tee, I nursed a cup of coffee until the movers had gone. Then I called the building manager, George Delos, and informed him I would be away for a week, left my cell number for emergencies, and asked him, please, to have the locks on the apartment changed.

No more Mr. Pepperell?

No more Mr. Pepperell.

The building manager sighed.

I poured a second cup and studied the items on my list for the lake. The weekend duffel was stowed in the trunk of my car along with a sleeping bag, blank composition notebooks, my laptop, electronic gear, and a stack of blank cassettes. Last in—flat packing cartons and rolls of tape: Nathan's leftovers. They'd be useful packing up the cabin. The roadster had a full tank—air in the tires—and I had a day of provisions to tide me over once I arrived until I could make a supply run.

I touched the postcard on the fridge for good luck and locked the apartment behind me. I pulled on a warm black turtleneck sweater for the mountains and tucked my guitar in the well of the passenger seat.

Here we go, I said to the empty garage. I adjusted my sunglasses and plunked a Martina McBride CD into the dash player.

I launched into "This One's For the Girls" along with Martina and slipped the Miata into traffic. The convertible was old, but she was fine. A trucker headed the same direction blast his air horn as he passed and I waved back. I opened the throttle and headed east on the Interstate, powered on by Martina, Reba, and McGraw. One helluva country road trip.

Sweeping through Rye Grass Pass into the Columbia

Gorge, It's "Just That Way" began to play and I swiftly hit the eject button on the Alan Jackson CD. A flip of the wrist and it sailed out the open window. Who needed the world's most perfect love song at a time like this? Give me vintage Cash. The glorious, heart-wrenching Patsy Cline.

After a pit stop on the far side of the Cascades and fueled on by another can of Red Bull, I crossed the empty sage plains toward Spokane, Washington. Exits to farm towns—distant pinpoints on the horizon—fell away as wind pressed the dried grasses into rolls of gold. Red-tail hawks, Buteo Jamaicensis, the common chicken hawk as Grandpa Kurt called them, sprang from their perches atop fence posts as I passed, rising into the blue.

I mulled the songwriting ahead of me and the theme of Andi's new album, *Baby Look Away*. What would country be, if not born of the need for, yearning for, grief over, soul-consuming fire of love? As for love's dance partners, loneliness and heartache, Andi had nixed that.

Were we four, five, when Donna began to take notice of the songs Andi and I sang in the back seat of the car?

What's that you're singing, girls? Donna asked, listening in on the silly rhymes I made up and taught Andi to sing as we drove back from the market, or the mountains, or home from the cold sand of the Oregon beach. That something new?

There must have been some charm in our off-kilter harmonies, or in the way we sang along with the radio. Something that led Donna to imagine a future bigger than any we knew. Donna Stone, daughter of a wheat farmer running a half a hundred Angus on the side, began to craft a musical duo out of her fatherless twins.

We fell into music as a sparrow finds a song, if you'll pardon the cliché. But from the beginning I hated the stage lights, the faces staring at me from the dark beyond the spotlights. The way my voice sounded as though I were singing in my own ear. My knees knocked together hard under the stiff skirts even as Andi beamed her big smile, her gold curls piled high above her tiny tiara—ready to race into those same hot and fiery lights.

It's just stage fright, baby, Donna said and pinched my cheeks for color as she pushed me forward.

Our mother was imagining a bigger universe, uncloseting a universe only she could see. Her search for handcrafted material for costumes led her to farmers' markets, and to an interest in organic farming. Between our vocal competitions and talent gigs, she worked the fields of a lavender and bee farm in Longview, compounding honey balms and lotions. In southern Idaho Donna learned to grow hemp. She hand-cut and dried the stalks herself, twisting the strands into macramé designs and adding unique and decorative beadwork. She sold her craftwork at the coffee shop near the university.

You knot like this, girls, she said, laying lengths of twine on the kitchen table. This is your base knot. See? A Larks Head. Isn't that a beautiful name for a knot? She guided our small hands through the shape of the knot as we wrapped the string around a metal ring. And this one, a square knot...here an alternating square. And this, a spiral.

In my mother's hands the twists formed shapes, intricate worlds we knew were not just pretty but strong.

Hand-sewing our kid costumes, choreographing vocal skits, teaching strangers the beauty of knots and to think with patience, each of these things led Donna Stone to find her own voice—a voice perfect for radio. The Donna Stone Show, a radio show on backyard farming and homestead crafts. And thanks to Uncle Ben, working at the time in Venice, California, in the back office of The Lawrence Welk Show, a shot at a television pilot. The pilot failed, but "stoned Donna Stone" jokes became the wisecrack of the late talk shows.

Radio syndication meant hard dates and yearly contracts, and for Andi and me, official sixth grade enrollment in a brick and mortar middle school.

But we don't want to, we chorused, standing in front of the pink middle school a block from our new house.

We might have missed chunks of the basics, homeschooled Donna's way, but we loved "table school" as Andi called it, and looked forward to our afternoon free reads at the local town libraries, heads cushioned on Donna's knees, books on everything from medieval knights to rocket ships at our feet. We were given the freedom to find and read whatever interested us, and it was glorious.

Don't you worry, Donna answered, the no-nonsense tone firm in her voice. She pushed us ahead of her through the double glass doors of the school. You girls need math, she said. Look at me. Still counting on my fingers!

Before high school Donna moved us again. We left Boise for the northern Idaho panhandle, settling in Paulette, a logging town at the foot of the Selkirks. The granite ridges of the north looked nothing like the rounded burnt hills of Boise. Paulette was more pickups than citizens. More forest than street.

When we asked our mother why—we had loved the little Boise house with its tattered gingham curtains—her answer, Fresh beginnings!

We sincerely hoped the same could be said of northern men. Donna's last boyfriend took our TV and the new Buick before disappearing into the dunes of Nevada. The old Pontiac, parked out back under a canvas sheet, was rolled back into commission. Donna had it tuned. New tires.

New men. Donna's men. Reiterations of some inescapable, original pining. All the words in the little desk thesaurus listed under "absent." Away, gone, departed, disappeared. AWOL. Like our father. Lacking, not found. Andi and I had a Mystery Date game at the time. We understood a Mystery Fred. We suspected this was the nature of things between our mother and men.

Donna had let slip once that Fred was an ornithology student—or maybe that was oratory, she seemed uncertain. At any rate, a Mayflower east coaster. Blond-haired and blond-bearded, a preppy fellow of boat shoes and wrinkled long-sleeved Oxfords rolled at the cuffs. The one picture she produced showed a rumpled college kid with gentle eyes, a J. Crew Jesus. Just a boy.

Andi and I understood we were somehow the product of an outdoor Grateful Dead concert and the rather potent dope Fred pulled out of his pocket during the final set. Kickass Alaskan Gold, he'd whispered, rolling a doobie.

My girls, Donna said, drawing us close in a hug. You never know when a big enough why brings you a big enough how, she said. I needed you in my life. And Fred…Well, here you are.

Fred never knew he'd left behind more than a dime baggie of weed.

This was her gift, our mother. A tristful whimsy. A startling idea embroidered to a common loss.

And that is what I know about love. Donna fell for a boy when she was eighteen and never fell for another in the years that followed. Men came but they didn't stay. Donna never asked them to. Somehow from this vocabulary of absence my sister grew up to ask every wrong man home, and then left them or they left her. I was the one to roost, nonetheless truant to love. My sister grew up to sing about heartbreak and moving on, and I wrote the music for her to sing.

I let the white noise of the road carry my thoughts for a while. After another hour, I pulled into a rest stop, used the facilities, and walked around the sparse bit of green to stretch my back.

I climbed back behind the wheel and cued Sugarland on the car stereo. Jennifer Nettles—a gravelly voice that reminded me of the tobacco and vanilla tones of a young Bonnie Raitt.

What I wouldn't give for a voice like that. While not a terrible alto, I was mostly—as Mrs. Trindle, the high school music teacher, put it—a Foghorn for the Almighty. Andi, a confident soprano, starred in the school musical, I played first chair euphonium. Yes, there was, and is, such a thing. There was a second euphonium, Johnny Marks, but Johnny drifted to the wrestling team and left me to go it alone on the oompah-oompah of the Paulette fight song.

Mrs. Trindle felt Baker's Dozen might better utilize my "capacity to project," and the small group size steady my nerves. And so I auditioned for the high school performance a cappella ensemble led by the handsome Mr. Carville, the spitting image of a young Mickey Dolenz of The Monkees.

Marley, Mr. Carville said. Stay after practice, if you would. Let's work on that harmony. You're coming in late on the refrain.

After correcting the timing on the refrain, there was work to be done on a new solo. And learning the fundamentals of music theory—I was not going to be allowed to wing it for life. We began preparations for the year-end state competition.

Marley, I'd like you to set key tone, Mr. Carville said after winter break. You're ready to be pitch.

Choir pitch was an honor awarded to the group member with the most perfect mastery of pitch; the person who would set the key tone before each song. I blushed, flattered Mr. Carville thought me good enough for the job. Maybe I wasn't destined to be the worst of the singing Stone girls after all.

Me? I said. I remember how stunned I felt. How special.

Yes, you, Mr. Carville said. He brushed his dark hair out of his eyes and smiled, amused by my gasp of gratitude. But it means extra work, he warned. Especially on the competition songs. You should plan on coming in early the days you can't stay late. I can drop you off at home afternoons—if your mother is concerned about you walking home after dark.

I nodded. It was January and dark by midafternoon. Andi studied voice after school every Tuesday and Thursday with a professional tutor, an elderly professor at the state college, and Donna drove her into the city and sat in the waiting room the entire two hours Andi worked scales and exercises, knotting and beading endless macramé plant hangers. Donna would be grateful to Mr. Carville for seeing me home safely, and I was relieved not to have to walk home in the cold.

Baker's Dozen took state honors my junior year. The group disbanded when Robby Carville abruptly left Paulette before the end of the school year, rumored to have left secondary teaching to take a community college post somewhere in Utah.

Everything I needed to know about music I learned from Robby Carville. My eyes watered and I blinked angrily and refocused on the road. The hell with Carville, I thought. The hell with everything to do with the man.

Not long after the choir disbanded Donna presented me with an acoustic guitar. A simple Takamine with a maple face, a slender neck, frets of dark ebony, and a handsome rosewood keyhole design.

My first guitar and the guitar beside me now.

Donna held the instrument out to me, her eyes bright with emotion.

You have a way with words, sugar, she said. How about you make up songs for Andi to sing? You always did in the car, remember back when you were little? She leaned in. Don't look back, she whispered. Forward, Marley. Always forward.

Singing, being a twin, having a mother on the radio— a mother who raided our closet, wore our jeans, and had more boyfriends than either Andi or me—these were things remembered from Paulette.

∽✵∾

What'll you have, ma'am?

Ma'am. Gone were the days of a cheeky "miss" and I missed them.

I glanced up from the laminated diner menu. A lanky, acne-faced kid wearing an MSU sweatshirt stood in front of my booth, holding a pencil and pad and looking at me expectantly. I'd taken one of a slew of roadside exits, identical to the others I'd passed. It led to a tiny main street flanked by a pair of gleaming metal grain silos, tracks for the railroad, an equipment repair shop, a white steeple church, and a cafe.

I glanced at the university logo, tilting my thumb at his chest.

Bozeman? I asked.

He looked down at the blue and gold basketball logo on his sweatshirt.

Yep, he said, slightly embarrassed.

Big Sky Conference, I said.

He grinned. Right.

So, what year are you?

Junior. I'm taking a semester off to save up the money to finish, he said. He gestured to take in the half empty restaurant.

I nodded. It had to be rough, I thought, being from the middle of the middle in a state like Washington, where the population aligned to the east and western borders. The middle of the state was largely scrubland, high desert. Tilled and irrigated when possible, cattle where it was not. Richer wheat lands lay east, the milled forests behind me and to the north. Our grandparents had lived south outside a small town just like this one.

Good school, I said.

Yes, ma'am, the kid nodded. He fiddled with his pencil and cleared his throat. Grilled cheese and chicken noodle soup are the specials today.

I'll take that, I said.

The Blue and Gold. Montana State University, the Bobcats. One entire state and three substantial mountain passes from my own small town of Paulette. I smiled at the memory of my acceptance letter, the way Donna and Andi grabbed my hands and the three of us danced around the table in excitement. There was a good school of music at MSU and I was going to be in it.

Baby's gonna be a songwriter! Donna whooped. Did ya know there's a Songwriters Hall of Fame?

I majored in music at MSU, finding my way to composition, and surprised everyone my senior year— none more than myself—by winning the Jerome Kepler Original Song Award, which came with a two-thousand-dollar prize. Along with earnings from part-time work at the Bozeman Nickel Ads writing radio jingles, I now possessed a veritable fortune—enough money to last a good nine months after graduation.

The waiter returned with my meal and set it before me, refilling my coffee cup.

What's your major? I asked. I was curious, despite guessing he would say Ag, or maybe large animal vet.

Theater, he admitted. His gaze slid away. His posture unconsciously stiffened.

I said nothing for a moment. I knew exactly what comment or put-down the young man anticipated, having suffered much the same fate as a music major. The well-meaning lecture from strangers on the pointlessness of the arts. The skeptical questions. How would he earn a living? Who did he think he was anyway, Brad Pitt?

Acting or stagecraft, I asked, taking a sip of coffee.

Stage, he said, releasing an audible sigh. I really like set design. His eyes brightened. They were a dark brown, I noticed, the color of good earth, and lighter than his black hair. But, he said, and here he shrugged, I guess it's not practical.

It never is, I agreed.

He looked at me, puzzled.

Doing what you love, I mean, I said, clarifying. It's never practical. You just do it. Because— I stopped myself. Who was I, giving free advice to a college kid slinging hash for tuition?

Yeah. The kid nodded. Because.

Something in the way he spoke, the doughy languid syllables, reminded me of Carter. I'd had but one boyfriend at MSU and picked Carter at the freshman mixer. Barberson Carter, a scruffy oceanography major from Yellowstone Springs. After graduation I stayed on in Bozeman and moved in with Carter, who then continued on in grad school. The recruiters at university career fairs advised me my music degree made me essentially unemployable, but Carter said he didn't care. He said he was okay with me on our secondhand futon, guitar in hand, trying new lyrics on the spotted cat, Lucy.

On completion of his master's I followed Carter on to

Alaska. He became part of the marine sciences department at the university in Anchorage, and I found temp work, again at an ad agency. It was well-paid, easy work. Creating jingles for things like disposable tissues and baby cereal. I worked on my own music on the side. I felt lucky. Andi had moved straight to Nashville after high school—Donna along with her, as sidekick and chaperone. Five years into the music business and my sister still struggled to make a living.

For a time, it was a great life. But Carter was often at sea on the university's research vessel and an unfortunate string of late-night callers finally pushed him to kick me out. Seven years. It took me seven years to understand how lousy I was at commitment. I liked the shape of commitment but somehow missed the essential construct.

The kid returned and laid a slip of paper on the table. Here's your bill, ma'am.

I picked it up and fished my credit card from my wallet. I put the card down on the bill and turned my attention to the last of the soup, thick with homemade noodles and chunks of vegetable and chicken.

I thought about the years that followed with Andi and Donna in Nashville, writing songs, playing backup, and doing whatever I could for Andi in her quest to break into the business. I stayed single and was okay with it. But then Andi eloped with Menlo, her band guitarist, and Donna, not a happy third, returned to Paulette. I threw a dart at the map and moved west, to Seattle.

I met Nathan at a wine tasting during the Christmas holidays. Professional, well groomed, courteous—Nathan Pepperell was a fresh change from the Pike Place "bar cowboys" I normally borrowed and returned in the morning. I liked his cool confidence, his big dreams for success, his easy way of making—and spending—jaw-dropping amounts of money. How sexy and sharp he looked in his bespoke suits and ties. I was in my mid-thirties, and again, game for love.

Separation without closure. Donna and Fred. Carter and me, and now Nathan.

You want a to-go cup? The waiter glanced at my half-full coffee before he picked up the bill and my card.

I shook my head no.

He glanced at the face of the credit card. Marley Stone? He read the name out loud. Your last name's the same as my favorite singer.

And who might that be? I asked, smiling.

Andi Stone! he said and grinned. She's hot! And a voice to beat all.

He colored and I coughed into my hand. I'm fond of her myself, I agreed.

You got a favorite song? he asked. I sure do. Has to be—

No, don't tell me. I held up a hand. Let me guess…

"Bayou Baby"! he burst out before I could say another word. Wow, I mean that song. Totally into it. You too?

I signed my name to the charge slip. Something like that, I said.

I owed the kid an apology for destroying his budding teenage taste in music. But I didn't get to pick which songs became hits. "Bayou Baby" was the worst stinker of the lot but I owed everything to Andi singing it. I'd even become known after a fashion, because of her. People who knew music knew who wrote the songs—that is, the ones that mattered.

You take care, ma'am, the waiter said.

He picked up the signed tab, about to place it in his order pad. He froze, blown away. Who leaves a hundred-dollar tip on a fifteen-dollar special of grilled cheese and lukewarm soup? He glanced over, clearly wondering if the card was stolen or going to bounce.

I'm good for it, I said with a hint of humor. I glanced at my watch. It would be dark soon. I put my card away and grabbed my jacket off the seat beside me. Stick that bit of pocket change in the back-to-school fund, I said. And personally? I'd love to see a fresh staging of Death of a Salesman. Awfully tired of those sofa sets from the late forties, aren't you?

He raised his order pad in a jaunty salute. You got it, he said with a grin.

Go Bobcats, I said.

I started the car and returned to the Interstate. The open range lay in shadow, smudged in muted grays and purples.

I accelerated and passed a line of trucks as I pushed forward, thinking about the cabin.

Donna kept the cabin key in a hollow log off the front steps. I would have to undo the front lock by flashlight.

Dapplewood. A ramshackle cabin more than seventy years old set on a small clearing by the lakeshore. Ours for the last thirty. A hunting shack, the two-bedroom bungalow had a massive central stone fireplace, and a covered porch that faced the lake. The trusses sagged in the middle, the tin roof matted with pine needles downed by the storms. On the porch stood a pair of benches hewn of one split log, aged and gray, and matching chairs. Under the eaves, iron hooks nailed into the wood held fishing poles and wet towels. The trappers before us had added an outbuilding in the clearing for stacked firewood, and inside the shed, hooks and cross beams held typical winter storage: an aluminum rowboat, two fiberglass canoes, and piles of life preservers –circa 1973.

Dapplewood, the last place Donna had been alive. And I would be entirely alone with her things. Her books and photos, the almanacs, the worn hand-pieced quilts. I'd have to sort it all, even the boat and canoes.

What we keep and what we do not.

Deep exhaustion swept over me and I let up on the accelerator. I would layover in Coeur d'Alene. Tomorrow was time enough to head north through the mountains to Lost Prince.

Beat and pause.

What came to mind then but the famous refrain of "Lucille," written in the late seventies by Hal Bynum and Roger Bowling, and a radio hit for the bourbon-voiced Kenny Rogers.

I could hear the crackle of the car radio still, the plaintive ballad breaking up in the canyons as the Pontiac thundered through the night.

These, the things we keep.

9

What'll you have, miss?

I glanced up at the middle-aged waitress with the pencil stuck through her ponytail. Eggs, scrambled, I said. And a side of pancakes.

The small diner on Sherman Avenue was a block from the mom-and-pop motel where I'd stayed the night, the modest motel lost in the shadow of a towering resort complex sprawled along the northernmost bay of Lake Coeur d'Alene.

Nice day, huh? The waitress smiled, revealing a gap where a tooth used to be.

It is, I agreed. It would be that much better if "Bayou Baby" weren't crooning over the cafe sound system, the darling moneymaker.

I flipped my laptop open beside me, hoping to catch up on email.

I'll be right back with your breakfast, honey, the waitress said, turning away.

I sipped the coffee the waitress set at my elbow and scrolled through a few industry alerts and promotions, read a rambling email from Andi expressing her faith in the upcoming November studio session, and scanned a PDF from Ben with the month's financials.

What's this, I said aloud. A note from Nathan. *Thanks for remembering the skis*, yadda yadda…*See you around, you could have kept the other stuff, rather you did*…Here he was again, ever the adult in the relationship. I hit Delete.

I noticed an email at the bottom of the inbox with the subject line, Paulette 25th Reunion. I frowned, remembering a flurry of emails forwarded from Andi earlier in the year. The school reunion committee was attempting to lure their most famous graduate to attend, despite Andi's touring schedule.

Bored, I clicked the email open.

Hello Marley. It's Robby Carville.

I froze. I slammed the laptop shut.

Here you are, hon—scramble and 'cakes, said the waitress. She slid a heaped plate before me and reached into her apron pocket to plunk down a squeeze bottle of maple syrup. She returned a second later to refill my coffee. She glanced at me, curious. Everything all right? she asked.

I couldn't breathe. I pulled a twenty-dollar bill out of my pocket and tucked it under the plate. Sorry, I said. I have to go. Keep the change.

I couldn't get out of there fast enough. I jaywalked Main Street and cut behind the motel to my car. Fumbling with the key, I slipped inside. Robby Carville had found me.

Hands shaking, I opened the laptop on the seat beside me and re-read the entire message.

Hello Marley,

It's Robby Carville. Paulette High School? Baker's Dozen and all that?

*I've been looking for you. Your record studio sent me
to your band manager, who I must say, left me hanging.
But I found this email through your music publisher. I
assume it's still good. Anyway. Hope you'll be at the
reunion. Been a long time.*
    RC

Fear, an iron band, tightened hard against each rib. My
heart bloomed in my chest, and I felt it pound, each beat
slow, slowing, booming inside like battle cannon.

I leaned over and hit Delete and exhaled as Carville's
email pixelated off the screen. I stared out at the parking
lot, seeing nothing.

I needed time. Time to think. I rested my forehead on
the steering wheel. Where would Carville take this if I
failed to reply? He could not know I was on my way to
Lost Prince. Ben would never give that information out.

The email was a shot in the dark. It had to be.

Straightening my shoulders, I started the car and
followed the road out of town to the highway. I drove
nonstop, and reached the Lost Prince Lake turnoff around
noon. A mile past the marina I turned the car onto the
gravel road of Dunscott Bay and ten minutes later drove
up a private drive. I parked in front of the cabin, sitting
there for several moments, absorbing the familiarity, the
solitude. The rush of safety.

I got out of the car and slowly walked up the plank
steps to the weathered cabin, pine needles crushing under
my boots. The quiet, and the implacable silence of
abandonment.

I found the key and jiggled the lock, nervously
whistling Kip Moore's "Faith When I Fall." When the
lock gave, I used my shoulder to shove the door open. I
flipped the light switch. The ceiling fixture in the center
of the room popped and flickered on, full of dead moths.

Everything was exactly as I remembered. The lake fishing map on the wall, the board games and paperbacks slumped on the shelves, the plaid couch and side chairs marred with burns and patches of melted marshmallow—even the braided rug, embedded with years of sand.

I glanced at the firewood bin on the slate hearth. Empty. No one had restocked the iron bucket with wood splits or kindling. Donna's longstanding rule echoed in my head: Fill the bin before you leave so dry firewood will be ready to warm the cabin.

Donna had been last out.

Covering my mouth, I bolted back outside, clinging for support to the car door. I couldn't do it. I just couldn't.

I shut the car door and leaned against the hood, aware of the wind creaking in the trees. I couldn't go back in. I couldn't go home.

The past, that nimbus of all worlds that have been, had found me. I was without options. I was here because I had to be.

A pinecone fell from the trees and clattered down the cabin roof, thudding to the ground. Squirrel chatter immediately pierced the still woods, scolding and alarmed. I straightened and stood, remembering Grandpa Kurt's practical advice. If you can't get into it, get out of it. If you can't get out of it, then get the hell into it.

So be it.

I opened the sliding door to shed and gathered an armful of loose kindling and carried it into the cabin, and then returned to the car for my duffle. As I passed under the beam separating the living room from the porch, a bit of straw, or string, snagged my hair and I stopped, peering up. In the trapper's snowshoes crisscrossed above the doorway mantle sheltered a tiny mouse nest—a gathering of feather and string and dry moss packed into the loop of a leather strap. I pulled back, batting wildly at my hair until I was certain no actual mouse had landed on my head. Unnerved, I shoved the curtains open to let in light.

The cabin had two bedrooms. Inside the larger room, Donna's room, a crazy quilt of calico blues, reds, and purples covered a full-size bed. In the other room, smaller quilts of embroidered stars and moons lay folded neatly on the twins Andi and I had slept in. Our room faced the wooded clearing, Donna's had windows on the lake.

I set the duffle in the doorway of Donna's room. Every horizontal surface was layered in yellow velvety pine pollen. Spider webs clotted the corners of the ceiling and there were dead flies flipped on their backs, legs stiff in the air like little expired warships lining the sills. Out the window at the edge of the porch I could see a broken pine limb snagged on the overhang.

I heard echoes of laughter and singing. Dusk falling blue through the forest as Donna yelled for us to come up from the lake. Supper's on, she called.

Ghosts. I was hearing ghosts. She was gone and yet everywhere. Her absence and presence like the play of light. I looked at the dusty bookshelves, the coat hooks by the door, hunting for any object, any sign, or mark that might explain why Donna Stone filled her pockets with bricks and stepped off the end of the wooden dock. It was impossible, improbable at the least, to consider Fred a realistic cause. Donna had been quite calm after they spoke, Ben had said. Curious, he said. She sounded curious.

Donna had left nothing behind. No heads up, no sorry here's why. No explanation. No goodbye. No teary phone call or odd behavior. The Donna Show simply signed off the air one summer Tuesday night.

Our mother was sixty-two the day she stepped off into

deep water. Ben told us she'd recently purchased an RV—hadn't even picked it up yet—and a high yield bond. That last truly made no sense, he said. Bonds were long term, for retirement planning. She'd talked to him about the tour. Ordered three-penny nails from Sam's. Finished a bottle of good California cabernet.

Twenty-four hours after her feet hit the water the radio in the cabin continued to blare KUZZ "Nonstop Country" out of Bakersfield, California. Annoying as hell. The Melznicks down the beach hiked over and knocked hard on the cabin door. Sure looked like someone was home. The lights were on, although the curtains were drawn, and there was a car parked in the clearing. But no answer. The next morning the Melznicks placed a call to the Bonner County Sheriff to do a welfare check on the Stone cabin. Place seems empty, they said, yet the lights are on. Music so damn loud you can hear the car ads clear across the bay.

It was the sheriff who found her. Wade Elkins, part-time officer, bass fisherman, and former Kootenai Community College chess champ. He'd walked to the end of the dock to inspect the tethered boat and looked straight down to see a curtain of graying blonde hair floating upward among the waterweeds. A body, six feet below the surface of the lake.

The Dunscott Bay EMTs and the county medical examiner were called to the cabin. They fished Donna out and zipped her into a body bag, loaded her into the back of the ambulance. Wade Elkins wrote up his report. No evidence of violence, intrusion, or theft. No criminal investigation recommended.

Neighbors around Dunscott Bay stood gathered on the beach, talking in hushed tones. Donna had been a superb swimmer. Every morning she stroked the length of the bay and back, pale arms flashing in the dark water. The

summer folk knew to fry their breakfast eggs by the sight
of Donna gliding by their cabin docks.

The coroner ruled, Intentional Drowning. On his
report, Wade Elkins noted the weights in Donna Stone's
coat pockets: chunks of broken masonry, the pockets
pinned shut. Effective, he thought. When they found her,
she was virtually standing on the sandy bottom, her body
swaying in the undercurrent like some strange water lily,
eyes wide open, mouth parted in surprise.

Go home, people, Wade said. He turned to the medical
examiner. Anyone know how to reach the kids?

Andi was in Munich on tour, I was on Maui,
vacationing with Nathan. Ben told us the news over the
telephone. I'm terribly sorry, he said. He waited out the
stunned silence. I'll take care of things, he said. Come as
soon as you can.

He arranged for his sons to close the cabin. The two
men emptied the perishables from the refrigerator,
dragged the boat and canoes to the shed, and locked the
place up.

Not a soul had walked through the door since. Not in a
year and two months.

Nothing here but cobwebs and the stale air of absence.

I stood in front of the fireplace mantel and picked up a
framed photograph of the three of us. The Stone girls,
gathered around a sunset beach fire, waving toasted
marshmallows at the camera. I set the photograph back,
face down.

Can't get out of it, get the hell into it.

I pulled off the black sweater and dug an old
university sweatshirt out of the drawers in our room, and
tied my hair back with a rubber band.

I threw open the front and back doors, dragged the
braided rugs onto the porch and banged the dust out of
them, draping them over the railing to air. I ran the

ancient Hoover hard, far into the corners and under the beds of every room, hunting spiders. Wildlife belonged in the wild. I wished them all—every last creepy-legged one of them—sucked, sealed, and bussed straight to their new lives anywhere but here.

Working through the cabin, I swiped a dust cloth over every surface, dug out clean linens, and made up the big bed for the night. I would sleep in the room with the view of the lake. I smoothed out the quilt and stopped. On the bedside table, Donna's reading glasses. The red framed pair from the drugstore.

Who was I kidding?

I crossed the hall and threw the sleeping bag on the nearest twin that had been mine.

Irritated, full of sorrow, furious, frightened. Pick a feeling. The sooner I got the cabin cleaned out, the quicker I could leave. I labored on in a bonfire of grief. I grabbed a trash bag and took it back into the room and threw the remaining contents of the linen closet on the bed—all the thinned and yellowed cottons.

No point in keeping any of this.

My arms were full of pillowcases when my cell phone rang.

You did not break up with Nathan and not tell me! Andi exploded over the phone. I just spoke with Uncle Ben, Marley! Spill all, and I mean all—and in case I forget to say so, what a jerk! Six years!

Andi, I said, my voice choked to a whisper. Oh, God. You were right. It's terrible here. I can't bear it.

Oh, sugar, she said, abruptly gentle. I was afraid it might be. A pause. Take a break...Tell me about Nathan.

I dropped the pillowcases and sat on the edge of the bed and filled my sister in on Nathan's departure, wondering if she guessed from my voice how much of everything I was feeling was not about Nathan.

So, you missed a party or two…I miss things all the time, Andi fumed. Why ever didn't you tell me this when I called? I can't believe you told Ben first!

Ben and I had kept more than one secret from Andi. We protected her. Or so we rationalized.

I didn't intend to, I said. I'm sorry. I'm such a fuckup with men. What is wrong with me?

Nonsense, Moo, Andi said. You couldn't possibly be as bad at men as I am.

Moo and Belle. The memory cheered me.

Andi laid out her rules of forgiveness: no men. No living with them, engaging to marry them, or otherwise pairing up with one. She made me pinkie-swear to avoid the entire male race. At least for the foreseeable future.

Likewise, you, I said.

We chatted a few minutes more, not talking about the album or Donna or the cabin. And I did not say a word about Robby Carville—the email had faded in importance of packing up my mother's life. I had real problems to address and Carville could not be one of them.

I was certain Andi had dismissed any interest in the reunion anyway.

Promising to check in during the week, I hung up.

I blew my nose. Renewed in determination, I bagged the remaining bedding and dragged the bags into the living room, making a stack under the window of things to junk, filling several cardboard boxes.

I brought out the ladder and pulled the broken tree limb off the eave on the back porch and swept the boards clear of debris. I banged the broom on the top step. Dust spiraled furiously into the slant of sun angling away through the trees.

Heading to the yard, I crumpled old mail, magazines,

and newspapers into the screened burn barrel at the end of the driveway and kept watch as the contents burnt quickly to ash.

The work felt, if not exactly good, at least cathartic.

I entered the kitchen then for the first time.

I stood, transfixed. A shingling of yellow sticky notes danced across the face of the refrigerator and the painted cabinets.

After the initial shock at the sheer number of them, I laughed out loud. Exactly the kind of notes we were used to. Donna's never-ending lists and reminders.

But good Lord, there were so many. Had Donna been coping with a new forgetfulness?

I would take the time to read them all later, but not now.

I opened the fridge, leaves of yellow stickies waving in the motion.

Two beers. I silently thanked Ben's boys. When all this was done, a cold beer would be my prize.

Out of habit I emptied ash from the wood burning stove in the corner of the kitchen and laid in wood for later that evening. The small black stove dried mittens and boiled water for tea beautifully. Andi had named it the Black Bomb for its squat shape and the ticking sound it made as fire heated the iron belly. As Grandpa Kurt's cuckoo clock marked the quiet hours at the farm, the Black Bomb groaned and creaked through cold lakeside nights.

At last, and completely spent, I propped back against the kitchen sink and opened a bottle of water, gazing out the front window. Long forest shadows sloped from the upper ridge down across the cabin.

Memories, like black and white film, flickered across my mind without translation. The shadows were blue. I was blue.

10

I glanced at my watch. I'd better get a move on. I needed basics, and Sam's Mart closed early in the offseason.

I grabbed my keys off the kitchen table, ruffling curls of paper as I passed. One of the yellow squares detached from a cabinet and fluttered to the floor. I reached to retrieve it, glancing at the handwriting. To my surprise, the note wasn't a to-do list or reminder as I'd assumed, but a phrase. I stuck it back on the cabinet and read a few of the others beside it. Collages of words, titles, even paired rhyming schemes.

Ah. Nashville, I thought.

The three of us had lived cramped together in the tiniest apartment, and it was impossible for me to find room to compose or the quiet I needed to concentrate. I'd frequently packed up my things and disappeared in town. An empty cafe or the park. And when I returned, I would find little notes on my bedroom mirror or dresser, or stuck to the wall, even taped to the light switch. Ideas for lyrics. Bits of imagery. Anything Donna thought would spark something creative for me.

One morning, Donna caught my wrist at the breakfast table and pushed up the loose cotton of my blouse.

What's this? she asked. This is new?

I colored. My tattoo?

She leaned down and read the script. *Don't Look Back*. What does it mean, baby?

You said it, I said shyly. It's from you.

Me?

Yes.

Sudden comprehension flit across her features. That man, she said.

She was silent for a long moment, holding my wrist between her hands. You're right, she said. What's the past anyway but things best left behind.

I love you, Mom.

Her eyes glistened. You don't say that often, she said.

Don't I? I think it all the time.

Ah, Marley. Grandpa Kurt was right about you.

Right? Right how?

He said you were tough, she said. But there's tenderness in there, too. Way down deep. There if you looked for it. She released my hand. Don't wait too long to look for it, Marley, she said. We need tender. Like rain. Rain that falls on a willing earth.

I patted the note on the cabinet one last time to ensure it was secure and the cuff of the sweatshirt slid back and I glimpsed the now faded tattoo. Perhaps it should have said, "a willing earth." It would seem I had waited too long.

Someday I would write a song about that, a song for my mother.

Crossing the main room, I passed the shelf of paperbacks and the 1983 *Farmers' Almanac*—more read in the Stone household than the Bible. I ran my thumb down the spine, thinking of Donna at the kitchen table in

Paulette, planning the garden, researching the perfect full moon to start seeds.

I heard a clanging of metal and turned to peer out the window at the clearing. A black Ford pickup had parked beside the burn barrel, and a man was lifting the spark screen, poking at the ashes with a stick.

What the hell? I thought.

I moved quickly to Donna's bedroom and swept my hand under the bed, feeling for the rifle the trappers had left behind with the cabin—an army surplus M-1, possibly from the '50s or '60s.

Donna had asked a local gun shop to show her how to clean and oil the mechanics of it, stocked up on .30 caliber cartridges, and spent the summer practicing, plunking lead at pine cones placed upright on half rounds of wood set across the yard.

Can't be too sure, she said, somewhat grimly. Best we know how to protect ourselves.

When we turned sixteen, Donna had instructed each of us in the use of the rifle. It was rather funny that Andi, who hated the loud bang and kick of the thing, was the best shot of the three of us.

When she had said protect ourselves, I had assumed she meant bears.

My hand closed around the stock of the gun and I pulled it out from under the bed, moving rapidly out the front door. I knew without checking it would be loaded.

I came down the steps—the gun, barrel down, at my side.

Hey, I shouted from the edge of the porch. What are you doing there?

The man dropped the spark grill back in place and pivoted around. A look of surprise passed across his face.

Why Marley Stone, he said. I did not expect to see you here.

Who are—

The stranger dusted off his hands. C'mon girl, pick up your jaw. You remember me. You'll break my heart if you don't.

Frank Lockford.

He dropped the stick in the dirt and approached the steps.

Frank leaned against the porch support in that easy way tall men have, hands thrust deep in the pockets of his jeans. Light eyes, square jaw. Salt-and-pepper hair. A slight cast to his features at the cheekbone and eyes, something sharp and refined smudged by age. The broken nose, Charlie Brown ears.

You aren't going to shoot me with that thing, are you? Frank asked. He nodded at the rifle. I know we broke up, but I hear time heals all wounds. He half-smiled. I hope.

I glanced down at the rifle in my hands and flushed. No I won't shoot you, I said. How the hell are you, Frank? Why on earth are you here?

Saw the smoke from your barrel, he said. He jerked his thumb backward toward the burn barrel pumping a thin trail of ashy smoke into the sky. Thought I should check, he said. No clue it was your place. Though now that I'm on your porch, things look pretty much the same as I remember.

It's been like, what? Forever?

Twenty-six years, he said, his eyes locked on my face.

Frank Lockford, I repeated, shaking my head. I tucked my hands in the front pocket of my sweatshirt. I heard you were in Salt Lake City.

Frank. My Frank. Track star, football center, Prom King. Not to mention Paulette High Mathlete four years running. Frank Lockford, my first ever boyfriend.

Frank was the only child of Maggie Lockford, a former navy nurse, who had served aboard ship in the

Pacific Fleet. She raised Frank alone, a single mother, after his Japanese father, a professor of English at a Tokyo language school, carefully and politely informed her that his family disapproved of their hasty union and nullified their civil marriage.

We had had that in common, Frank and I, our absentee fathers.

I bore the mark of my unknown family in my tawny hair; Frank in the subtle epicanthic fold at the inside corner of his eyes and his shock of jet-black hair. A remarkable thing, Frank's eyes. That startling color, a hard gemstone blue. His father's name, Kaito, his mother said, meant of the ocean and constellation. Frank did somehow seem more of the sea than the forest. But his height and jawline were all Lockford, his mother's people.

Frank had graduated the year ahead of me and the last time we saw each other was the summer before my senior year, the day he drove his pickup off to college.

I could see not much had changed but for the slight gray threaded through his dark hair and a wornness about the eyes and mouth.

Going to invite me in, or what? He kicked a pinecone off the step with the toe of his boot.

I just got here, I said. Everything's a mess. I stood back and let the cabin speak for itself.

He stepped over the threshold and surveyed the stacks of half-filled boxes and trash bags.

Whoa. He whistled. Break in?

I propped the rifle in the corner behind the door and raised my hand to my hair, picking at the cobwebs and dust.

Cleaning, I said.

Remind me not to inquire after your services.

I was on my way to Sam's, but it can wait. Get you a beer? I do have that.

I felt the crack of ice in my ear, a sling of lead, a sounding. My brain blurred somewhere between 1988 and the man standing in the doorway.

Sure. Why not, he said.

He followed me into the kitchen and stopped in his tracks. He twisted, taking in the masses of sticky notes. What in the—

Don't ask, I said.

I took the two beers left by Ben's boys out of the squat fridge and handed Frank both, along with a bottle cap opener. He uncapped one and handed it back to me, keeping the second.

Sorry about the burn barrel, I said. And the rifle, I added as an afterthought.

No problem, Frank said. Not many folk up here this late.

He tilted his head in a way that reminded me of an afternoon at The Stoplight Diner. Frank and the school quarterback, Billy Nelson, ordering root beer floats from Darla, the waitress. He'd bent his head in that same charming way, fully expecting Darla to give in and make it two real beers. Darla, a grandmother, was having none of it.

Frank bent over the toaster to peer at a sticky note. *You tossed me to my fate, the designated driver at a hot time, last date, rodeoin' tailgate*, he read aloud. He peered over his shoulder. You're kidding, right?

I smiled but said nothing, embarrassed; unwilling to defend Donna or explain. I made a mental note to axe that one, although it had a Kenny Chesney swing to it I rather liked.

You scared the crap out of me, I said.

Beg pardon. He took a swig of beer. Wasn't expecting you either.

I pulled a pair of cane chairs up to the kitchen table and shoved the packing tape and wrapping paper to one side, gesturing for Frank to join me. Take a load off, I said.

He stretched out in the chair closest to the door and unzipped his baffled down vest, exposing doubled, long-sleeved moss green Henleys—the same style shirts the moms in Paulette bought their boys at the beginning of every school year. He pushed his sleeves up and my attention was drawn to the length of his forearms and a heavily inked tattoo of an eagle breaking free and springing upward from a tangle of barbed wire. The marines? I wondered.

Heard about your mom, Frank said. Sorry.

How'd you hear, if you don't mind my asking.

The papers. Your mom was pretty well known. And her death was, well…unusual.

I nodded. There had been stories on the AP wires, in the entertainment news, and the tabloids. Every report tied back to The Donna Stone Show, and to the band, and Andi, of course. Ben shielded us from most of this.

You're okay? You and your sister? Frank asked.

Yes. Thanks, I said.

I'd run out of words. It felt as if I was standing below the surface of things. Parsed from reality in some time-bending way. And I couldn't figure out how to rise clear. Be clear.

You here for long? Frank asked.

Nope, I said. What about you? You live up here now?

I laced and unlaced my fingers, finally letting them fall in my lap. A lifetime had passed between us since the night Frank Lockford had given me my first kiss under the gnarled elm in our front yard in Paulette. I glanced at his left hand. A gold band.

Here? At the lake? he echoed. I wish. He half-smiled. No, you heard right. I live in Salt Lake. Teach high school science. He rolled his beer between his hands and then set it on the table and settled deeper in his chair. Lynette—that's my wife—we have a cabin not too far up the road from yours. At the moment I'm here alone.

I raised an eyebrow. Hard not to give that last sentence more weight than it probably deserved. Separate lives and separate wives, that old saw.

Long drive, Utah, I said.

Winterizing, he said. He held my gaze. He gestured at the living room then. Yard sale?

Selling the place, I admitted. But don't spread it around. Not yet. We're listing with an agent in Coeur d'Alene end of the week and I don't want people snooping around before then.

Sure. Got it.

It's good to see you, Frank.

Been awhile.

You and the wife have a family?

He nodded. A daughter, he said. High school junior. Runs track.

Like you, after football season, I said. Wow, a daughter. Now I feel old.

He chuckled. We are old, girl.

What've you been up to besides firing up Bunsen burners? I asked.

I stared at his tattoo. Looking for history, a roadmap on his body between destination points. It had been more than half our lives since we'd seen each other last.

Nothing fancy like you girls. Frank peeled back the edge of the label on the bottle. You recall, I left Paulette for Boise State on a ROTC scholarship, he said. Joined the marines, served in Iraq mopping up after Desert Storm. Lynette and I, we married after. Couple of years and Tallyn came along. The usual. Split-level, minivan. You went east to school, that right?

Tallyn, Lynette—the "Lyn" carried on. I got it. Cute.

I pointed to the university logo on my chest. If you consider Montana east, I said.

Frank grinned. East enough.

I rolled my eyes.

He spun the wedding band on his finger. You married? Kids?

He looked surprised when I shook my head. Beats and lyrics, I said.

Right. Probably would've read about that in *People* magazine, he said. You mean music?

Been at it more than twenty years, Frank, if you can believe it.

Twenty years. That's as long as I've been married, he remarked idly.

How'd you meet your wife? I asked, curious. Not that it's any of my business.

He shrugged. Caught shrapnel in the shoulder in Iraq. Lynette—she's a surgical nurse. Met her at the VA hospital.

He was her hero. Or was it the reverse.

Glad you made it back in one piece, I said. Well, mostly one piece. I tipped my beer at him. And here you are. A whole family, a whole life. Golly.

Frank had a wife, a daughter, had gone to war, taught school…He had the footprint of a solid adult life. What did I have? A condo. A *GQ* ex. One horrible hit song.

It's not like you and your sis are slackers, Frank said and chuckled. Every time Access Hollywood comes on, there you are. Saw you both on television at the CMA awards last year. Lynette says I ought to bug you for tickets to a concert, but I wouldn't do that.

Why not? I said. Everyone does. Just call Ben.

What in the world was wrong with my hands? I couldn't seem to figure out a good place to put them. They moved like airplane flaps off the ends of my arms, tilting up or down on every word Frank spoke as if I were testing the wind. Finally I sat on them.

Andi's not nominated at the CMAs this year though, I said. She's a presenter. She hates that. Second fiddle stuff. And one of the reasons this new album...I was babbling. I pressed my fingertips between my brows. Shut up, Marley, I thought.

Must be great, that kind of success, Frank said. He ran a hand across his chin, scratching the stubble.

Our eyes collided and I had the oddest feeling we were each judging the world to the other's advantage.

He bumped his beer against mine. Never forgot, you know.

You graduated and left.

I'd have waited.

Everybody believes that in high school.

But not you, he said quietly.

Not me, I agreed.

Frank set his beer on the table. He stood, zipping his vest. I won't keep you, he said. Really great to see you, Marley.

I rose. Here we were, dropped right back into our last conversation, on the last day of June Frank lived in Paulette. He kept talking but I heard only that day. The way we stood by the side of his pickup, the truck loaded with boxes for his college dorm room.

I'll write, I said, knowing I wouldn't.

Frank, in his track shirt and jeans, reached out for me. We don't have to break up, Mar, he said. I'll be home breaks. And you can visit me at school.

My heart squeezed in my chest. I looked down.

I'll write, I said.

I never did.

I walked Frank to the door, lost beside his six-foot frame. I wanted to grasp his arm and squeeze hard, see if the feel of the man were different than the boy I'd known. The years would all be there, wouldn't they? Embedded in the muscles of his shoulders, the ruggedness of his hands?

I followed him out onto the front steps in the late afternoon sun.

I heard there's a reunion coming up, I said. You around for that?

He shaded his eyes and shook his head. No, he said. Hadn't thought about it, honestly. But there is a party at the lodge this weekend. Just the old gang. You interested?

What, and leave all this? I waved at the mess behind me.

Might do you good, he said. Have some fun.

I made a face.

Okay then, Frank said. Water down that barrel. You need anything, I'm up the road. Look for the sign, Twin Pines.

You're not mad? I asked suddenly.

Why would you think that?

Well, the last time I saw you...

You said you'd write, Frank filled in.

And I never did, I said.

Nope, you did not, he agreed.

He jumped the two steps off the porch, crossed the length of the yard and swung up into his truck.

I survived, he called through the open window. Although when you came out with that rifle, the thought did cross my mind I might finally be out of luck.

He grinned, backed the pickup around, and headed up the gravel road, one hand stuck out the driver's window in a lazy wave.

11

Why, if it isn't Marley Stone! Bud Jenkins's voice boomed across the dockside convenience store.

He rounded from behind a stand of Little Debbie snacks, his hands full of packages of batteries, two of every size. He dumped the packages on the counter and threw both arms out, drawing me into a crushing hug.

Mr. Jenkins. How are you? I pulled back to breathe. His mustache tickled and his breath had a peppery smell.

Fine, fine, the older man beamed. He released me, taking me in. Gosh, if you Stone girls don't get prettier every year! Near pretty as your poor Momma. He colored then and his gaze swiveled sideways to the batteries on the counter and back. Been a spell, he said. What you up for?

Looking after the place, I said. Winterizing.

The Stone girls. The exchange with Bud slipped back to the days when the lake folk simply called us collectively by our last name. I'd known Bud Jenkins from the day he and his sons took over the grocery and bait shop from Sam and Alice Watts, after the couple retired to Arizona not long after Donna took possession of Dapplewood. Even now I half expected Andi to pop up behind the ice cream cooler, two nutty, chocolate-dipped drumsticks in each hand. Bud was a good soul, if a total gossip. Then again, everyone at the lake had his or her nose in everyone else's business. It was the nature of things.

I picked up a wire basket and began to hunt for the items on my list, circling away to a different aisle. Under no circumstance would I let Bud know we were selling the place. Just the mention of a cabin on the market and his hunting friends and flannel-shirt relatives would come knocking on the cabin door, ready to bargain before I'd had my first cup of coffee. An out of town buyer—that would be ideal. No history, no stories, no explanations. A quiet pocket sale that could be orchestrated through Willis Webster, the realtor I'd spoken to from Coeur d'Alene.

Bud followed me down the aisle, picking at his teeth with the edge of a matchbook. Andi with you? he asked hopefully.

Just me, I said. Toilet paper, work gloves, a couple bottles of red. Across the marina the silvery light thinned, the sun dipping below the granite ridge of the Selkirks.

That Andi. A firecracker, that one, Bud said, his eyes in their pockets of plump wrinkles inquisitive as a blackbird's. You need any work done on the cabin, call my cousin Vince—

Thanks, I said. I think we're okay.

Lucky then, he said. Big blow down here a couple weekends ago. George Baldwin, the Forest service guy? Says half-thou acres hit. Took out Harry Schultz's front pines. And wouldn't you know, blew their dock pert near quarter mile south. Vince and Schultz's boys had to tow the thing back up the lake with two fishing rigs.

Any fresh smoked salmon, Bud?

He shook his head. None left but what's in the can. He disappeared down another aisle and came back with two dusty tins of King's Bay smoked salmon and dropped them in my basket.

Thanks, I said. I hesitated. Hey, I ran into a friend from Paulette yesterday, I said, casual, as I trailed Bud back down the aisle toward the register. Name of Frank Lockford, I said. Ring a bell? Says he has a place on the bay, Twin Pines. You know it?

Lockford? Bud shook his head, then his eyes brightened. Oh, you mean the Mitchell place. That's the daughter's husband. Lynette's her name.

I nodded. Oh, the Mitchells, I said. The Mitchell place was well known. The Twin Pines sign Frank mentioned must be new. Couldn't place the cabin, I said. Around the point then.

Her folks have had that place for years, he said. He spit a sunflower shell into his hand and pocketed it. Ralph and Adele, he said. Winters got to be too much for 'em and they moved south nearer Lynette I think. Only see the family summers now. You know, he said. There was a guy in the store not long ago asking about you. Heard you had a place here and did I know it. Ha. Just like you, everybody asks ol' Bud.

I knew without asking Bud had given the stranger excellent directions. Another fan, asking after The Stone Tour. For years Donna had routinely shooed away the occasional star-struck fan who wandered up the beach.

Two cans—charge you for one, Bud said. Winter hours start end of the month, you know. Them snowmobilers more a jerky 'n' six-pack crowd.

I added a box of crackers, light bulbs, a small jar of mustard, a box of instant oatmeal, one bag of rock hard marshmallows, and a bar of chocolate.

Bud eyed the marshmallows. Only hot cocoa's gonna soften those suckers, he said. He tossed a package of flashlight batteries off the counter into my basket and two emergency cans of Sterno for the camp lantern. Best stay prepared, he advised. Got candles?

Think so, I said. Expecting another storm?

Radio's going on 'bout more wind. He tugged the corner of his mustache. Don't usually get this kind of wind in October. Brings the cold.

He rang up my purchases and handed me the grocery bag. I can send Vince anytime, you need somethin'. And lock your trash bin, he said. Black bears been tearin' through the cabins along the shore road.

Will do, I promised.

The dusky shadows had lengthened. The car's headlights picked through the pines and I kept a wary eye out for the deer. A Jeep passed heading the opposite direction and I felt comforted, knowing I wasn't the only soul on the road.

At the cabin I dropped the grocery sack on the top step and replaced the burned-out bulb in the porch light. Heeding Bud's warning, I dragged the power generator out of the shed and onto the back porch. I hefted the gas can used to power the generator. Good, full. Thank God, Donna had purchased a generator; if the power lines went down, it could take days if not weeks in these mountains to get a crew up to repair them.

I unpacked the groceries and crossing to the fireplace, lit the crumpled paper and moss layered in the grate. I blew gently on the spark, waiting for the kindling to catch. The flame took hold and firelight skipped against the cabin walls. Beyond the dock the lake had flattened to a dark gun-mental gray and I watched the last of the light sink behind the Selkirk range. I had forgotten how serene the wilderness was, how remote and still.

Restless, I began sorting more of the cabin drawers, in the back of my mind wondering if I'd find anything that might be a letter. Nothing. I boxed the books worth saving, adding in the Almanac, and then propped a ladder against the wall and gingerly lifted the ceiling hatch to the attic. I pulled the chain on the overhead bulb. Still dark. I fetched yet another new bulb, screwed it in, and this time, the attic flooded with brightness. Poking my shoulders up between the cross beams, I looked around.

More mice nests. I tied a bandanna over my nose and mouth and hauled out the loose folding chairs, sifting dust on everything below. I pulled out a stack of moth-eaten beach blankets and a box of mismatched rainbow thongs—the rubber soles pocked with embedded glass. I hand-swept the attic clean.

I surveyed the main room. Boxes of things to be shipped home stood stacked under the front window, including the hand-sewn quilts Donna had made. The basic dishware would be left in the cupboards for the new owners. It was like that with cabins. Furniture and kitchen things conveyed. As for Mystery Fred, still a mystery. My emotional first reaction to Ben's revelations seemed vastly overplayed now. Understandable but silly. There would be nothing. Not even a secret. Just a literal nothing.

Propping open the front door, I dragged the bags for the dump out two at a time across the clearing and left them at the side of the shed. I paused, struck by the silence of the deep night. Above the silhouette of the trees the black sky shimmered with stars. Resplendent and pristine and as far away as far away could be. So dark I could see the Milky Way just looking.

A thousand times I've counted stars, wondering where you are. I'm standing here—you're standing there. Somewhere under stars. I shivered and closed my eyes.

Another lyric. Another song I would not get paid for.

Back inside, doors locked for the night, I put something mellow and instrumental on my travel speaker and uncorked the bottle from Nathan's stash, a fine French Bordeaux scored off an online collectors' sale. How Nathan had gloated.

Shouldn't have left it, big guy, I said, and toasted the Bordeaux's original owner.

Cross-legged on the rug in front of the fire, I shifted the logs with the iron poker and warmed my shins by the flames. I opened my laptop and checked for emails. Just one. I glanced at the name. It took me a minute to place it.

Hey, Marley,

Bart Owens here. I'm partnered with Amelia Parleur. We're songwriters. You might have heard of us? Or not. We're based in LA, not Nashville. At any rate, I'm writing because your manager, Ben Stone, suggested we get in touch and introduce ourselves to you. He seemed to think there might be an Andi Stone Tour writing gig down the road, a new album, or something, and as you were in charge of all that, we should hang sometime. Have to say, would be absolutely thrilled—thrilled!—to write for the Stone Tour. Y'all are LEGEND.

Let us know. Happy to meet, anytime.

Sincerely,

Bart Owens

Jesus H, I swore softly. No pressure, Ben.

I shut the laptop and downed more of Nathan's good wine. It had been a long, hard-ass, surprising-as-hell day.

A familiar painted wood box of playing cards caught my eye on the shelf beneath the table lamp. I knew that red diamond box. The Chiefs. The card set had belonged to the north-country trappers. We'd loved the painted portraits of the Indian Chiefs on the back of the cards, admired the elaborate headdresses and fancy beadwork.

There was something else shoved under the card box, a spiral-bound notebook.

I scooted over and tugged the book out, realizing it was one of my teenage sketchbooks. I set it on the rug in front of me and flipped the pages open. Tucked in between the colored pencil and charcoal sketches were photographs. Discolored Polaroids mostly: Andi and me, our dog Pete, even the old station wagon, loaded for a trip.

The prints were creased and dog-eared, dates in Donna's handwriting in pencil on the back. I remembered I had been trying to recreate the photographs with charcoals on paper. I had sketched everything in those days. Lost in the peace and concentration of the process, the pale blank page. I loved the feel of the charcoal in my hand, the small silky motions, the shading that made each broad foundation line supple and suggestive of character or emotion.

I studied a sketch of the three of us, arm-in-arm on the beach. I remembered the late August day perfectly. Our legs tanned and bare, bodies wet after a swim and zipped into hooded terry sweatshirts. We clowned for the camera and I'd caught something of that silliness in my sketch. Andi, her hair in tangles to her shoulders, stuck her tongue out and kicked a foot sideways like a cartoon crow. Donna, her wet hair in a single braid that fell to her waist, laughed and smiled.

I looked at my own face, scrunched up as if I had a good joke to tell. One stroke of charcoal had captured my hand in Donna's, as I, too, hopped on one foot mimicking Andi. Just kids on the beach. Who wants ice cream?

Donna had called. Me! Me! Andi and I screamed in reply, dashing up the sand.

A rumor of belonging. A golden slant of light, close and familiar. We might in our lives have many thresholds, but this one, these sketches, held more discovery than the ordinary.

I thumbed through the drawings, remembering the moments, the soft charcoals. How irritated I felt when the side of my hand smudged the lines and made the paper blurry and black.

A photograph slipped from the sketchbook, a photograph I had not sketched.

I caught my breath. It was a group shot, taken by Donna from a sleepover at the cabin the end of junior year, the weekend of our seventeenth birthday.

Silently, I named the friends of my high school years.

Aggie Wilson, six-foot-two Paulette High volleyball star. Andi's hand gripped Aggie's braids in a mock pull. In front of Aggie and Andi, stood Mindy Hernandez and Elsa Jennings, arm-in-arm, the school's radical "girl" couple. They posed, bold in shredded shorts, heavy black boots, and matching Green Peace jerseys.

To the other side of Aggie, Tom Shultz, the pulp mill owner's son. Large and awkward, Tom had had a crush on Andi before Aggie. But then everyone had had a crush on Andi at some point. Next to Tom, in a Spock T-shirt, stood our class valedictorian, Royal Morton.

Could there be a more awkward teen in those black glasses? His brown legs and arms bent out from his T-shirt and PE short-shorts like Gumby. But Royal's dad had the best comedy album collection ever, and this we appreciated. The Firesign Theatre, Monty Python. Even Tom Lehrer—the math professor guy with the hilarious monologues. My favorite, "Poisoning Pigeons in the Park."

To the right of Royal stood Bill, and perched on his shoulder in a solo one-armed cheer lift, his girlfriend, Lorrie. The quarterback and the cheer captain. Bill and Lorrie had married after graduation, and the last I'd heard, there were five little Nelsons running around the football fields of Paulette. Last, the group's newly graduated senior, Frank. Hair slick from a swim, he stood with one arm around my waist, the two of us wrapped in striped beach towels.

Well, Frank Lockford, I said under my breath. We meet again.

The autumn of my junior year a senior boy named Frank Lockford walked up to where I was hanging by the concession stand, watching the pregame warm-ups for the state championship football game. No preamble, no hello. He smiled, uncertain but bold, and asked me out roller-skating Saturday night. Frank Lockford—football center, state track star, and drop dead gorgeous math whiz.

He must not know which twin he was speaking to, I thought.

Marley, he repeated. Saturday night?

Too flustered to answer, I pumped my head up and down like a bobble-head doll. Even now I felt the rush. Andi got the boys, not me.

That year we became Lock & Stone—a school hallway fixture. Paulette's 1988 yearbook was sprinkled with pictures of the two of us leaning against the lockers or in conversation at the water fountain; necking at the Sadie Hawkins Dance, smudging the brown ink freckles on our faces, matted straw falling out of our matched plaid shirts. That spring at the senior prom, Frank was named Prom King—the Prom Queen our school's Darryl Hannah lookalike, Sally Klemper. After their official yearbook picture was taken, Frank put his crown on my head and the cameras snapped once more. I felt like the queen of the world.

I looked at the two of us standing with our friends on the beach, remembering the terrible fight after that picture was snapped. How I'd stepped away, shaking off his arm.

Why? Why won't you let me hold you? Frank protested, his expression pained.

I crossed my arms over my chest and looked down. Frank was always drawing me in close, reaching for my hand, sneaking up behind me to pick me up by the waist. Yet now I felt nothing but a well of panic. I hated that he grabbed me, and hated that I hated it.

Just don't hold so tight, I whispered. It makes me...I can't breathe.

Frank turned and toweled off his hair. He was angry. I could tell from the way he wouldn't look at me. You're my girlfriend, he said. It kind of goes. You never minded before.

I can't, okay? I fired back, backed into a corner. I can't.

Frank stared out at the dark island across the lake as our friends set up for a bonfire. Without looking at me he said, I don't know why you don't trust me.

I do. Please, Frank. Please understand.

Frank, the boy who once said to me, I get how you're so close, you Stone girls.

I had asked, Why did you change your name, Frank? Why are you and your mom both Lockfords now?

He was quiet before answering. Your dad never knew about you, he said. Mine did.

That was how we understood each other. Frank and I were sure of what we were not. A knowledge different from discovery. So he took his name from the grandparents who raised him, who clothed and fed him until his mother could leave the military and come back from her assignments at sea. His sense of belonging rested in those who loved him.

Just as Andi and me, the Stone girls.

I hoped Frank's wife was kind.

I set the picture to the side, along with the one of Donna, Andi, and me.

I grabbed Donna's coat and knit hat off the hook and lifted the flashlight off the mantle. Pushing open the back door, I made my way down the steps and through the trees, crossing the hard sand to the boat dock.

The structure sagged, waterlogged here and there, but felt generally sturdy underfoot. The boards creaked as I picked my way to the end to where the dock formed a T with an iron ladder for swimming and twin pairs of boat ties. The structure heaved on a roll of low waves from the wake of a distant motorboat headed down lake, marked by pinpricks of red and blue light from the fore and aft night runners.

I took a breath. Drawing cold, clean air into my lungs.

I had no idea where Donna went in. But I felt her.

I'd learned to dive from this dock. Still a little afraid of the water at thirteen. Donna lined my toes up at the edge of the boards, crossed my shaking hands above my head in a V, and tipped me gently in, letting go only as I touched the water. My body felt slippery as a sunfish as my hands sliced into the cool wet. Andi and I were soon playing daredevil games off the dock. Our favorite dare—to dive into the lake weeds and swim beneath the dock from its widest side to the opposite end. I calculated the width. Thirty-five, maybe forty feet across. A daunting distance at that age.

The game had scared us. The water beneath the dock shadowy and deep. We were afraid of the muskrats that nested below deck in the floating logs, and scared of the possibility we would run out of air, that we might tangle in the fronds of the waterweeds and not be able to come up. We could die down there, Andi whispered, eyes wide. You first!

Exhilaration. Popping up to the surface on the other side. Triumphant.

We were Trout Queens. The mermaid rulers of the water world.

I tucked my hands in my pockets, balancing on the rocking motion of the dock. Where had that reckless confidence, that abundant daring gone?

12

I stood on the back porch wrapped in a quilt, rubbing my neck with one hand and drinking warmed-up coffee. I'd fallen asleep on the couch, and by dawn developed a crick in my neck, my feet numb with cold. Lake fog, a gown of ice and light, draped among the trees and furled across the surface of the lake.

I loved this place, felt its peace in my bones. Knew every corner of lake and sky. And yet, and yet. Something terrible had happened here. Donna had lost her place here in these woods, found no comfort in their embrace. Unpersuaded by the same mountains I looked at as looked back at me, their crags and canyons as familiar as the back of her own hand.

How could that be, I wondered. How could you stand under these ancient pines, guardians of the northern waters, your own belonging as complete and sincere as that of owl, young deer, the last summer moth?

Donna had drowned herself in the depths of all that I found fair and tranquil. Allowed. Witnessed. Hushed by these very waters. Her death but a ripple in the quietude of the day.

I shivered. I set down the coffee mug and squared my shoulders. Somewhere out there, somewhere in the lake fog, was a man who used to be my best friend. Also, I suspected, alone on a porch with a cup of coffee. I owed Frank an apology. Even twenty-five years too late he deserved to hear it. And if I could articulate the dark of my own heart, an explanation.

I would go by canoe.

I ate an apple for breakfast as I dressed, layering a jacket over a warm jersey. I pulled on a knit cap. The shifting weather had what Grandpa Kurt called an "itch"—a premonition even the smallest of critters could sense. How the cows filed in from the far end of the pasture and huddled against the barn before storm clouds even shadowed the valley. The way birds stilled before the winds hit. How to tell a storm was barreling down from the high deserts by the way the air smelled. The pestering of the rooster by the back door.

The summer I was fourteen I stayed alone at the farm, along with our cousins, Ben's boys. Donna was on her way to Spokane, Washington, with Andi, who was to sing in an interstate fair "Tribute to Starlit Stairway," in honor of a local television kid talent show that had ended in 1972 that Donna remembered watching as a child.

By mid-morning, the sun blistered hot in the absence of any breeze. Sweat trickled down between my shoulder blades as I picked vegetables in the garden. Grandpa Kurt hollered my name and I popped up out of the beanpoles.

Storm's coming, Marley Anne. Help Grandma with the chickens, he called.

I glanced at the sky, confused. Nothing but cloudless blue.

Get moving! he yelled.

He and Kurt and Joey jumped in the big truck to locate the calves while I scrambled to round up the chickens.

Afraid of the white rooster, Foghorn, I armed myself first with a broom and pulled my hat low to protect my face from Foghorn's spurs if he flew up and attacked. I ran, yelling and waving the broom, herding the chickens toward the backyard coop. They bumped and squawked loudly, but even Foghorn seemed to think the coop a good idea, pecking helpfully at a laggard as he strutted inside to safety.

Minutes later a great wind rushed the bluffs, raising a wall of dust as high as the windmill pump behind the barn. A cold front had arrived, driving an incoming thunderstorm of dry lightning.

More unusual than a dense fog in October, or animal paw prints dimpling the early frost, the coincidence of Frank's presence at the lake was not to be ignored.

The door to the big shed squeaked with rust as it trundled open. Inside, an aluminum canoe rested on the ground on wood rollers alongside a bigger boat on a lift used for water skiing, a fine old Chris-Craft in dire need of a new coat of varnish. A second canoe hung from ceiling hooks. I tugged the lead of the canoe on the ground and it slipped forward off the rollers easily, poking out of the shed. I stroked a hand along the gunnel, feeling the chipped green paint missing along the sides from frequent scrapes against the dock. The paddles lay tucked beneath the seats. A life jacket in the bottom next to the paddles.

I dragged the canoe across the soft dirt and down the sand path to the beach, leaving it at the edge of the water. I returned to the cabin for a thermos of coffee, and as Donna had drilled into our heads, left a note on the table as to my intended whereabouts.

Mitchell cabin by canoe, I scribbled, adding the date and time, *9am*. Not that anyone would find it, but I left the note on the table anyway.

I shoved the canoe into shallow water and it bumped lightly against the dock. I contemplated the narrow seat. Getting in was the hard part. I had no desire for a cold-water dunking and stepped in gingerly, directly into the center of the canoe as Grandpa Kurt had shown us. I let the canoe balance and then lowered onto the back seat. I reined the lead in, picked up the paddle, and pushed off.

Within minutes I was floating within a cloud of white mist. I began to stroke, keeping the bow pointed slightly left and parallel to the shoreline, the only sound on the lake that of water sliding past the sides of the canoe. The Mitchell place was north beyond the tip of Dunscott Bay. I would be fine if I kept the shore in sight. I dipped in straight and pulled the paddle down and behind me. The canoe cut forward, silent and quick. The lake steamed, the warm surface water kissed by cold mountain air, a smell of wet rock and evergreen. The shoals were not deep but I easily navigated between downed logs and boulders, glimpsing the slow-moving fish beneath. Rounding a tree stump, I surprised a pair of loons feeding along the shore.

Dunscott Bay was not expansive, more wilderness cove tucked away at the northern end of the greater lake. There were no more than twenty families along its shores. I passed a handful of boat docks, unable to identify any recognizable landmarks or cabins, but not lost, not in a geographical way. I was adventuring through strangeness, experiencing the familiar without recognition, aware of fleeting small things—the drip of water from branches, the shift in the current or in the mist around me.

I fell comfortably into a rhythm of strokes as the old canoe traveled under the pull of the blade. There was peace on the water. I had my place among things. The trees, the deep boulders, the green water frilling against the pebbled shore and out again.

I pulled the paddle up, resting it across the gunnels as the canoe drifted beneath the overhanging branches of an alder, and blew on my hands to warm them. My thoughts returned to Donna.

Was this why?

There was comfort in this peace. This tender stillness that poured from silence in the morning light. My thoughts reached back and back. Back to the day before, the moment before, the split second before. Until I found her. Found her laughing at something silly, dancing by herself in the kitchen to "Box of Rain."

Donna vanished. Her memory a wave upon the lake.

The canoe bumped against a pine tipped low over the water and the bow swung out sideways. I picked up the paddle and shoved beyond the entanglement of branches.

Ribbons of cloud surrounded me with scents of nutmeg and cinnamon bark and I remembered a wild grove nicknamed "the spice woods" along the banks of the shallow thoroughfare that linked Lost Prince to its smaller, uninhabited upper lake.

Could I have paddled that far up shore?

I pulled the paddle hard through the water. The canoe shot forward and smacked roughly into an object at the waterline.

The impact reverberated through my arms and I wobbled forward off the seat, gripping the gunnels for balance as the canoe shuddered. On my knees, I plunged the paddle straight into the water to brake the backward rebound, steadying the canoe's position.

Before me, a black semicircle at the watermark. A tire sawn in half and nailed to the side of a dock to cushion boats tied alongside.

I released my breath. Lucky for me, I'd smacked right into the tire. If I'd hit the dock I might have damaged the canoe as well as the dock itself. Half-rotted as most were, season after season in the water, one good hit might sink the corner of someone's landing.

Yo there! a voice called out. Everyone all right?

I twisted on the seat. Sorry! I called back. Smacked your dock. All good!

Footsteps echoed across the water as someone strode the length of the deck. Looming from the white mist stood Frank.

Marley? Frank reached for the bow and tugged the canoe in, steadying the craft as he brought me in alongside. He looked at me in genuine surprise. What are you doing? You can't see five feet in this!

I know, I said. Otherwise I wouldn't have hit your dock.

You know you're a mile up lake?

Absorbing Frank's puzzled expression, I realized now wasn't the time or place for a meaningful conversation. Frank didn't need me unbuttoning the past. No one did. Look, sorry I whacked your dock, I said. Give me a push and I'm off.

I raised the paddle but he held fast. I fixed my gaze on his hands as he kneeled beside the canoe. There were wood chips on his leather gloves.

You look wet and tired. It's a haul back down the bay, Marley. Let me drop you off in the truck, he said.

Just push, I said.

He studied the lake. Sure that's wise? Getting thicker out there by the minute, he said. Wind's picking up.

I'll be fine, I said.

I flipped the paddle to the opposite side of the canoe and stroked deep, not thinking of Frank. The craft shot forward, ripped from his hands, and he fell backward on his heels with a shout of surprise. I raised from the seat in alarm and the canoe collided with a corner of the dock in a sickening metallic crunch. I flung out my arms instinctively for balance, sending the paddle flying, my hands grabbing air. The canoe rocked hard and flipped.

Cold water closed over my head.

Marley! I heard Frank shout my name. My shoulder bounced gently against the sandy bottom.

A strong hand plunged through the water and grabbed me by the wrist, pulling upward as another hand collared me by the jacket as Frank hauled me out and over the edge of the dock in one heave. He held on as I crouched on the wet planks, coughing up lake water. Then he turned his attention to the canoe listing on its side and filling with water. It had begun to sink.

Sit! Stay! he snapped as I struggled to my feet. I'll get your canoe, he said.

I did sit, pulling wet hair out of my mouth. A shoe was missing, my clothes sodden and puddling under my bottom.

I wrung out my knit cap as Frank used a boat hook to draw the canoe closer. He dragged it on the dock, flipped it upside down to drain, and lashed it to the boat ties.

He pulled me to my feet.

Inside and out of those clothes, he ordered. You'll get hypothermia at this temperature. That water can't be more than fifty degrees.

The man taught science, and yes, it was cold. I untangled my jacket and lake water poured from the pockets onto my socks.

Okay, I said, unable to mask the chatter of my teeth.

Can you walk on one shoe?

He looped an arm behind my back and under my armpit, and I hobbled off the dock beside him. We headed toward a log house set back in the trees.

cscs

I came out of the bathroom wearing loose gray sweat bottoms, stamped BSU, and an enormous hooded sweatshirt frayed at the cuffs. The sweatpants were short and wide at the hip and I guessed they belonged to Frank's wife. But the hoodie was clearly his, as the arms hung a full six inches below my fingertips. I rolled up the sleeves to my elbows and made my way into the main room of the log house, a bigger and fancier version of Dapplewood.

Frank looked up from the fireplace where he crouched, kneeled on one knee, laying in splits of cedar on an already crackling fire. He glanced, amused, at my mishmash of clothes.

Sorry, he said. Best I could do.

Thank you for the use of the shower, I said. I tugged my wet hair into a ponytail and opened my hands to the warmth of the fire.

Coffee's on the stove, he said. Help yourself.

I did so and carried back two mugs of coffee, handing Frank one. He lifted a pair of logs with iron tongs and a cascade of sparks fell through the grate as he exposed the bed of coals.

Stand here, on the stone, he said.

He was right. The warmth of the slate thawed my toes and the mug of hot coffee brought life back into my fingers.

He returned from the bathroom with my wet clothes and draped everything off the hooks along the mantle used for marshmallow sticks and wet towels. Water dripped from the hem of my jeans, sizzling as it hit the flagstone, and Frank matter-of-factly unballed a wet sock, hanging it beside the jeans.

I grabbed at my underthings. I'll do that, I said.

Frank crossed to the kitchen and removed salami and cheese from the refrigerator, sliced it, pulled a box of crackers from the cupboard, and efficiently arranged everything on a plate.

You realize you're a terrible boater, he said, setting the plate on the table.

I ignored that and helped myself to a chunk of cheese, taking my first real look at Frank's cabin. I circled the room, examining the pictures and memorabilia tacked to the pine-paneled walls. Twin Pines was a log home, outfitted with the typical stuff of any lake place. A crate held flip-flops and boots by the door. There were hooks for coats, snorkel gear, and snowshoes. Cross-country skis hung on pegs, racked with their poles. I noted the water ski photos, the woven-straw carpet squares underfoot, and the outdated magazines on a coffee table fashioned from sawn logs.

Sawn anything was lake chic. That, and mounted fish.

Frank watched as I made my circuit, his expression inscrutable.

These the gang? I asked. I tilted my mug to indicate a framed photograph of Frank and a petite and curvy dark-haired woman, along with a girl of maybe nine or ten with a short pixie cut showing off her trout catch.

He nodded. That was taken seven years ago, he said. Up at Elk Pond.

He pulled out a chair and sat down. The table, large enough for eight, stood between the kitchen counter and the main room, and faced a wide picture window overlooking the lake. Above the table hung a light fixture of twisted antlers. Dense cloud obscured the lake so that only the nearest pines remained distinct and visible.

Your daughter looks like your wife, I commented. Pretty.

I returned to the fire and angled my back to its heat, cupping the coffee mug in both hands. I felt completely out of place with this mash of high school Frank and married-with-kids Frank. What had I been thinking? Dragging up the past was pointless.

I ought to get back, I said.

Canoe's in the pickup, he said. I'll run you down when your clothes dry.

I hid my surprise. Grown Frank was far more efficient than the high school boy I remembered. In those days, life was one litany of missing running shoes, lost jerseys, and misplaced schoolbooks. The frantic phone call the evening before class. Marley! Have you seen my chem book? You have the notes for the exam? Once I'd found his track cleats in the back of my locker, although neither of us had a clue how they'd got there. Maybe the coach had dropped them off.

I relaxed. There was no power in such memories. That Frank had pulled me out of the water and not left me there to drown was proof of that.

He pushed the plate across the table, and glanced at his watch. Eat something, he said. It's past noon.

I took a seat opposite him at the table. Look, I'm sorry about hitting your dock, I said. I was an idiot down there.

He tipped back his chair and reached behind to pull a bottle from the wine rack built into the lower half of the kitchen counter. He added glasses, half pint jars in the Italian style, opened the wine and placed the bottle between us.

Hope you like northern Italian, he said. He poured a glass and handed it to me. It's five o'clock somewhere, he said and grinned.

Thank you, I said. I bit into a cracker and brushed the crumbs off my chin. Honestly, I am sorry, Frank.

He got up from the table. He'd shucked the vest and plaid jacket, and besides jeans and trail boots, wore the same moss-green shirt of the day before. He pushed his sleeves up and bent to rake the coals. There it was, the eagle tattoo. And a large complicated watch—one of those professional pieces with dive meters and a chronograph. I studied Frank's face in profile. A thin scar sloped from the outer corner of his right eye to the base of his cheekbone. That was new. Iraq?

He caught me staring. It's okay, Marley, he said, smiling faintly. What were you up here for anyway?

To see you, I blurted. I can't get over running into you like that. I mean, isn't it weird?

Slipknot in the universe, he said.

At my look of puzzlement, he explained. Lynette says a slipknot is when something serendipitous happens that maybe should have happened all along, but didn't, then finally it does.

Slipknot or not, I said, this whole thing's got me to thinking. I'm not much for speeches, but I'd like to say something to you I should have said years ago.

I met his eyes, their dappled lights and darks in the firelight like the lake in shadows.

I'm sorry, Frank. Really sorry for how badly I acted at graduation. You deserved better.

Water under the bridge, he said and waved his hand. He closed the fire screen and came back to the table. We were young.

I'd like to tell you why, I said. Are you free later? Can I make you dinner?

He propped his feet on the chair opposite him and refilled his wine glass.

Speaking of your place…Why isn't someone up here helping you?

Andi's got the CMAs next month, I said. Always lots to prepare. Music, dresses…

I took another sip of wine and glanced at the bottle label. A Barolo—a Brunello in fact. Nathan had raved about Nebbiolo grapes, but the Frank I'd known preferred

Dr. Pepper. Or a Bud in a tall-neck bottle left by one of Donna's boyfriends and filched from our fridge. Again, the many changes. Had I changed as much?

He pressed. Nobody can help? No boyfriend? Ex-husband?

No, I said.

He cocked his head, assessing me with an expression I couldn't quite read. You seem sad, he said. If you ask me.

Well, I didn't.

Sorry, he said.

Lots of sorrys, I thought. We were a duet of sorrys.

I broke up with someone last Friday, I said. It's kind of raw, so—

Not good?

We were together six years. It just never…worked.

He accepted this. Can I ask—were there signs? They say there are.

I thought about this. Were there signs? Would we know them if we saw them?

Maybe, I admitted, not that I was going to confess my bar cowboys or the tour stagehands. Not to Frank. Nathan and I weren't in love, I said. We just, I don't know, got too comfortable with each other. I downed my glass of Brunello. Lucky me. I don't get brokenhearted, I said. I gave Frank my best tough chick grin.

He snorted. Everybody gets a broken heart. Even the Tin Man.

Somebody's got to stay above the fray. Be the designated thinker, I said. I thought about that and laughed. That would make a great country title, I said.

Just that right touch of melancholy and wit, I thought.

I giggled then and hummed a riff of experimental notes. Like this, I said. *I've been living in the dark, blind in the heart. Now nothing could be clearer. You're gone*

*and won't you come back. Oh, babe, I'm your designated
thinker.*

You just came up with that? Frank asked. Right here?
His eyes crinkled.

I felt Frank watching me, his expression thoughtful as
he refilled our glasses. I glanced at the bottle. Nearly
empty. Unaccountably awkward, I got up and checked on
the drying clothes.

The jeans were stiff and nowhere near dry but I
collected them and my shirt anyway. The jacket was not
going to dry before tomorrow. I crushed the bundle in my
arms and faced Frank.

I really should go, I said.

That jacket can't be warm enough to wear. Half an
hour more, he said.

I hesitated. A few minutes, I agreed. I flopped back
down at the table and looked at him curiously. You like
being a dad?

Live for it, he said. Having a family helped me refocus
after combat. Lynette had to put up with a lot from me in
those first years, he admitted slowly. T's my little bud,
although not so little anymore at sixteen I guess.

You said she's a nurse? Lynette, I mean.

Yes, he said. I dropped in at the VA hospital to see a
buddy and she was the floor nurse. So pretty, gentle-like.
She was still there when I came off deployment six
months later for my own shoulder surgery.

Were you discharged?

I recovered, Frank said. Served out my time.

And Salt Lake City? I asked. Why did you move?

Lynette's parents are there. And her sister. After the
marines, we moved and I took a job as a high school
teacher. My folks—You know my mom remarried? Nice
guy named Phil—They're both retired and into an RV

lifestyle. Never in one place for long. We wanted Tallyn to grow up around family.

He leaned back, staring out at the lake. The mist had not lifted but thickened, pushing up through the trees to the cabin.

This matter of signs, he said, his eyes fixed out the window. Is one of them getting too comfortable? Or do you just stop seeing things, the obvious things?

How so? I asked.

Maybe I shouldn't be telling you this, he said. But as we're new old friends again, he gave me the ghost of a smile, I somehow find I have a need for a friend. He looked down into his wine glass. Last week Lynette said, and I quote, You know what you are, Frank? You're a traffic light that never changes. I'm plain tired of waiting on you. And then she asked me to leave. He glanced up, coloring slightly. Traffic light that never changes? Now that's a country song.

I straightened up. I could not have heard him right. For real? I said.

He nodded.

I let it sink in.

Frank picked up the wine bottle, working the edge of the label loose with his thumb. There's more, he said. But then he shook his head, changing his mind. No, he said. I shouldn't be dumping this on you.

I shrugged. Try me.

A month ago, he said, speaking as if every word pained him, Lynette came home from the hospital after her shift and told me she had breast cancer—serious breast cancer. She had the tests and everything without telling me. His expression darkened, crushed, a wounded mix of confusion and disbelief. He cleared his throat. She said she wants a divorce. And, primary custody of Tallyn.

My mouth fell open. What? But why? None of that makes sense, Frank. My God, I'm so sorry.

He rubbed the back of his neck. Dunno why, he said. Guess she'd rather live what days she has left without me. However long that is.

She's going to—she's not going to recover?

Not likely, according to the docs, Frank said. Barring a miracle. Don't have much faith in miracles, lately.

He left the table and wandered to the fireplace. Both elbows on the mantle, he dropped his head in his hands. I shouldn't have said anything, he muttered. He straightened then, shoving his hands in his pockets. Everything in me wants to be home, Marley, he said, shoulders stiff. To be there for Lynette—help her deal with this. To care for her and comfort my daughter. Is it wrong to want to fight for my family?

I rose and crossed to his side. I laid a hand on his arm. I'm truly sorry, Frank, I said. The offer for dinner still stands. If, if you'd like the company.

And I meant it. What I had to say could wait, had already waited more than half our lives.

He turned, his eyes full of anguish. Who does this? Who ends a marriage this way? What could I have possibly done that was so wrong?

I dropped my hand. I had no answers.

Frank turned away, withdrawing into a private chamber of himself. I could not begin to guess why his wife had abruptly spurned him. But I bet it had everything to do with Lynette, and not so much Frank. Perhaps she'd decided that if only a limited time was left to her, she would live the road not taken. However briefly.

But leave with Tallyn, too? A teenager? That seemed cruel. And not just to Frank. The young girl would by default become her mother's prime emotional support.

No child should be forced to navigate both divorce and death.

I understood now why Frank had driven the two days to the lake.

He took a deep breath. Let's get you back to your place, he said.

I leaned in and hugged him, tucking my head against his breastbone. Lock and Stone, I said, my face muffled in his shirt. I leaned back, looking up at him. Remember? Get through anything? State Champs? Gotta win Ro-sham-bo?

He smiled faintly and fished out his truck keys. Consider the duds a gift, he said.

I crossed to the fireplace to collect my one shoe, frowning.

I can fix that, Frank said. He dug a pair of clogs out of the basket and handed them to me. I slipped them on, draped my damp clothes over one arm, and waited as Frank pulled on his vest.

All set? he asked. He shut the door after us, handed me into his truck, and took his place behind the wheel.

I'd like to take you up on that offer of a meal, he said.

13

I switched on the lamp, lit a fire, and put the coffeepot on the Black Bomb, stoking the coals. I dragged two chairs to the fireplace and hung my damp things off the backs where they would dry but not scorch. I swapped Lynette's borrowed sweat bottoms for flannels of my own but stayed in Frank's sweatshirt. The cotton fabric smelled of him, the familiarity a comfort.

I checked my phone messages. One from Andi. I texted her. What's up?

CMAs! she texted back. Come. I've guest seats and Josie found dresses. The album will be done. We'll have fun! She dangled the evening of glitz before me.

Take Marco, I replied.

Ben would kill me, she responded.

You'll never guess who I ran into. Frank Lockford.

Lock? What's he doing there?

Remember Mitchell's place? Wife's family cabin. Married and a kid.

Too bad. You know, Marco has a lovely cousin named Raoul…He adores me, he'll adore you.

No, thanks, I typed. Andi's men assumed twins meant

double the pleasure, double the fun, like the old chewing gum ad. That I was a perfect copy of Andi, or as Rita Hayworth put it, They go to bed with Gilda and wake up with me.

Send songs! Andi texted. Can't sing 'em if you don't write 'em!

I flopped onto the sofa, bundling the quilt around my knees and stared into the hearth. I missed the Andrea Rose who snorted bubbles in her milk when she laughed. Who innocently thought Aunt Charlotte's Alzheimer's was called Old-timers. Grown-up Andi was about to fire my ass, and then what in the hell would I do?

I moved to the table and stared at the yellow notes in the kitchen. I pulled them all down, dug a notepad and a pencil from my backpack, and began to copy what I liked. *Like so much water under the bridge I am so over you.* Song title, "Bridge to Nowhere"?

I underlined one nearly perfect line. *Don't come in. Your bed's in the barn and your dinner's in the dog.* Good bet Donna had used that one.

Drinking a fresh cup of coffee, I surveyed the other possibilities. *So love poor, all my hope's in the drawer* might work with *Stone on a riverbed all gone dry, you skipped me a wish, then left me to cry.* I repeated the phrases under my breath, played with new linkages and sang the lines out loud. There was something coming together here, an invisible ink revealing a hidden song.

So love poor not a hope in the drawer, stone on a riverbed all gone dry.

You skipped me like a wish and left me to cry.

If you say you're gonna—try, baby, try. Knock, knock, knocking ain't goodbye.

I remembered a summer night, Donna sitting in the farm kitchen with Grandma Leila.

Weren't no singles on God's ark, Grandma Leila

declared. She glared pointedly at Donna. And, daughter, water's rising. She stacked some guy's mail in front of my mother, marked "Forward." Choose, she said, her tone testy. And for the girls' sake, choose smart.

Wouldn't real true love sweep you away, Andi? I remember whispering, stretched out in the dark on our twin beds, sweltering in the heat. Like that day in Santa Monica? Rolling in the waves? Like that?

Real true love, I fervently believed, should tumble you around. Set you down different than you were before.

I just want to be adored, Andi said with a long sigh.

Maybe it wasn't so much about choosing as finding, I thought. Finding that someone who made you feel you were body-surfing the sea.

I looked down at my penciled notes. "Wishbone of My Heart," I'd call it. Men had skipped Donna like stones across the river, wishes on a riverbed gone dry. Her song. A song for my mother from her own words.

I took the pages back to the couch, pulled the guitar out of its case, and tuned the strings.

Two hours later I put my notes away, aware I was running out of afternoon. I had three-quarters of one song chord-blocked on paper, a damn good feeling. Washing up at the sink, I poured myself the last of Nathan's wine and started a chili with the ingredients from Sam's Mart and spices and beans from home. Frank would be over at six.

Dinner simmering on the Black Bomb, I sat back down with the guitar and picked through the barebones of "Wishbone" one more time. I liked it in 6/8 meter: a rocking chair beat, the slow rhythm of the ballad. I imagined the song as a blend of honeyed harmonies, vignettes of solo instrumental among the guitar, bass, and mandolin. A throwback ballad to an earlier time, the smoky-voiced melancholy of a grown woman singing her years of heartbreak.

Andi's voice had deepened with age, acquiring a patina in the lower registers that would serve the plaintive solos perfectly. I could imagine her, slender under a single spot in a sequined midnight gown, her scarlet hair loose on her shoulders, the band in shadow behind her. She would open a cappella, joined by soft vocal and instrumental harmonies, drop back into the solo lyrics, and then rock away in lilting harmony. All slow. An easy waltz through a failed romance, like a single tear down your cheek. She'd knock it fucking out of the park.

I knew I could convince her on this one. Felt it in my bones. It was her song, straight from the heart of Donna.

I had my three, I realized, stunned. "Wishbone" could go straight to Ben and the band could begin to play with arrangements. I had a concept for "Dinner's in the Dog," and maybe as a third, "So Over You"—the line I originally pulled as "Bridge to Nowhere."

I could do it. I could really do it.

I toasted Donna in the flickering light. Maybe, just maybe, I'd keep my job after all.

A pinecone hit the tin roof and rolled off the eaves, followed by a gust of wind that pushed at the porch door until the old latch creaked. The patter of rain beat against the window.

Bud's predicted weather had arrived.

I unplugged my phone from the charger and stood near the window for better reception. Four voicemails. One from Andi, two from Nathan, and one unknown. I deleted the unknown and Nathan voicemails. No, Nathan would not be getting the espresso-maker back.

The message from Andi had garbled together, something about flying up to Nashville in Marco's

private jet for an impromptu gig at Tootsie's Orchid
Lounge.

Classic Andi, generous to the bar owners and studio
execs first willing to front her. She dropped in on
Tootsie's whenever she could, honoring the tradition of
its legendary proprietress "Tootsie" Bess, who had
welcomed new musicians for decades, years before we
were old enough for a drink or a Willie Nelson set. Andi
believed in paying it forward, and lent her fame to the
humble honky-tonks that had given many of country's
own their beginning.

She'd still be in Nashville if not for the wrecks of ill-
fated romance.

Donna had tried to save her, more than once, but had
finally returned alone to the little house in Paulette after
Andi had eloped with Menlo.

Listening to the creak in the trees, "Wishbone" swirled
back into my thoughts. *You think wishes are things that
don't come true, but, baby, when I wanted love, I wished
for you...*

I shook my head, recalling Menlo's bellbottoms, his
Devil Loves Mambo tattoo, the fluffed locks like he was
one of the Bee Gees. We had no clue what Andi saw in
the skinny Oklahoma guitarist. There was no accounting
for love—or lust that looked like love.

I put away the dried clothes from the morning,
changed into jeans and a plaid shirt, and set the table with
paper napkins and cabin plates, rinsing out the wine
glasses and setting them beside chili bowls. I dug out my
"emergency" Christmas brandy from the duffle—a gift
from Uncle Ben. This would be dessert.

I placed a candle in the center of the table and lit it.
Not much in the way of hospitality, but enough.

A knock rapped the front door. Frank.

He stood there under the solitary porch light, his hair

plastered to his head from the rain. A gust of wind flared his coat open and he held out a bottle of wine. Italian, he said.

Perfect. I grinned. We're having chili. I took his jacket and hung it on a peg by the door. Bud predicted a storm, I said. Guess it's here.

That's a definite, Frank said. Branches down all over the road. He brushed the rain out of his hair. Hey, thanks again for the invite. I'm glad of the company.

Dinner's easy, I said and laughed. At least I don't owe you a whole dock.

I dished up bowls of chili for each of us as Frank uncorked the wine and filled the glasses. He took a seat as I set a half of baguette on the table and thumped it hopefully.

No guarantees, I said.

Frank seemed to find the chili pleasing, going into the kitchen for seconds.

Today on the dock was kinda surreal, he said, soaking a chunk of bread patiently to soften it. Meant to run into each other I guess—like literally.

He grinned, the thin scar on his upper cheek disappearing in laugh-lines.

This is nice, he said. I miss this.

He stopped and a flush rose from the throat of his shirt to the rims of his ears.

I studied Frank over the rim of my wineglass. This man was my road not taken. Even the smell of him, the smell of good clean soap and pine, filled me with memories. One could drown in so many memories.

No, I get it, I said. You're lonely. I am, too. There are things to say.

Marley, I wasn't coming on to you, Frank said.

I know, I answered. I just mean we used to be friends.

I miss that too. I pointed to the fire. If you'll put more wood on, I'll get dessert, I said.

I came back carrying Ben's brandy and two juice glasses. I poured Frank a good portion of the liquor, fragrant with ripened peach, and handed him the glass before pouring my own. I gestured to the couch and sat facing him.

I promised you an explanation, I said. About graduation.

None of my business, Marley. Don't worry about it, Frank said. He settled back against the cushion. That was a lifetime ago.

I rubbed the knuckles of one hand, cold despite the fire. The interior of the cabin felt as if it had plummeted to ten degrees above nothing.

Recently, very recently like yesterday to be honest, I said, I made the decision to change some things. This might surprise you, but I've lived a life of secrets, Frank. Done stupid, often hurtful, things. I want to clear the decks—make amends—beginning with you.

He raised an eyebrow.

You were the first to knock on my door. I half-smiled. Frank, talking about that last summer is important to me.

We all have stuff, he said, swirling the brandy in his glass thoughtfully. I wouldn't be so hard on yourself.

Secrets become regrets, Frank. I don't want any more regrets. I sipped my drink, holding the fiery liqueur on my tongue, silently begging for its courage.

I don't mean Mystery Fred, I said. Or my mother's death, or even the fact there may be a letter here in the cabin Fred might have sent Donna before she died.

I paused at the startled expression on Frank's face. Yes, I said. Ben told me. And for the record, no, I haven't found it. But it's possible it had something—

I broke off and looked away.

The fire popped and spit an ember at Frank's feet but he ignored it.

I stood and leaned back against the mantle, facing Frank on the couch.

I steadied my breath.

I can count on one hand the good things in my life, and you, Frank Lockford, are one of them.

He opened his mouth to speak but I shushed him. No, I said. Hear me out. Please. You complete a part of me I never even knew was missing.

He waited.

I never expected to see you again, Frank, and now that I have, I can't imagine my life if we hadn't run into each other. I hesitated. You bring back a part of me I thought I had lost.

The innocent self, I thought. The girl that wore a cowbell and danced under stage lights plastered in glitter.

I set my glass on the mantle and stared into the fire, watching flames skip the length of a cedar split.

I refuse to do anything anymore that isn't genuine, Frank. That's what I'm trying to say.

Okay, he said slowly.

I straightened my shoulders. Here's the deal. You love Lynette, Frank. I heard it in your voice. Yes, things are a mess for you right now, and probably have been better, might even be over, as she says. But I know you—or at least, who you used to be—too damn well to let you lose faith in that love. I can be a friend…if you need one.

He shook his head. I didn't tell you about Lynette because I'm feeling goddamned sorry for myself, Marley. This is not your problem.

I'm the one that needs a friend then, I said, and shrugged. The truth is, I admire your commitment. Your courage. Things I would like to learn.

I fell silent, thinking.

Finally I said, Nathan left me, Frank, after I missed a hundred events I'd given my word I would attend—events that mattered to him. No big deal to me and easy to do, but I never made the effort.

Frank stretched his legs toward the fire, clearly curious.

Six years together, I said, and I never made one genuine from-the-heart effort. The last time I was a no show? I was in bed with a college kid I picked up in a bar. And not the first, I might add. I watched Frank's face as my words registered. I sleep around, Frank. Not because I like to cheat, but because I don't commit. My voice cracked. I don't treat good men well. Beginning with you. You deserve to know the reason why.

I'm listening, he said.

He won't believe me, I thought. It won't mean anything. He'll be glad we broke up. I'll have exposed my entire life for what? Indifference? Ridicule?

But Frank was not looking at me with either indifference or ridicule. He was waiting. Frank was looking at me without judgment, with something that felt like unconditional acceptance.

My mouth felt dry, and I instinctively cast a glance at the door.

Tell me what? he nudged gently.

I closed my eyes briefly before staring hard at the floor.

I was assaulted in high school, Frank, I said.

He set his glass on the floor.

It happened two weeks before I turned seventeen, I said. Before your graduation.

Who?

Robby Carville.

Frank half-rose from the couch. Robby Carville? he said in disbelief. The choir teacher? You're saying the choir teacher raped you? His face reflected his shock. Where? When?

At the state a cappella competition, I said. I tucked my hands tight under my armpits, unprepared for the starkness of the truth spoken aloud. Carville left the school afterward, I added, barely audible. Before the end of term.

But you never said a word, Frank protested. Not one word. Did you report it?

I didn't, I said. I shook my head. I didn't tell anyone. Just Donna. Donna knew.

What he did…That's not just wrong, it's criminal, Marley, Frank said, his voice hoarse.

I wrapped my arms tighter about my body, cold, so cold.

I was too afraid, I said.

But we—

We broke up right after, Frank.

I watched him digest this, connect the events in our young relationship that year. His expression changed. Turbulent. Severe.

That son-of-a-bitch! he exploded. He jumped to his feet and paced to the door and back, full of fury. God damned. God damned, he said. He enunciated it, said it twice.

He stopped in front of me. You kept this a secret all these years? he asked. He shook his head. His shoulders tightened as his hands unconsciously made fists.

I thought I'd done something wrong, he said. I couldn't figure out what. It drove me crazy! My God. No wonder you wouldn't let me touch you… He pressed a hand to his forehead.

Jesus, he said. I was such a shit to you.

No Frank, no you weren't, I said, close to tears. I know nothing made sense when you left for college. Why

I promised to write and never did. I'm not proud of how I handled things.

He stood still in the middle of the room, bereft. Sorrow pooled between us, deep with the taste of water drawn from an iron cup.

I remembered what a traveling preacher had said, sharing dinner with us one August night at the farm, welcomed in by my grandparents in the old way of country people and preachers. Dimensions and stages, the elder man said, touching the corners of his snowy mustache with the cloth napkin. Life is dimensions and stages.

Death is not real, he said, merely another dimension of life.

So too, the history between any two people. The book of the heart, its many inked pages falling open to one recollection or another.

Here we were. Another stage, another dimension. The same heart.

I touched his hand. I've hurt you telling you this, I said.

But finally, finally, Frank knew that day on the sandy beach I was not rejecting him but Robby Carville.

I—I don't know what to say, Frank said.

I could see the dark thoughts bombard him one after the other. He was himself a high school teacher, had a daughter the same age I had been…

He leaned down and cupped my face in his hands, like you would a stunned bird, hoping it might live. He let go, collected his coat, and walked out the door.

Act Three

Accidentals

"Not Enough Whiskey,"
Kiefer Sutherland

14

A resounding crash, the bash of metal on metal, woke me. I opened my eyes, face down in the orange and brown couch. Immediately there was another crash, this time followed by a thud, the racket coming from the clearing in front of the cabin. I rolled off the couch and jumped to my feet, running to the window.

A black bear stood on its back legs, paws locked around the trash bin. Jaws open, the bear attempted to pry off the locked lid. When the lid wouldn't yield, the animal rolled the can onto its side, smashing it against the shed like a cantaloupe.

My car stood parked a few yards from where the bear tossed the can.

I scooted to the door and pulled on my jacket and boots in the predawn gloom, the bear repeatedly thrashing the can against the shed. In the corner stood Donna's rifle. I grabbed it and ran out the door.

Go! Shoo! I yelled. Scram! I dashed across the clearing, wet sleet pelting my face. The burly shaggy-coated animal swat the can one more time with the broadside of its paws and then turned and circled on all fours to face me, baring its canines. The animal hissed, a sound somewhere between a guttural rumble and a spit.

Get out of here! Go! Scram!

My ears tingled with danger. I was nearer the bear than the cabin. Perhaps forty-five yards separated the two of us. I rest the butt of the rifle on my shoulder and pointed the barrel at the animal.

In Donna we trust, I muttered, and cocked the trigger. I couldn't hit the broadside of a barn, let alone a pawing, plunging bear.

But the bear didn't know that.

The animal trundled slowly forward, its yellow eyes fixed with what I could only think of as extreme animosity. I held my breath and stood my ground, holding the rifle steady.

Bear and elk were nothing new, I reminded myself. Every winter a bachelor moose grazed the backyards of Paulette. But this bear seemed to view me as a competitor for the trash can. A dangerous turn.

The animal reared up on its hind legs and let out a snarl, claws raking the air.

I lined the rifle sight on the trash can and pulled the trigger. My body jerked backward at the kick and pain ripped through my shoulder. The bullet clanged hard into the metal framing of the boat shed, the brass skidding at my feet. I fired again, this time hitting somewhere nearer the ground. And a third time. Again the *ping!* of metal.

I aimed one more time closer to the bear and the bullet pounded the dirt at the animal's feet. With a roar the bear scrambled backward onto its haunches and, in a mash of broken branches, plunged sideways through the pine trees.

I clung to the rifle and waited, listening until I could no longer hear sounds from the wood.

I approached the trashcan and quickly righted it, my

eyes on the trees. I tested the lock on the lid and pushed the can back against the shed, aware the bear could circle back and charge at any time.

I made my way around the perimeter of the yard, the rifle aimed in the general direction the bear had taken.

I returned to the cabin and propped the rifle in the corner, making a mental note to swap out the old magazine and load a new one.

I cast another long glance around the clearing before locking the door. Adrenalin coursed through my body. How stupid, I realized, shocked. Had I stayed inside the cabin, the bear would eventually have given up and moved on.

I crouched at the hearth, steadying my breath, and blew on last night's embers, and, within seconds, new flames kicked up. I hooked the poker on its nail off the mantle and brushed my hands on my jeans.

A wash of gold and blush spiked through the trees, filling the room with light, the lake a molten sheen of color. The light swept up the sand, gilding branches into carnelian skeletons of fire.

I took a long shower, washing away the difficult conversation of the night. Leaving the small bathroom, I crossed to the kitchen, toweling my hair, and glanced outside. The early radiance was now gone, obscured by flint-colored clouds.

Flecks of white tapped the glass. Snow.

I cranked up the baseboard heaters in the two bedrooms and double-checked the generator on the porch, the extra candles and the flashlight on the mantle. Ten to one, the power would fail.

I glanced across at the hearth. I was low on wood.

I shrugged back into Donna's jacket and zipped up. After a precautionary glance at the woods from the doorway, I jumped off the porch and held out my hand, catching snowflakes like petal blossoms. Slipping on the new work gloves from Sam's, I began to fill the wheelbarrow with kindling and split pine. I made three trips to the porch, stacking the wood two splits deep under the eaves.

Listening to the melancholy call of an owl drift through the trees, I wondered if I would hear from Frank again. It was possible I would not. I knew he'd asked his principal for two weeks' personal leave, originally intended for Lynette's doctor's appointments but instead spent here at the lake. I had no idea how much time he had left before his return to Utah.

I refilled my coffee mug from the camp pot on the potbelly stove and made a simple omelet breakfast, kept company by the snap of the fire crackling in the hearth. Despite the chaos of boxes underfoot and the hours of sorting and cleaning, life on the shores of Lost Prince had once more settled in my bones.

My thoughts drifted on the bar blossom melody as snow fell silently and aimlessly through the thin blue light.

The temperature continued to drop.

Branches scraped the roof of the cabin like nails on tin as the wind drove in hard, bending the pines in a slow synchronized dance around the perimeter of the bay. Lake chop broke in white spray over the wave-soaked boards. The dock creaked, singingly, mournfully, a landlocked buoy.

I sat down at the table and picked up the guitar. I strummed a few chords experimentally, concentrating on "Dinner's in the Dog."

I penciled out a fourth set of stanzas and reworked the refrain. The key was to deliver the lyrics like a Texas two-step, *Dinner's in the dog, dog, dog*—marry the word repetitions with a bridge to the refrain.

I thumb-picked a guitar riff, imagining a shaggy blond Keith Urban, in tee shirt and jeans, holding the duet with Andi. If we could get backup singers to bounce back the echo bars, the piece would have the throaty, rich complexity of something Patsy Cline might have sung but with the kick of early Urban. *Like a note out of tune, tune, tune, this fool's need for you. A pair of broken shoes, shoes, shoes, another something I ought to lose.*

I concentrated on the counter rhythm, shaking up the chords. What if I added a sharp twang? An accidental? And why not a funky beat as a break between stanzas—a syncopated finger tap on the soundboard? *Don't come in the house, O love, love, love of mine. Bed's in the barn, my stray Valentine. Chicken 'n' biscuits, little Mama's gravy train, ah sweet, sweet, sweet baby, you've only you to blame—dinner's in the dog.*

I stretched out "dinner" as I sang it, imaging how Andi would find the high break.

I repeated the stanza, and again the refrain.

It stood. The song had voice, rhythm, and muscle—all three legs required in the anatomy of a hit. "Dinner's in the Dog" was something a real woman might say to a man who'd let her down once too often. Another, better, "Bayou Baby"—and the younger set could dance to it.

I stretched and placed the guitar back in its case.

I crossed to the kitchen window and pressed my nose against the glass, my breath making a little circle of condensation. The snow had begun to form shallow drifts across the road.

No sign of the bear, or Frank.

I ran my mental checklist of things left to do. Lists. The enemy of free-range time, the barbed architecture, the scaffolding of a quotidian life. One day I'd write a song about lists.

My cell phone rang and I answered it on a sigh, Hello?

Everything all right there, Marley? It's Ben.

Oh, hey, Uncle Ben. Busy morning. One bear and a snowstorm, I said. But I've got some good news for you. Without mentioning the email from Bart Owens, I filled my uncle in on the progress I was making on the album.

You'll get what I have this week, I promised. I'll FedEx a package from town.

Excellent, excellent, Ben said. Heard from your sister?

Quite a few times. Why?

She's not answering my calls, Ben said. Her divorce to that tennis player is final next week and I need to go over press release details.

Soccer, Uncle Ben. Stephan is a soccer player.

Yes, yes, that's a detail right there. Can you get a message to her? Get her to call me?

Last time I heard from Andi, Ben, she was on her way to Nashville.

What? he barked in my ear. She's supposed to be keeping a low profile!

Something about singing at Tootsie's. She flew up with Marco.

Have I taught you girls nothing? Nothing? Ben scolded. I heard him gulp, he was that livid. Your press is only as good as your last tabloid headline!

I'm sure it's just good ol' boys and music, I said.

He let out a spent sigh.

Right, he said. Fun. Fun in the spotlight.

More of a dark bar, Ben. C'mon, you've been there.

You think she's okay, Marley Anne? he asked. That Marco fellow hasn't made much of an improvement in her mood from what I can tell. She's always cocktailing, no matter the hour.

I caught my breath. Ben was right. Maybe the divorce mattered more than she'd let on. So much for "twin radar."

I'll call her, I said. Oh, and that letter? No sign of it. I've been through everything.

Thought sure Donna would hang on to something like that, he said. The boys mentioned sticky notes everywhere—with strange stuff written on them, so who knows.

They did notice, I thought. Did they think Donna was crazy?

Ben cleared his throat. What a mess, he said. I waited too long to tell you about your mom and the letter.

She made you promise not to, I said.

Thing is, Marley, I regretted not saying anything way back when your mom dropped out of school. I thought it was a terrible mistake, terrible, not to let that boy know she was pregnant. To quit her education like that. When she called out of the blue and said she'd heard from the fella and what should she do…

I waited. I had never known Donna to ask for help or advice.

I let her down, Ben said finally. I had the chance to say something and I didn't. His voice wavered, indistinct. I can't help but feel her death had something to do with that letter. What if I was wrong to caution her, he said. I mean what was this guy offering? Was he married, did he have children? What did he want? Acknowledgement? Most important to my way of thinking, how would you girls feel about it? How would this affect you? He slowed his words. Charlotte told me to stay out of it, he admitted. But seemed to me you three'd done pretty darn well on your own. That's not something to toss by the wayside.

Did Donna—I hesitated.

Did Donna what? Ben asked.

Did she give you any indication what she was thinking?

No. He sounded frustrated. I don't know what she

decided and I guess I never will. Did she buy a ticket? Meet him anyway? Did she love him? Hate him? Did it even matter? Who the hell knows?

In his anguish, I heard the love he felt for Donna, for us, and the depth of his guilt.

I should have let you girls know earlier, Ben said. I see that.

Well, there's nothing any of us can do about it now.

One more thing, he added. I just remembered this. I asked her at one point if she intended to tell this man about you two and she answered, No need. He seems to already know. So. There's that.

Fred knew about us? I repeated.

Suddenly my situation was more like Frank's than a charming game board mystery. Had Fred considered our existence and rejected us?

About those demo tapes, Ben said, striving for a light note.

Soon as I can, I said, dazed.

He hung up and I stood at the window, thinking.

If Fred had known about us from the beginning, Donna was guilty of a darker betrayal in pretending otherwise. Would Fred's letter hold the answer to her suicide? And what if it did? Donna would still be dead. We might have someone to blame or a story to tell, but the facts would not change.

Family is family, Donna had said. We're the Stone girls!

I was forced to wonder. Was our threesome by choice and not chance?

I thought back to the last years we had lived together, the three of us reunited in Nashville.

Andi dropping back in yesterday on our old stomping grounds, back to the days before stardom, had to mean something. Was she searching for an answer or simply saying goodbye?

Andi had left Paulette for Nashville immediately after high school, and Donna followed. Donna rented out our house, closed the cabin, and arranged with a Nashville studio to record her radio show remotely. She became indispensable to Andi, managing her bookings and covering the lion's share of apartment expenses.

There isn't a thing worse than the music business, Donna said to me shortly after her arrival, on the rare call to Anchorage. Good thing the show's still making money in syndication or it'd be nothing but grits and sequins for meals around here. Your sister's knocked herself out cold-calling studios, singing at open mic joints, sending out demos.

She sniffed. They'd be lucky to have her if they had the sense.

Turned out the only thing worse in the music business than a newcomer was a former child star. The kid circuit was considered cute, if not downright trite.

Door after door swung shut and Andi stopped mentioning our vocal past. Depending on the age of the studio exec, she might bring up her appearance at the Grand Ol' Opry and Dollywood—the old guard had a soft spot for Miss Dolly. But the only advantage she truly possessed were her looks and her demo CD, and she knew it.

After college, after Anchorage, after Carter, I joined Donna and Andi in the tiny apartment on Merle Haggard Drive.

We were dreamers on a shoestring, Donna armed with her glue gun and box of costume bling. A splurge was pizza, served on a carton flipped over as a coffee table, and now and again, ribs from the place on Belmont when we got paid for a gig.

Donna had seemed carefree then. She wore her blonde hair in loose ripples down her back, pinned with the ridiculous flower pins she still made from brightly-colored beads scavenged from the local bead shop. She dated a bar manager down on Seventh.

She never mentioned regrets, if she had them, over her decision to backpedal the *Donna Stone Show* to a bimonthly gig, or if she missed her days back in Idaho as a celebrity sensation. Once again she was hand-sewing Andi's show costumes, happy to be backstage again around the music she loved.

What we need is one hit song, Donna mused, her hands stitching an intricate bodice of silk and velvet. One hit song, that's all it takes.

In Nashville, the Stone girls united, I set my sights writing that magic hit song. I took on shift work at the Bluebird Cafe and composed nights, plunking on a second-hand electronic lap-piano and my guitar.

I ginned sheaves of music for Andi, much of it terrible. Bright, belt-busting tunes that we hoped would catch someone's—a record producer's—roving eye.

A good day was a day recording. A rented studio with a backup band hired by the hour.

Weeknights Donna and Andi gossiped celebs in the tabloids and painted each other's toenails. Weekends were solid gigs—wherever the music was live.

It was some kind of weird. But we were happy.

One hit song, Donna said. And I delivered "Bayou Baby."

15

I was humming "Dinner's in the Dog" and rummaging around for a thick sweater in the back bedroom when I heard a knock.

Hey, I said, surprised, opening the door. You're back.

May I come in? Frank proffered a bag of groceries. Went to Sam's, he said. Stocked up double for you, too, when I saw the snow.

He removed his coat and dropped it on the peg by the door.

Thanks, I said. Since you're here, I've leftover chili on the stove. Hungry?

I'm starved, Frank admitted. Long morning. That sweater suits you, he said in passing. Unusual color.

I fingered the hem of the flecked pullover. Donna had given me this sweater.

Help yourself to coffee, I said. It's hot.

I unpacked the groceries and put things in the fridge. That color frames your lovely hair, Donna had said our last Christmas together as I held her gift against my chest, stroking the soft wool. And those Pacific Ocean eyes.

Pacific Ocean eyes? I'd wondered. The Pacific was a cold ocean. Did I have cold eyes?

As I dished Frank his chili, my thoughts turned to a family car trip south to Point Lobos, California, when we were twelve or thirteen—Donna on a mission to find the exact beach Edward Weston photographed his beloved Monterey shore. She'd told us one of her three dates with Fred, besides a Grateful Dead concert, had been to a campus art gallery displaying a traveling exhibit of Weston's black and white photographs.

South of Carmel-by-the-Sea we finally located Weston's beloved beach and wandered the edge of the ocean among the driftwood and kelp thrown high by the tides.

Andi and I collected abalone shells and broken Japanese fishing floats, hunting in the tide pools for stranded crabs. Donna sat apart on a rock outcropping, the ocean misting her in spray. To Donna Stone, the Pacific remained the ultimate untamed beauty. Fierce and unpredictable.

A few years later, Donna spent an entire month's paycheck on a 1937 Weston photograph, printed by Weston's son, Cole—the photograph a nude of Edward Weston's young lover, Charis. Weston had lived his life outside his marriage in the company of four different lovers, Charis the last, her photograph taken against the weathered panels of an old barn. Charis sat in closed pose, her face averted and tucked into the bend of one knee. In contrast to the milk-whiteness of her skin, a rough serape. Black, gray, tonal whites. An image of simplicity. And secrets.

The photograph hung in a place of honor in the foyer of our home in Paulette. Now, wrapped and crated, the Weston leaned against a wall in a temperature-controlled storage facility in West Seattle.

Pacific Ocean eyes. It had been a compliment, I realized, touching the sweater. I only now understood. Had Donna felt some kinship with Charis? Weston's muse, not his keeper. A lover, not a mate.

I stole a glance at Frank pouring coffee and my heart contracted.

He came up beside me and handed me a cup. I owe you an apology, Marley. That's why I dropped by.

For what? I asked.

For not responding better than I did last night. I apologize for bolting like that.

I shook my head. No need, I said. We're square.

His eyes, their washed silken blue, steel like the sky, searched mine. You're sure?

I am. I handed him the bowl.

He relaxed on the sofa and stretched his stockinged feet to the fire. Took your advice, he said. Called Tallyn.

I curled up at the opposite end of the couch, holding my coffee in both hands. I know nada about kids, I said. You know this, right?

You pushed me to reach out to her, he said. Glad of it, too. She was on her way to a track workout. He dug the spoon around the bowl, scraping the bottom. She said she wasn't so much mad as scared. Worried I'd bail for good. I told her I was here, at the lake. That in no way was I cutting out on anybody—especially her. He looked at me. Is this weird for you? Talking about my family like this?

Of course not, I said.

Anyway. I feel better, he said. I think T does too. He considered me. One thing bothers me from last night. Well, many things. But if what happened with Carville is squared away, as you say, why'd you live with that guy Nathan if there were always going to be these other guys?

It was a good arrangement in its way, I said. We were

into our work. He traveled, I was in studio a lot. We had an understanding.

After six years the guy didn't want to marry you? Close the deal? Maybe you're not the problem here so much as the guys, Frank said. Men who don't ask anything of you.

I gave it some thought. There had been friendships, passion. Hopeful future in-laws. But no, no offers, no proposals. I was aware I had a type—outdoorsy athletic guys—but was I myself a type? Donna, Charis…women who were lovers not wives.

No commitment meant no responsibility. I wasn't required to be vulnerable. That had never seemed as curious or worrisome to me as it did now.

Possibly, I said, my tone noncommittal.

Frank rubbed the back of his neck. That's symbiosis of a sort. Yet neither party has their needs met.

How's that different from you and Lynette? I asked. You're all about teaching. The kids and coaching, right? What if your passion for education, the time spent with Tallyn, left Lynette feeling cut out?

She doesn't feel a connection…and still wants it, he filled in slowly.

But now time's running out, I added softly. I gazed at Frank over the edge of my cup, but Frank was lost to me, following the threads, considering the hard choices ahead.

I'm only guessing, mind you, I said, thinking of Donna. But disappointment might be the hardest unhappiness of them all. You run out of road and what do you have? Nothing.

The cabin creaked under another onslaught of wind.

Marley, why did your mother— He stopped.

Kill herself? It was a fair question. I'd brought it up

myself the night before. No one knows why she stepped off the dock, Frank. No one.

Too many memories, I believed privately. I had no basis for thinking so, no letter from Fred as proof or contradiction, but I couldn't help but feel it to be true.

Why do you girls call her Donna anyway? I always wondered that, Frank said.

I raised an eyebrow. Is that odd?

Yeah. A bit.

I don't suppose we did when we were little, I acknowledged. Donna made Andi and me the center of attention when we were kids but things changed when she had her own show. Everywhere we went it was *The Donna Stone Show*. Doctor's appointments, grocery stores, even school. Donna Stone! Donna, mother, mom. The words meant the same to us. I shrugged. Since there was no dad in the picture, leaving the mom out made it that much less of a minus, I said. You know, like pepper no salt.

What about your dad? Frank asked. He must have known your mom became famous. Not to mention you girls. He ever attempt to find you?

Mystery Fred? I laughed. Never knew we existed. They never knew each other's last names.

How untrue that might be, I thought. But still, the story I knew.

My father knew exactly how to find me, Frank said.

Our eyes met.

Never heard from him, he said.

The wind howled down the chimney and the coals flared. I leaned back, staring at the pine ceiling.

This is why I love country music, Frank. Zero bullshit. Hank Williams said it—country music is sincere. When a man sings a sad song, he knows the sad.

I glanced sideways. But damn, why is it always so sad?

We listened to the porch screen door flap against the doorframe. Whisper and a thud. Whisper and a thud. I got up then, leaving Frank to contemplate the fire, and collected my phone from the kitchen. I spun through the inbox. Delete, delete, delete.

And there it was.

Dear Marley,
Did you receive my email?
The PHS 25th reunion is next week. Hard to believe that many years have gone by. I plan to be there—Mrs. Trindle is hosting a current and former faculty fundraiser for the Music Department.
Anyway. Will be in the area for a few days. Let's connect.
I think about you.
RC

Delete.

Should I mention I was receiving these emails to Frank? Tell him this mess with Carville was not "squared away" or close to over, might never be over?

The black potbelly steamed the window glass and I rubbed it with my sleeve, gathering my thoughts. The clearing was strewn with broken branches, snow flurries alternating with hail and sleet.

No, I decided. I was a grown woman. Carville was my problem.

When I returned from the kitchen, Frank was standing in the center of the room, his head tilted, listening.

Damn, he said. That's hail hitting the roof. Moving to the window he surveyed the bend of the trees. Might be smart to back the vehicles nearer the shed for protection, Mar.

I'll get my keys, I said. Do you think we'll lose power?

He took the keys and pulled on his heavy jacket. Likely, he said.

The taillights of the Miata lit up as Frank backed my car next to his pickup, leeward of the boatshed. I scooted to the front door and flung it open, and Frank hustled back inside, his backpack over his shoulder and his arms full of split wood.

Hey, there's bear tracks out there, he said. And bullet holes in the shed!

I opened my hands. What can I say? The bear got away.

He snorted. The shed wasn't so lucky?

I handed him a beer.

I recommend you leave the bullets to the pros, he said. Why not join us Friday at Macklin's? He nudged me with his elbow. Come as you are. Single, not single. No one cares. Half the old group's divorced, half kind of married. Me too now, I guess.

Kind of married? I asked. What's kind of married?

A work in progress, he answered lightly. Bill and Lorrie started counseling but are still together. Elsa and Mindy are back together again after two splits of almost a decade. And Aggie is sleeping with Tom Schultz—who is, or was, still married to Beth Sinclare.

Kind of Hollywood for a place like Paulette, I said.

He chuckled. Oh, you have no idea.

Plan a breakup reunion next year and I might come.

Bargains from the damage bin?

Dude, you could have a whole career in country music if you wanted.

I'll leave that to you Stone girls.

Thanks anyway. I shook my head. Work to do.

Believe it or not, Royal Morton texted he's on his way up from Portland.

Wait a minute, I said. Bio class Royal? What's he doing in Portland?

Making bank. Million-bucks-a-year neurosurgeon, Frank said.

I did not attempt to hide my shock.

Life is cruel, isn't it? Frank chuckled. Look at us, the beautiful people...total failures.

How much fun we'd had in high school together, I thought. Group dates down to Lewiston to the roller-skating rink, everyone crammed into Tom Shultz's parents' 1976 rust-paneled Suburban. I smiled, thinking of Tom's dashboard hula girl, nicknamed The Baywatch Babe. Tom had painted nipples on her plastic bikini top. To be more precise, Xs. He winked. X marks the spot, Tom said.

I remembered how the guys had out-pranked each other with crack the whip, the girls shimmying in close to their boyfriends during Couples Skate. I had loved the *whish* of skates across the polished wood, the wash of colors playing under the strobe lights. There were ski trips, too; hot chocolate and bonfires at the winter lake.

A square of cheese hit my cheek. Frank had bombed me, beer in one hand, the other on his stomach in evident contentment.

Penny for your thoughts, he said.

Remember the roller rink?

Ah yes. He nodded. They tore that down years ago. Car wash now.

Shame. Speaking of work, I said, I need to do some recording. If the roads are at all passable tomorrow, I owe

Ben an overnight to LA. Thought I'd try Branch Creek, if it's open.

Frank nodded. I'm fine by the fire. Need to push off once the hail quits anyway.

Armed with recording gear, song notes, and guitar, I closed the door to Donna's bedroom. It was colder back here than in the front room, and the baseboard heater clicked on and off to no effect. Sometime later I came out of the bedroom rubbing my shoulder, now quite definitely sore.

I leaned the guitar by the bookshelves.

Frank occupied the couch, his backpack on the floor beside him, and in his lap what looked like lab reports he was grading.

Go okay?

Think so, I said, dazed by the hours of concentration. I wandered into the kitchen, helping myself to another beer, seeing Frank already had one.

It was like Donna was in there, I said, coming back into the room. Listening to me lay down tracks. Humming along, like in Nashville.

I became aware of the shipping boxes parked against the wall, the knick-knacks and books emptied from the shelves, the bubble-wrapped photos, the stacks of folded quilts. I was taking my mother's life apart, photo by quilt by book. It hurt. It hurt like hell.

You miss her, Frank said.

I edged in at the end of the couch, careful not to disturb his stacks of papers and stretched my socks toward the fire. The flames cracked and hissed as snow dropped down the flue.

I do miss her, I said. Andi does too, though she won't say so. Donna loved music. She'd cry over Hank Williams or Johnny Cash on the radio. And while she liked The Grateful Dead, and Neil Young, it was always old country she came back to.

What about you? Got a favorite? Frank asked.

I gravitate to certain voices. Always have. Jennifer Nettles—you know, Sugarland? Her song "Stay" breaks my heart every damn time. She wrote it herself, which impresses the hell out of me. Montana State, Anchorage—the Barberson Carter years, I thought. Vince Gill's "Go Rest High on That Mountain." That's an oldie I love, I said. And Miranda Lambert's "House That Built Me." That one defines about everything.

What do you mean, Defines everything?

Whatever there is to say about love. Building a life, growing old together. I shifted to a more comfortable position. What about you?

Frank smiled. Anything Alan Jackson, he said. Give me a pickup, a fishing rod and a girl—I'm set.

I fell silent and after a while Frank returned to his papers. When I awakened, my head was nestled in the couch cushion, angled to the ceiling, and I had the uncomfortable feeling I had been snoring. I absorbed the intimate silence, the crackle of the fire, the blue-gray twilight.

Hello, sleepy head, Frank said.

I brushed the hair out of my eyes. How long have I been out?

Not long.

The hail has stopped?

Seems so, Frank said.

He leaned forward and began sliding papers back into his backpack.

I need to get back to my place, Marley, he said. But thank you for the company—and the things you had to say. I've a lot to think about. I'm not certain my marriage can be saved, but I'm grateful for the reminder not to walk without a fight. Whether Lynette boots me out for good or not—I owe my daughter that.

Lynette may not have meant what she said, I responded. People say strange stuff when they're in crisis. My hands were resting in my lap, and I noticed Frank staring at the tattoo above my wrist. *Don't Look Back.* How apropos.

He closed his backpack. She meant it, he said. Although I don't get why. I'd like to know where I screwed up. Fix it if I can. If she'll let me. I can't just abandon twenty-four years as unfinished business.

I leaned forward, the swing of my hair sheltering me from his gaze. I feel that way about my entire life, I said.

Lock and Stone, Frank murmured. Imagine, all these years later. He stood and collected his jacket. One of us must have done something right.

16

I stirred, woken from sleep by the ebb of silence. The quiescent calm around me was profound, heavy, still. I heard no ticking sounds from the electric baseboard heater, no hiccup-and-grind from the old fridge in the kitchen. A silence so thick you could fork it.

I sat on the edge of the twin bed, shivering. My watch read one forty-five a.m. Why was it so quiet? Grabbing clothes from the chair, I pulled on flannel bottoms and Frank's hooded sweatshirt in the dark and padded in my stockinged feet across the cabin. Out the front window a waxing moon clung high in the trees. The hail had stopped hours before, but somewhere in the night the wind too, had ceased. Every silhouette, from the black calligraphic pines to the pale scimitar of lakeshore, sparkled, sequined in ice.

I tucked my hands under my armpits for warmth and turned the switch on the sofa lamp. The switch clicked, but the room remained in darkness. The power had gone out. The remains of last night's embers glowed in the fireplace, and I crouched low and blew until the coals brightened, adding a few sticks of wood. I stood, warming myself. The silence was both unnerving and inviting, like the deep of the lake. This strange and tender quietude of an unguarded world.

I lit two candles and placed one on the fireplace mantle and the other on the table. I helped myself to a heel of bread left over from dinner and settled with my pencils and notebook at the table, alone with the crackling fire.

I drew circles on the yellow pad, bone-tired.

Life had to be more than the stemming together of lyrics, the skid of one-night cowboys across the nights. It must be more.

I thought of the crushed blossom song; an accidental art, a melancholy. The "brandy of the damned," Shaw once wrote. I felt the pull of the music in my hands. That working loom of harmonic and narrative. This, my wordless euphony. Blossoms on a barroom floor. The distance from where one stood and where the heart cries out in joy.

My music, my *aria da capo*. I could feel it, the answer locked in this one melody.

Night Train. Maybe we all had one.

I doodled with the pencil, sketching Frank from memory as he'd sat earlier that night, grading papers on the couch. I studied my lines and shaded in details— Frank cradling his chin in his hand as he concentrated on his work, the faded eagle tattoo on his forearm, the way he held a pen with just his thumb and index finger. The pale scar like a crescent moon above his cheekbone. The gold ring on his left hand.

As I drew, the pencil became a shelter for my thoughts, a place to step over the threshold on the current of the night, beyond the storm-marooned cabin and its dark and tender secrets.

I blew eraser shreds from my sketch across the table

and thought of an odd conversation with Donna years before, the two of us seated at the plank table in the house in Paulette.

Donna's table was Command Central, the Oval Office, the Round Table of King Arthur's court. We'd fought with Donna over curfews at that table; worked out math problems and written history papers. Left cocoa rings on the wood, discussed boys and then men, the music business, Ben's investment advice.

After Donna's death, Andi and I put the table in storage along with the other furnishings we couldn't yet bear to look at but would never sell or give away: The Weston photograph, her sewing basket, *The Donna Show* scripts.

I remembered coming into the house and setting down my luggage. How it felt to sit at my mother's table again. We were drinking margaritas from the blender, the screen door thrown open to the night, setting loose the heat of the day. Wood moths bat against the porch light, percussion beats on wings of dust. Chips and guacamole in red bowls sat between us.

Donna, then in her late-forties, wore a teal halter and cutoff jeans patched with old shirts. She had diamond studs in her ears—a gift from Andi after the band's second album went platinum.

This was my first visit from Seattle since Andi had eloped with her guitarist and Donna had returned to Paulette. Alone now for several years, I'd never said much after the breakup with Carter, and Donna was coming off a relationship with someone she'd dated off and on in Nashville.

A lull after every storm, the Stone women without men.

It was the hot part of July, a week after Andi and I celebrated our twenty-seventh birthdays halfway across the country from one another. I was about to purchase my first home in Seattle and I described the condo to Donna, the view over the water, the ferries at night, what it was like to hang out with the area bands.

I like Seattle, I said. It's open, good for starting over.

Don't you fret about Carter, Donna said. She shrugged lightly. It is what it is, my darling. You can't make a dragonfly into a bumblebee, now can you?

Andi and I laughed when Donna said things like that. What did it mean anyway?

Mom, don't you ever want to settle down? I asked.

She gave me a startled look, I supposed because I'd called her Mom, not Donna.

Settle down? she said. I am settled. Oh. You mean marry. She tilted her head. Marley, she said, a set of matching china and a shared sock drawer mean nothing to me. I'd rather be happy. And I am happy, she said.

She tucked a wisp of loose hair into her messy bun and re-secured the twist with Wong Chen Take-Out chopsticks.

Take Harvey, she said, meaning Harvey Campbell, her last boyfriend from Nashville. Harvey made me laugh. He knew everyone I knew. And now it's over. That's what happens.

Doesn't anyone find someone and…you know, stay together? I asked.

It was as if my mother were describing travelers sharing the path to oblivion.

She patted my hand. We three girls stayed together, she said, her smile sunny.

I mean couples.

Donna laughed. What's gotten into you?

She sucked the ice from the bottom of her margarita, then rose and brought the drink pitcher to the table, setting it between us.

Here's what I know, she said. You go with something as long as it works. When it stops, you change. Surely I've shown you that? She rested her chin in the palm of her hand. If you want to get married, Marley, get married. You've got your own money, a career in the industry. You want a husband and kids? Go get 'em.

I stared at her. Go get them? I echoed. Like the Family Pack from a Wal-Mart? I shook my head. Things don't work out for me.

Is this about that teacher? Back in high school? Donna asked softly.

I flushed. I never talked about those days and I wanted it to stay that way.

It's about commitment, I said. You know, someone for the long haul. Not just for fun—the tough times, too.

Donna stopped to adjust a chopstick that had slipped.

Sure, I think about it, she said. I'm getting older and more inclined to the idea. But we're on our own in this world, Marley. If you let yourself count on something— or someone—you're bound to fall apart when they're gone. That's just facts, sweetheart.

I broke a tortilla chip into small pieces, dropping the crumbles back in the bowl. Had a man likewise broken my mother's heart?

And was that man Mystery Fred? Had she given her east coast boy her world and watched as he dashed it? Or, and this thought bothered me even more because I recognized myself in its shadow, had she been so afraid of the uncertainty and risk that she'd never given her heart to anyone at all—even the man it was meant for.

Donna refilled our margarita glasses, overfilling hers and spooning up the overflow from the rim of the glass with one slender finger.

If you ask me, she said. When you want something too

much you're bound to crush it with all that pent-up wanting.

A log crumbled in the grate, sending a shower of sparks up the flue. There it was. Desire will crush the very thing. I balled up the sketch of Frank and opened the last bottle of red and brought it to the table.

Remembering that conversation had clarified two things. Donna did not step off the dock because she was alone. And remarkably, I was equally alone by choice.

I had played it that way with Carter, and I had never treated Nathan in a way that said, Stay, I love you. We had gamed one another, their cool to my casual. Then there was my career—my life in music.

I thought of Donna's warning. Don't love it too much. Don't want more.

I had poured that bottomless hunger into the tour.

I peeled the wine label off the bottle and flicked the paper toward the fire, watching as it curled and blackened to ash.

I stoked the potbelly in the kitchen and left the kettle on top to warm for morning coffee.

I decided to take on one last look at the lake before going back to sleep. All that beauty and I was the only one on the bay to see it.

I pulled on a jacket and boots and made my way down the back steps, crossing the frozen sand.

The pine branches hung low, embedded in sculpted ice and lustrous snowlight. A low moon glimmered across the black water and the landscape glowed with a peculiar brilliance, the more profound for the silence.

Not a creak of tree or murmur of wave against the dock.

Stillness.

I felt Donna at my side.

I had to be imagining this.

Wondered where you'd gone, I said.

Isn't it beautiful? She leaned against my shoulder.

And cold, I said.

I stamped my feet, the crack of frost breaking the quiet.

Tell me what you see, sweetheart, Donna said.

Ice.

And?

I gazed at the glistening lake, the luminous mountains.

That moonglow is fractured light, I said, my words slow. Frozen particulates suspended in the air. And iced condensation made those shapes in the branches and on the sand. That pebbly stuff on the ground, that looks like hail? It's graupel—snowflakes frozen at a lower level in the atmosphere than hail.

I sounded like Frank. Delivering the science report.

It's only October, so you know this won't last, I said. It's too soon.

A small sigh.

What do you see? I asked Donna.

I felt her smile.

No matter what we do to the world or ourselves, she said, nature remains capable of this.

She waved her hand the length of the shore. A storm, she said. Thrown across the lake like jewels.

Ice storms will always remind me of you now, Mom.

I looked one last time at the mountains.

Donna was gone.

17

The power hummed on around seven that morning. Frank stopped by to make sure I was back on the grid. He stood in the entrance of the kitchen.

Hey, answer your phone, he said, scolding gently. I called twice. Everyone on the lake lost power.

The water tank had gone cold during the night's outage and I was using warm kettle water to wash my breakfast plates.

I glanced at my phone on the kitchen counter, thinking of the email from Carville. I used the back of my wet hand to brush the hair off my face.

Sorry, I said, I powered off. Saving battery.

Anyway, you won't need that generator, Frank said. He patted his backpack with his laptop and the folder of papers from the day before. I'm off. Need to find an internet connection to send in these quarter grades. The lodge, you think? They have satellite, right?

They're open all year—it's a good bet they have some kind of link. I dried my hands on a dish towel. Frank, I really appreciate your offer to take the boxes into town in your truck. I'll be ready whenever you are.

And, I had my package for Ben. Third song or not.

By the way, I'll pick you up on my way to Macklin's. Frank smiled persuasively. Four o'clock?

I'll think about it, I said. I hadn't stayed in touch with anyone from Paulette. It would be nothing but awkward.

Everyone wants to see you.

They know I'm here?

Frank scratched his chin. I may have texted something to Royal yesterday, he said.

I made a face. They want The Andi Stone Tour, not me, Frank.

We're still who we were before, he said. Old friends.

I'll think about it, I repeated.

I watched from the kitchen window as Frank laid his backpack across the seat of his pickup and climbed in. He started the engine, letting it warm for a minute. I could see he was on the phone. Tallyn? Lynette? In three days, I would be gone. It would be as though neither of us was ever here. Frank looked up and touched his fingers to his forehead in a salute goodbye. I drained the dishwater from the sink, watching his truck disappear down the lane.

സ

I rounded up the gang. Patsy, Hank, Johnny and Loretta, some Merle and George Strait. I pumped up the volume on the speakers and dragged the remaining boxes to the center of the room and dug out packing tape. I was hollering along with "Ring of Fire" and lobbing plasticware into trash bags when I heard banging on the front door.

I looked at my watch. Noon. Frank? I scampered to the door and flung it open.

Standing on the top step, zipped into a white leather

jumpsuit and turquoise fur shrug, her red hair teased up in a Pebbles "do" straight out of The Flintstones, stood Andi, popping her gum and smiling broadly.

I dropped the plastic jug in my hand, thunderstruck.

Gonna let me in, she said, or just stand there with your mouth open, catching flies?

Andi! I cried. What on earth are you doing here? How did you get here?

She swept in, tossed her leopard bag on the counter, and did a quick survey of the cabin. She leaned in to air-kiss me on both cheeks. Why checking on you, darling, she said. What else?

She wiggled out of the blue fur, revealing tanned arms. She waved her hand toward the red car in the clearing. Silver bangles clattered around her wrist. Hertz, sugar, she said. Marco flew us to Coeur d'Alene last night. Once he spied that golf resort he was a whole lot happier than he was in Nashville. Geez, Marley, she said, wrinkling her nose. The place is a mess. And what the heck happened outside? Roads are terrible.

You came here from Nashville? I said, stunned. Why?

To help! She threw her arms around me, hugging me tight. I drove myself up, she said. Aren't you proud of me? Left Marco sunning his buns at the spa, the rat.

Why didn't you call first? I said. My nose twitched from the perfume she wore—something green with a citrus note. Shalimar? Or was that one a floral note? I never knew. The only notes that mattered to me were auditory. I sneezed.

I did call. Multiple times, Andi said. She raised an eyebrow. You didn't answer, mi amiga. Had me worried.

We had a heck of a storm, I said. Power outage.

Andi's attention shifted to the music on the speakers. Oh! she exclaimed. Now there's a blast from the past! She twirled around the cabin, dodging boxes, gyrating to

"Crazy," sung as only Patsy could. She grinned at me, shimmying to the beat, and danced off toward the back porch. She stopped and flung open the door, taking in the lakefront view. My God, she breathed. I forgot how beautiful it is. Everything is so green and blue…and white.

Your basic crayon colors, I said. We got slammed with snow and ice yesterday.

Andi glanced over her bare shoulder. We?

Figure of speech, I said.

She lifted the wool coat off the hook by the door with one manicured finger. And this, size XL, would belong to? she asked. She waited, her eyes bright. I blushed, and Andi laughed. Oh, come on, Marley. Who was here? Frank?

You here to help or just quiz me? I said. I scrutinized her white leather jumpsuit. You did bring real people clothes, right? I hope?

Can't brush me off that easily, baby sis, Andi said. She shut the porch door and shivered. Let's build a fire and you can tell me all about it, err, him. She skipped a glance around the main room, noting the barren shelves, the boxes. Place is still kinda sweet, she said, her expression misty.

Andi looked thinner than usual. Her mouth tightly gathered at the corners. Beneath her perfect makeup and the tan bronzer, shadows marred the delicate skin beneath her beryl emerald eyes. But beautiful. Staggeringly beautiful. I stepped close and hugged her tight.

Andi leaned back with a laugh, studying me. Lonely, sugar cakes?

Just glad to see you, I said.

Andi changed into my last pair of clean jeans and the MSU sweatshirt. She came out of the bedroom with her Pebbles bouffant brushed out and her long hair pulled back in a simple ponytail. Gone was the polished celebrity, the road-hardened performer. In her place the sister I knew and loved.

She looked down at herself and then at me in my flannel bottoms and Frank's enormous hoodie.

We look like a hillbilly moving crew, she said. She selected her latest album from the music player. You mind? She cranked up the volume.

I made a mental apology to The Greats and handed her a stack of shipping labels.

Here, I said. Address these. This box is linens, and this is books, and those over there, knick-knacks. The photos we'll take with us.

Address to whom? Andi asked innocently.

No, I said, blunt. This crap does not come to my house. You have the six-car garage. I have a teensy condo—remember?

You know I can't keep track of anything, Andi said. She pouted. Surely there's room at your place now that you've thrown out Nathan and all those suits?

There had been a preponderance of bespoke Nathan-wear. An entire closet filled with the custom dress shirts and suits from the Hugo Boss label Nathan loved. And sweaters, at least two dozen on the shelves above. Folded dark wools in flocks like low clouds.

I burst out laughing. Fine, I said. Send to me then. I'll drop it all in the storage locker.

We chatted as we worked and it felt as though Andi had been there beside me all along. As if we were teenagers again in summers never ending.

Andi pawed through a box of things under her twin bed and pulled out a ratty stuffed duck, old yearbooks, and cassette tapes of the Bee Gees and Journey—absolute contraband in Donna's "country" house. If you weren't listening to country music—the people's music—your only option was the other people's music. Neil Young. The Grateful Dead. Donna made her rules clear the day I tried to bring home the Pet Shop Boys. Garbage, she pronounced, frisbeeing the CD toward the trashcan. Brain rot.

Andi sat back on her heels, clutching the stuffed duck to her chest. We had such good times here, she said, nearly inaudible. And Nashville—Donna loved Nashville! At Tootsie's last night all I could think of was the fun we'd had together. Why do you think she did it, Marley?

I shook my head. No clue, Andi, I said. She seemed so small and lost, cross-legged on the floor. Is that why you flew to Nashville? I asked softly. Because you miss her?

Andi buried her face in the stuffed toy.

I threw a set of cardboard coasters, classic mountain views ringed with stains, into the trash bag. You remind me of her sometimes, Andi, I said. In the best way. You're clear about things. Determined.

I held up the Indian Chief playing cards. Want the cards? I asked.

How can you be so businesslike about all this? she said. Tears welled up and she looked away.

I kneeled beside her and gave her shoulder a squeeze. I've been here awhile, I said. That's all.

Afternoon shadows leaned through the trees, the clumped needles and branches dripping melting ice. In a few hours, the Paulette gang would be meeting at the lodge for drinks. Should I mention the mini-reunion to Andi? Would it cheer her up?

I handed her a tissue. We don't have to sell the place, I said.

She blew her nose. Look at me, she said with a sniffle. I've ruined my makeup. She pulled out a compact from her leopard bag and dabbed at her mascara and re-powdered her nose.

I spread a stack of land surveys, homemade soap recipes, old Nielsen radio rankings, and phone bills from the 90s across the table. What to save, I wondered. I glanced at Andi. She had moved to the couch, flipping through yearbooks.

This is wild, Andi said, looking up. Did you know these were here?

No, I said, but I'm not surprised. We always had the year-end party here. Are they moldy?

Not a bit! Andi laughed, opening a book to show me pictures of the two of us in safety goggles in Mr. Merken's chem class, Andi gawking like Thelma from the cartoon, Scooby Doo. And another from the year Andi tried out for cheer, with her then best bud, Lorrie. Look at that skirt, Andi marveled. It's practically up to my bellybutton. I can't believe Donna let us wear these.

Those were Grandma Leila's, I reminded her, thinking of the steamer trunk of woolen knife-pleat skating costumes we'd discovered in the attic at the farm. We'd pounced on the plaids and colored skirts immediately. Every one of them aired out and hemmed by Donna, thrifty to a flaw—but sadly before our growth spurt in the eighth grade.

Andi winced. This one is so short you can see my underpants, she said.

Remember the Vice Principal, Mr. Marks? He wrote me up for one of those skirts and I burst into tears and he tore it up, I said.

You patsy, Andi said.

I smiled. No detention.

I returned to the receipts and papers on the table. Andi interrupted again, this time waving a crumpled sheet of college-ruled notebook paper. What's this? she asked.

What's what? I didn't glance up, immersed in sorting.

This, she said. It's in your handwriting. She began to read aloud. *Bust me up, break me down, bust my world in two. I barely knew the world was mine, barely given time. Busted, broken, barely grown, forever broke in two. Forever is forever, broken by you.* Is this a poem? she asked, puzzled. No, wait, there are chords in the margins. These are lyrics! Am I right?

Give me that, I said, reaching out.

Andi pressed the paper to her chest. What gives?

Nothing, I said, my voice sharp. Just give it to me. It's mine and it's personal. I felt the heat in my cheeks.

Andi handed it over reluctantly. Fine. Take it, she said, pouting. I wasn't snooping, you know. It was in the yearbook.

Without looking I balled the page up, flinging it into the fireplace. It's nothing, I said. Just crap from English class. Neither of us said a word as the crumpled paper smoked and burst into flame.

Andi shrugged. Depressing stuff anyway, she said. She flicked her ponytail, turning away. Gotta keep it upbeat. Not for nothin' they call me Queen of Country Sass.

And that makes me Johnny Cash? I demanded.

Pretty much, she said.

Then I just incinerated some serious Johnny. I began to giggle, my eyes watering. Going down, down, down in a burning ring of fire, I choked out. Get it? "Ring of Fire"?

Freak, Andi said. Yawning, she dove back into another box of junk from our room. What a slog, she complained. Is there no end?

I stretched out a kink in the back of my shoulder. Way too much *Donna Stone Show*, that's for certain, I said.

Andi glanced at the box of Andi Stone flyers and press

columns and radio ratings. And too much me, she said.

I'll remember you said that, I said.

She glanced at her diamond Cartier, a fortieth birthday gift from Stephan. Her eyes widened. Gosh, I forgot to tell you— She grabbed my wrists —there's a get-together at Macklin's tonight. The gang from Paulette, can you believe it? Bill and Lorrie, Aggie, Tom, Mindy and Elsa. You must come with me! I promised you would.

You know about that? I said.

Royal called. Finagled my number out of Ben, Andi said. Did you know— Her eyes widened —Royal's a muckety-muck brain doc in Portland now. Royal Morton! The Elvis Costello glasses? All pole-cat skinny?

I blinked. Royal called you?

She shrugged and giggled. All work and no play makes Andi a dull girl, she said.

I should have known, I said and made a face. This is as much help as I'm going to get from you, isn't it?

Look, sugar beet, Andi said with a grin. I'm gonna dash back to Macklin's and get cleaned and prettied. She saw the look on my face and pinked up. Yes, I booked a room at the lodge. So sue me. I like ample hot water and a good mattress. Come, she said. Bunk with me at the lodge. I mean, why stay here?

I shook my head. It's okay, I said. Go.

I suspected Andi was feeling the same onslaught of emotion I had among Donna's things. The rush of memory without interval of time, the plumb of her presence in these spaces. I could sense from the tightness in her shoulders, the way she held her arms close about her body, that being this close to Donna was nearly too much.

You will come tonight, Andi insisted. We haven't seen these people in forever. She flew around the cabin, gathering her stuff. She waggled a finger at me. And I intend to find out why Frank Lockford's jacket is hanging on our door hook, mark my words.

Maybe later, I said. Like never, I thought.

She winked. Tell me or I'll spill the beans there's been a very private Lock and Stone reunion.

She disappeared into the bedroom and changed back into her leather jumpsuit. She returned, three bobby pins clamped in her teeth as she twisted up her hair. Can't go into Macklin's like something the loggers dragged in, she said. She examined herself critically in the window reflection and adjusted her turquoise shrug. Like it? Got it in Dallas.

You look like a Smurf.

You'll come?

I hate crowds.

Frank will be there. Andi fished her keys out and headed to the door. You'll come, she said.

18

Marley,
Lorrie Nelson posted an update you were at
Lost Prince. If true, please confirm.
RC

They wouldn't stop coming. A third email. The bite of
salt and politeness. I was sitting at the kitchen table, a
glass of water between my hands, when Frank's truck
pulled in the yard. C'mon, girl, Frank said, standing in
the threshold. Time to rock 'n roll.

Go away, Frank, I said, waving a hand at him. Have
fun with the Class of '89.

He pulled me up out of the chair. Come on, grumpy,
he said. Get cleaned up. You look like Cinderella—
before the magic part.

I headed to the bedroom and pulled on my cleanest
jeans and a scoop-neck black lace blouse, adding a pair of
gold hoops. A touch of mascara and lip-gloss, and done. I
surveyed myself in the bathroom mirror. It would have to
do.

Your glass slippers, miss. Frank handed me my beat-

up Frye's. He spun me around with an amused smile.
Excellent, he said. Much more 'rella than cinder.

We drove north toward Macklin's Resort, two bays up
from Dunscott. A pair of loons bobbed at a distance from
shore, tiny black boats against the sinking sun. Andi's
here, I said, glancing sideways.

Frank shift gears. Heard that, he said.

You knew Royal asked her up?

Didn't expect she'd come.

It complicates things.

So don't let it.

I frowned at my hands folded in my lap. Frank, I
really don't want to do this, I said.

There were so many reasons. People who knew us
might ask about Donna. And I didn't want to field
questions around our plans to sell the cabin, or, frankly,
deal with the brouhaha wherever Andi made an
appearance. And if I were honest, I was feeling uneasy,
given the proximity of Robby Carville.

It's only a party, Marley, Frank said.

He turned onto the graveled road that led to the lodge.
Macklin's was unexpectedly crowded. The abrupt shift in
the weather signaled the end of the boating season and
trucks and boat trailers were double-parked the length of
the winding drive, cars stacked two deep in the parking
lot.

Frank handed me out of the truck. Let's just have fun
tonight. He smiled. For old times' sake.

Do they— I hesitated. I mean does everyone know—

He nodded, pulling open one side of the double glass
doors to the lodge. Yes, he said. The Paulette grapevine
works exceptionally well. They know about Lynette. He
squeezed my arm.

Frank! A high female voice sailed out from deep
inside the noisy bar. Mindy Hernandez threw herself

across the room and tackled us at the entrance in a bear hug. I fell backwards into Frank as he steadied the three of us. At five feet, two inches, and 175 pounds, Mindy was a cannonball to be reckoned with. Oh, my God. Oh, my God, Mindy squealed. Look at you two! Just like high school. The blonde and the warthog!

I beg your pardon? Frank objected. Who's a warthog?

Mindy's round face split into giggles. She jammed her glasses up her nose but in her enthusiasm knocked them off the back of her head. Frank caught them midair in one hand.

He handed them back to her. Easy there, he said. He looked through the crowded room. We have a table somewhere in there?

We do, Mindy said, bobbing her head vigorously.

I looked around. Nothing about Macklin's had changed since the summer Andi and I had turned twenty-one, laid our driver's licenses proudly down, and ordered our first tequila.

The main room, dominated by a horseshoe bar, faced an expanse of windows overlooking the marina and the lake. Summer boats, rigged and tarped for winter, rocked in their berths under their protective blue canopies; the volleyball pit empty of tourists, the summer folk gone. The dance floor had two Ping-Pong tables on it, the stage cleared for band equipment.

I touched the smoke-stained paneling, noted the heavily pocked dartboards, the same sawn-plank lunch bar over the oyster tank. The only nod to the new century appeared to be an espresso machine installed near the martini shakers.

Come! Mindy ducked to one side for a man wearing a Cabela's Big Game sweatshirt, plunking coins into the cigarette machine. She pushed us ahead of her toward the very back of the bar—past the flat screen televisions broadcasting a Seahawks-Vikings game on ESPN.

Got us tables by the windows, she said. Oh, this is gonna be epic! Her face squinched in the exact overwhelmed way as that time she'd irretrievably frozen all the fruit flies we were supposed to be breeding in science class. We received a C on our lab report. Mr. Claussen flatly dismissing Mindy's hastily fabricated explanation we'd been able to investigate long-term cryofreeze fertility even when unable to reanimate our subjects.

Mindy plowed ahead in her studded bolero jacket and peg jeans, her black hair bouncing down her back. Elsa! She called to a slender blonde pouring a pitcher of beer into glasses. Guess who? Lock and Stone!

Elsa Jennings looked up and her flat Norwegian face opened in a wide smile. She waved. Hey there, kids. Want a beer?

Elsa, I said, busting a grin. Wow, girl. You haven't changed except to grow more beautiful. I took the beer Elsa handed me and leaned in to exchange air kisses with the 1989 Idaho State High School Debate Champion and respected family practice lawyer out of Boise.

Nor you, Elsa said, and swept me with a glance. I see you hooked up with our Mr. Lockford. She coughed into her hand. Ran into each other, I mean. Hey, Lock.

Frank took a beer.

Look who I found smoking on the porch, Mindy announced, dragging a couple in from the outside deck. She had one arm around PHS's former football quarterback Bill Nelson and the other around head cheerleader, Lorrie Babcock, both now in their forties, married, and thirty-five to fifty pounds overweight. Lorrie'd kept the bottle-blonde hair whereas Bill had none.

Smoking! Elsa shook her head. Stop that this instant, she said. You'll kill yourselves.

We're trying, dammit, Lorrie said. To kill ourselves that is—you've met our kids. She shook her head. Seriously, we've got patches on. She pulled up her sleeve and revealed a square nicotine patch. She smacked Bill on the shoulder. He has one, too.

You're smoking and using a patch? I asked.

Prep and back-fire, Bill answered with a grunt. That's us. He grabbed a beer off the table. Coach Culbert— remember that cussed bastard? Coach called it wallpapering over paneling. Long story short, babies one and two arrive using her diaphragm. So yeah, babies three and four require the rubber bonnet, gel, and a condom. His beer wobbled in his hand. Ouch! He glanced at his wife.

TMI, Lorrie hissed.

Nothing wrong with being certain, Bill protested. Insurance is what I do for a living.

I smiled. The two were a rumpled version of their former high school selves settled into family life. The moment felt as if I'd never left Paulette. As if twenty-five years spooled by in a single summer over a pitcher of beer.

Bill moved over to stand beside Frank. Hey, you hungry? Let's order oysters and fries at the bar.

The guys left and Mindy, Elsa, and I sat down at the big table with Lorrie. I looked at them. I had no idea you guys got together like this, I said. Who're we missing?

Um, Royal, Lorrie said and snagged Bill's unguarded beer. And Ricky's not here yet. Tom Schulz and Aggie are driving up together. She turned a big smile on me. And your sister! She is coming?

Andi? I just found out she was here myself, I admitted. She's staying at the resort.

Lorrie let out a breath. Oh good. I have concert tee shirts for her to sign for my girls, she said. And you of course. If you would.

No worries, I said. I'll make sure Andi takes care of you.

At that moment, Aggie Wilson and Tom Shultz strolled in. Stunning at six feet in height, and athletically fit, Aggie had kept her hip-length blonde hair—and a very Gisele Bündchen bang-cut brushing her blue eyes. Tom, thickened through the years about the neck and waist, wore a crisp Tommy Bahama Hawaiian shirt and pressed slacks. He placed his hand under Aggie's elbow as he guided her to the table.

He bellowed, This the party of Paulette's best and brightest?

You mean fun and fastest, corrected Lorrie.

Make that least and lightest, I said.

Hot and horniest, said Elsa.

The cream de the cream, Mindy boasted, offering no effort whatsoever at correct French pronunciation. How was the drive?

Aggie nodded languidly and folded her long frame into an empty chair. She crossed her slender legs in their tight black boots and ignored the pitcher of beer and instead asked the bartender for an appletini. Good, she said. I flew from Tacoma to Spokane, and Tom picked me up from the airport.

Tom beamed. My pleasure, too, he said. His ancient torch for the Paulette volleyball star glowed in his chubby cheeks.

Tom paid for Aggie's drink and Mindy leaned over and whispered in my ear that Tom's divorce had been final for a couple of years. He was desperately hoping to hook up with Aggie again, now a nationally franchised fitness instructor, with videos, infomercials, and a chain of workout places up and down the west coast. Tom, a banker, still lived in Paulette.

It appeared Aggie was less smitten back.

Frank and Bill returned to the table with platters of appetizers balanced in their hands. We cleared a space amongst the empty pitchers and Tom headed to the bar to order refills. I stuffed two twenties in his shirt pocket. Don't argue, I said.

Lorrie was full of dating questions, and soon I was skimming over Histories of Men. Nathan, the Abridged Edition.

Six years? He left after six years? I mean who does that? Lorrie said. At least if you marry, and then get divorced, you've done your time. She pointed directly at Tom. Am I right?

Exactly, Mindy interjected. What's cohab, but splitting the rent and skipping the in-laws?

Sounds good to me, Tom said.

Frank had remained quiet, but stirred slightly at Lorrie's "done your time" comment. So far no one had mentioned Lynette or his situation in Salt Lake.

Bill leaned forward. Lorrie and I hardly do it anymore and split bills. What's that? Live-in, zero benefits? His eyes brightened. We're in counseling though, he said. Think it'll help?

Oh, my God. Bill. Lorrie glared at him and then shrugged. Oh hell, we have no secrets. All of Paulette knows. Small town, big ears. Just ask Tom. She winked at Tom Shultz, who nodded.

Tom had married Beth Sinclare, the egg farm heiress and State Fair Queen. Whole town knew about Beth divorcing me for the carpet cleaner, 'fore I ever got wind of it, Tom said.

Carpet cleaner? Elsa echoed. She choked into her fist, trying hard not to laugh. As in Out, out, damn spot?

What's that? Tom asked. Some new ad?

Shakespeare, Aggie said, and swept her long hair over her shoulder. Mrs. Milton's English Lit class, Tommy. You'd know, if you hadn't spit-balled Spud Henson the entire time.

Tom pursed his lips. It was clear he couldn't quite figure out what was so funny. Anyway, he said. Beth and the Carpet Express guy took out a second mortgage just last week, so, hmm, maybe the carpet business has—

Worn a bit thin! Mindy and Elsa chorused in a howl of laughter.

What'd I say now? Tom demanded. Aggie leaned in and whispered in his ear and his face flamed. Nothing lasts anymore, he lamented.

The problem isn't the I do's, it's telling lies, Elsa commented. She had her arm draped over Mindy's shoulder, rubbing the other woman's skin gently with her thumb. In my practice, she said, those are inevitably the worst divorces. Where there hasn't been honesty in the relationship for a long, long time.

Bottom line, for sure, Tom said. He gazed at Aggie, who toyed with a French fry. Beth didn't want kids. I did, he said. She liked farm, I liked town. I was faithful…she was not.

Mindy patted his hand. She was a bitch, Tom. Everybody knew it.

Coulda told me, he said.

We did, Mindy retorted. Remember the beach party at Andi and Marley's?

A swim party none of us would ever forget. Least of all, Beth. Spring break, junior year, and the gang had come up to the cabin—Donna giving us the key with an admonition to behave. It had been too cold to swim, but we'd had the boat for fun, and as darkness fell, built a beach fire. We got way too wasted on pot and beer, and before long Beth stood up in the fire circle, stoned out of her gourd, and informed Elsa and Mindy that they were lesbians and totally going to hell.

She deserved what she got, Mindy said complacently, taking a drink from Elsa's beer.

Lorrie widened her eyes. Couldn't believe you picked her up in that fireman's carry we learned in PE, Mindy. Tossed her in the lake like a sack of potatoes!

Beth had been livid and took Bill's car—dripping wet—to drive herself home. Frank had to give Bill and Lorrie a ride back to Paulette.

You guys were right, Tom said, morose. He shot a look around the table. Frigid, too, he blurted. Got off using this vibrating contraption called a Sure Thing she ordered from some catalog.

Mindy and Elsa looked at each other and Mindy collapsed in silent giggles, clinging to Elsa's arm. Oh, my God, she choked. Maybe we could've been friends.

The Sure Thing? Aggie asked, bemused. About yeah big and so round? She used her hands to circumscribe an obvious shape in the air. About ninety-nine dollars and ninety-five cents? I sell it. Great shoulder massager.

Frank, seated in the corner, paid no attention to our laughter, checking messages on his phone.

Marley, come with me, Lorrie said. I gotta pee. She lurched up out of her chair, knocking it backwards. Tom caught it, and balanced it upright.

What is it with you women? Can't pee by yourselves? he asked.

I steadied Lorrie with one hand as we jostled through the crowd toward the restrooms. I glanced out the windows. Beyond Macklin's beach, the lake was dark. Andi had yet to arrive.

Can't hold my pee at all, Lorrie grumbled as she washed up. That's what four kids does to you. She put on a dash of red lipstick, observing me in the mirror. How's Frank, Marley?

I was threading my fingers through tangles in my hair but stopped. What do you mean?

She closed her lipstick case. My sister in Salt Lake works with Lynette at the hospital. You know his wife has cancer?

I said nothing.

Listen, doll. Her face softened. Love the guy. And you. But I gotta say, it's probably not a good idea to get mixed up in what's going on between her and Frank.

I'm not mixed up in anything, I said, shocked. What do you mean?

I don't know details but my sister says Lynette kicked Frank out. Lorrie fluffed her hair. Who knows where it's headed, but I wouldn't be throwing any gas on that fire, if you get my drift.

Why would Lynette push Frank away? I asked.

Lorrie shook her head. Could be the cancer talking. Some people react real bad after news like that. They want to break things. So, Lynette breaks Frank. It happens sometimes, between married people. Who else is there for an anger that big? She gripped my hands. Be careful is all.

Lorrie left me outside the restrooms and detoured to the bar for a gin and tonic. The band was beginning to warm up in the back room, the sound of drums and amplifiers skittering over the metallic screech of the Ping-Pong tables as they were dragged off the dance floor. I rounded the corner and bumped into Bill leaning on one arm, gazing into the cigarette machine.

You realize this thing sells only breath mints and condoms? He looked at the mound of change in his hand. I was looking for menthols, he said. Not Ribbed Extra Large.

I turned straight into a familiar black turtleneck. The scent of wood smoke and pine.

Hey, Frank, I said, stepping back.

Ladies and Gents, interrupted the band's lead singer through his mic. Look who just sashayed into our little watering hole! Why the one and only—Miss Andi Stone! The stage lights strobed wildly and around us the room shifted and broke into cheers. Whistles and the stomp of boots thundered in my ears.

From the corner of my eye I saw Andi sail up to the stage, her arm in Royal Morton's. At least from the back the man in the tailored white jacket resembled Royal—he had the same warm nutmeg-colored skin and hawkish leanness—although this man had filled out and grown a few inches since high school. Sleek titanium glasses had replaced the plastic black Costellos. And Andi...My sister had outdone herself.

She let go of Royal's arm and scampered up on the stage in a skintight black dress, two feet of fringe hanging from a tiny gold bolero dancing about her hips. Her scarlet hair teased out in fat curls beneath a gold-sequined Stetson.

Hi ya, Macklin's! Andi waved and pirouetted around the stage.

The bar hollered back, Hi ya, Andi!

The room started to spin. Easy, Marley, Frank said in my ear. He caught my wrist. Get some air? He guided me to the back of the bar toward the open deck. He grabbed a lap throw from the basket by the door and tossed it over my shoulders as we stepped out into the cold.

Above us the indigo sky held a million pinpoints of light, a velvet cloth confetti-gunned with stars. Out here beyond the muffled bass of the band it was quiet; the only sound the rhythmic slap of water against wood.

You okay? Frank asked. You seemed overwhelmed in

there. He searched my face. That glam stuff? That's just Andi being Andi, Marley. We all know that.

I know, I said, fixing my eyes on the deck railing until the waves of vertigo subsided. Andi's splashy entrance hadn't bothered me. Who better than I to appreciate my sister's knack for the show. I pulled the blanket close. I'm fine, I said. I just…dislike crowds.

We stood against the railing, watching colored boat lights crisscross the lake.

It's strange seeing everybody again like this. How much has changed, I said. How much hasn't.

Another moment of clarity, nested in another loss. Lorrie's words of warning haunted me. Frank, kind and honest Frank. He was my friend. And that was a problem. I took a deep breath. People are going to start talking if we hang out together, Frank. This is Paulette we're dealing with here.

Let 'em talk, Frank said.

I'm serious, Frank. You have more to lose than I do.

He glanced at me, amused. I think I can handle it, he said.

I don't know, I said. Trust me. People can be cruel. I left it at that. Celebrity, even the faintest dust of it, fueled gossip and sold stories.

You're the serious one tonight, Frank said.

I shrugged.

After a time, Frank stirred and hooked his boot over the lowest crossbar on the railing. What's with you and The Andi Stone Tour if crowds aren't your thing? he asked.

Good question, I said. Sometimes it's as if life just happens, Frank. One day you realize you're not where you thought you'd be.

He looked sideways.

I'm talking about music, I said.

You're not happy about all this? He gestured toward the bar—Andi holding court behind us.

Pushing the next big hit isn't the reason I made music my life, Frank. Yet somehow, that's the life I live. Does that make sense?

He shook his head. No, I don't get it.

You're a teacher, I said. What you do always matters.

He chuckled. If you mean teach the Table of Elements and test the little idiots on the parts of a molecule, well, sure, he said. He spun me around, holding me by the shoulders. Look, Marley. If you're doing what you believe in, and somehow it adds to the world and doesn't subtract from it, in my eyes it's all good.

He glanced over his shoulder. Look at our friends in there, he said. They're crazy and happy—and good people for all that.

Yes. I get that. But, Frank, I want to know what music is. I emphasized the word. The colors, do you see them? The shift in the air when someone sings or sinks into a note? But instead I write songs that are honestly a step away from a jingle. An Andi Stone hit is not serious music—it's an earworm on the radio I get paid handsomely for.

I looked at my boots. Why was I pouring out my soul to this man?

Back in college I thought I'd be writing my own music one day, I continued, my voice quiet. Not chasing the Billboard Top Forty. I glanced sideways. Does that sound arrogant? Like a stupid fantasy?

Frank tilted his head back and looked up at the stars. Marley, he said. From the time you stepped onstage at school and sang that solo you wrote in competition choir—everybody thought you had a gift. You wrote music about the world in a way the rest of us couldn't find words for. He lowered his gaze and met my eyes, gentle. I know things have been difficult—with losing your mom and all. But you have a gift for music. That means something. Don't tell me it doesn't.

The tops of the pines danced with bats, their spiky silhouettes flickering in and out against the rising moon.

Remember, Frank said, after that terrible earthquake in Haiti? When the images of destruction were beamed around the world? There was this video clip I'll never forget. This old woman standing in the rubble, singing from a book she called *The Songs of Hope*. There she was, in barely audible French singing to no one and anyone who might hear, around her the dead and despairing. This stunning human spirit amid that terrible disaster gifting comfort. The gift of hope.

I bowed my head, moved by how well Frank understood. I wondered if he would also understand if I told him about the crushed blossom song. The first music from my hands that had sung itself to me in a very long time. Music not conceived to win accolades or radio time but that came from somewhere inside. And that somewhere felt authentic, a wider, freer room to roam in.

Tell me, Frank said. Why did you write your first song?

Immediately I had a lucid mental image of Andi and I, maybe four or five, in the back seat of the Pontiac. A hard rain streamed down the windows, and Andi was crying. She wanted to sleep and laid her head, exhausted, on top of her stuffed duck across my lap. Donna drove furiously through the dark, the windshield wipers thumping back and forth, back and forth.

I remembered this detail clearly because of the rhythm and the sound of each blade as it swiped right and then left.

We took car trips when I was little, I said slowly.

Mostly at night. I made up traveling songs to keep us company.

Frank nodded.

The noises of the car, the rhythm of the road, I'd listen, I said. I looked over. You know how tires on concrete sound different from asphalt or gravel? Those were melodies to me. I made up words to go with the sounds and taught them to Andi, and we would sing to each other when we got scared, I said. But that's not really music. Just—I spread out my hands.

Singing from the rubble? Frank asked. He leaned an elbow on the railing. One of your early songs, "Sundown," saved my sanity, Marley, he said. *One day's end holds the promise of another day to come*, he quoted. That line alone got me through the days after Lynette's diagnosis.

He turned to face the bar, crossed his arms, and leaned back against the rails. Those words got me to where I could talk with Tallyn, Marley, he said. To where I could face my class again, after the collapse at home. Sure, maybe they won you a Grammy, or whatever, but to me they were important and personal. I've always wanted to thank you for that.

I laid a hand on his arm. Briefly, just a touch.

There are unbreakable links between each of us and everything else, Frank, I said. Music is the language of breath, of the sky, even two little girls in a car. A melody—one pure note—and those who wander near, who listen, feel infused with belonging. Joy.

What's stopping you then? Frank asked. Do it. Write your own music.

Here you are! I've looked all over for you, baby sis.

Andi stood bathed in the light from the bar, Royal behind her. Our little joke, you know, Andi said, and peeped up at Royal. I'm a teensy few minutes older than Marley.

Frank straightened off the railing, catching someone's empty beer bottle with the toe of his boot and sending it spinning off the deck into the grass.

Andi smiled. Nice to see you again, Lock.

You too, Andi, Frank said.

She turned to me. Marley, I've agreed to a couple songs for Macklin's after the band's next set. Off the last album I think, and maybe a classic or two. I need you on backup, sugar. Be a peach? The band will lend you whatever you need.

I nodded unhappily. This I had not anticipated. Although Andi had yet to bring up the last songs I owed her for the new album *Baby Look Away*, distracted by the cabin, I knew she was in full diva mode tonight. I needed to show up and not let her down.

Work means we play when the play is paid, Andi chuckled. That's how it goes in this business. She patted Royal's cheek. Be a doll and fetch me a Mountain Dew from the bar, would you? No ice and bring it to the stage?

She swept back inside, Royal trailing after her.

19

Someone called my name from the lobby.

I turned and a man in his late fifties stepped forward out of the shadows. Shoulders rounded in middle age with a slight paunch in the midsection, the man's salt-and-pepper hair brushed his shoulders in the style of an aged rocker. I normally would have assumed the stranger was an Andi Stone fan, mistaking me for my sister, but something about the horn-rimmed glasses, baggy cords, and button-up shirt, rolled at the elbow, suggested otherwise. Very few music fans knew me by name.

I paused, preoccupied by the music set I was unprepared for and loathe to do. May I help you? I asked.

Marley Stone! The man smiled broadly, extending his hand. Damn, it's good to see you.

It was the smile that triggered recognition. The Mickey Dolenz grin that had once made the girls in Music Appreciation class swoon through lectures on five-part harmony and The Jazz Age.

You recognize me? the man asked. He dropped his

hand as I stared back at him in shock. It's me, Robby Carville. Paulette High. Your choir teacher?

Time telescoped as if no time stood between my high school years and now. I was again sixteen. The end of junior year. The last day and minute I stood in front of Robby Carville after music class.

That was fine, Marley, Mr. Carville said, after I finished the vocal solo from "You Fascinate Me So," the same arrangement made famous by Blossom Dearie. We were alone in the music room, rehearsing one last time before the class trip to the state competition. He got up from the piano. Now maybe you could relax your hands?

I looked down, startled. My hands were balled into fists at my sides. I stretched them open. Sorry, Mr. Carville.

Are you nervous? he asked. You needn't be. You nailed that.

I'm not good on stage, I said. I get kind of freaked out.

I'd always hated the faces, the lights. Donna, for all her back-stage cheek-pinching and encouraging words when we were kids had changed none of that. What if I croaked under pressure and let the ensemble down?

Mr. Carville studied me a moment. I have some ideas, he said. He walked out and sat in the front row in one of the auditorium seats. Can you see me, he asked?

Yes, I said.

Look up, he directed. The last row of seats. Do you see that red EXIT sign?

I nodded.

I want you to sing to that sign, he instructed. Don't look here, where I'm sitting. Look there.

He got up then and flicked off all the auditorium lights but those directly over the stage. I blinked, blinded by the shift in spotlights.

Now. Sing it again, he said, and this time focus on that sign.

I frowned. I didn't see how any of this would help. I began again, singing not to the darkened auditorium but focused on the red EXIT sign. I sang my heart out to that sign, forgetting about the lights in my eyes, even that I was alone on the stage.

Near the midpoint of the song I became aware of a warmth, a presence. As though someone were standing directly behind me.

A pair of large hands gripped my shoulders gently and I hiccupped a note before the hands relaxed but rested there, lightly. Keeping singing, Carville said softly. Imagine that I am your group. Here, for you. Ready to step up and carry a note. Rescue any song if you falter. You are not alone, Marley. Not like it feels.

He dropped his hands.

I gulped for air and swung up to the high C, hitting it perfectly, Mr. Carville's comforting presence unseen in the dark behind me. I repeated the coda and let the last note hang, as we discussed, waiting for the group to join in and handle the refrain to the end.

The lights flicked on. Mr. Carville was back in his seat in the front row. He clapped silently. He beamed at me. Awesome, he said. You got it. He walked to the stage, looking up at me. Remember those two things, he said. Look up. And you're never as alone as you feel.

The crash of glassware behind the swinging doors to the lodge kitchen broke the suspended moment. No exit. Not here, not now. I pulled myself together, staring in shock at the now older man in front of me.

A couple passed between us, edging by gingerly as though the air itself were barbed.

Sorry if I startled you, Carville said, and pushed his glasses up. The gesture betrayed his nervousness, the slight tremor of his hand. I did email, he said. You never responded.

He drew close and clasped a hand on my shoulder.

I flinched at his touch.

I know who you are, I said, shaking off his hand and stepping back. What do you want, Robby?

I used his first name deliberately, unwilling to give Carville either the respect or power he'd once had over me as a teenager.

I'd like to talk, he said, warm and hopeful. His smile deepened and he sighed, expressing an emotion somewhere between nostalgia and delight. It's been a long time. I've missed you.

You've got to be kidding, I said flatly.

No, I'm quite serious, Carville protested. I've followed your career for years—always hoped we'd run into each other someday. You can't imagine how proud I am of you. You were my best student.

You and I are not friends, I said roughly.

He leaned in. What was that?

You're a goddamned stalker, Carville. Get out of my way or I'll call the cops, I said. I turned.

Wait! Don't go. There are things to say, Carville burst out. Five minutes, Marley, he begged. And then, I promise, I'll leave.

He watched my face, anxious, suddenly less sure of himself.

I weighed the situation. Five minutes and no more emails? What was there to say anyway, a rushed confession, possibly an apology? I could handle that.

Over there, I said.

Carville followed me into the empty restaurant at the backside of the bar. Dinner seating had yet to begin so I chose a table in a corner, signaling the waitress for coffee. She poured two cups and set down a pitcher of cream.

Neither one of us picked up our cups.

Line of sight, line of sight, I reminded myself. Breathe.

Carville removed his glasses, rubbing each lens with the hem of his shirt as he considered his next words. He set them on the table and spun his coffee cup around by the handle.

Let me start over, he said. I apologize for coming up on you like that. From the ruckus in there, he tipped his thumb toward the bar, I gather your sister's here and you two have a gig tonight? He waited, but without any reaction from me, he sniffed nervously and plodded on. Gosh, your talent blossomed, Marley. I mean the accolades, the awards!

My pulse thundered, echoed in my ears, a pump of sound. I stared at Carville, forcing myself to dismantle the monster in my memory.

The man before me was older than the music teacher of high school, his beard, gray and clipped close to his jaw. A tall man no longer athletic, frayed at the edges and somewhat abused by time. I took notice of the telltale flush across his nose and cheeks from too much drink. The teeth tarnished by caffeine.

You should be in jail, Carville, I said without emotion.

He exhaled. As if the batter had hit the opening pitch back in the direction expected, if not exactly hoped for. A hit he'd prepared for in the many ways he'd played the conversation out in his head.

I never looked at what happened between us back then as anything but the highlight of my life, Marley.

It wasn't a relationship, Carville. It was rape.

Oh, dear girl, he said. He leaned forward, his hands inching toward mine. Do you not understand how deeply

I felt about you? All that special tutoring? The after-school sessions, just you and me? We were made for each other. I knew it and I think you did, too. It's just… He paused and fiddled with his glasses as he searched for the word. …unfortunate, we shall say, that I was married, and you were so young.

His expression was tender, no sign of regret in his eyes.

I'm sorry I left Paulette, he said. I was afraid of what such strong feelings would do to my career, my family. I had to think of them.

He spread his hands in a what-can-you-do gesture and smiled at me as if we were comrades in our responsibilities and troubles.

You were my teacher. I was a teenager, and I trusted you, I said.

He shrugged. I really don't think high school was as innocent as you make it sound. You were dating. A senior, if I recollect.

I held myself in check.

Why did you contact me, Carville? I asked.

To see you, he said. I'm a huge fan! I've kept track of the albums. I've got one of each framed on my office wall. I sent a card once to Anchorage—got your address from the alumni office but it bounced back. Drove over to a concert in Portland even, he added. His gray eyes lit up. Took my daughters with me. Afterward when I tried to see you, security wouldn't let us backstage. His face fell. They didn't believe me when I said I was your friend. Guess a ton of creeps must hang around you girls.

Then I read about your mom, he continued. Learned you were living somewhere in Seattle.

He paused. Not far away at all.

I felt hardly capable of breath. Carville had been this near for years.

I visited Seattle bars with your picture, even sent around a yearbook. Nothing. It's taken awhile to finally get a good email, he admitted. Very uncooperative manager you have, by the way. Not helpful at all. He allowed a conspiratorial wink. A bit of detective work, the help of the reunion committee—I found you.

He picked up his coffee and took a sip. I left secondary teaching after Paulette. You heard? Moved up to college-level. Chaired the department of a private music school in Utah. Eventually we returned to Idaho, to Boise. In fact, I retired last year. I'm running a private adult studio now, he said with pride.

Robby Carville had left teaching in secondary schools. The news gave me pause. Because he was aware he was on thin ice or to expand his range of opportunities with women still young but of a legal age?

The thought was horrifying. I felt heavy, aware of the weight of my silence, the moral consequence of not telling someone in Paulette years ago what Carville had done.

The bastard belonged in jail for God's sake. Far, far from children, even his own.

Carville folded his hands, relaxed. I'm still married, not much to say about that. But the kids are grown. I feel—freer—to do what I want now. You're single. I'm sure you get that.

You disgust me, I said.

Carville straightened and squinted, mildly confused. As if these weren't the words he had expected. You're upset? About us? Look at you, he protested. You're beautiful! What did you expect, I'm just a man. He shook his head. Your life is a success. You have it all—fame, wealth. What do you have to be so angry about?

He placed his glasses back on, both elbows on the

table. His expression altered, became concerned and empathetic, professorial. The counselor, the coach, the man you could trust.

Marley. Dear. Yes, you were young, he said, sentimental. I was your first, wasn't I?

The truth flamed in my face.

I thought so, he said. That's why it was so special, you see? He lowered his voice. I've thought about you every night, he said. Bet you didn't know that.

I stood. We're done here. I want you to go. I insist that you go.

He opened his mouth to protest and reached across the table, dropping his hands, empty, as I pushed back my chair. We can't be friends? he asked, incredulous.

Listen. Listen carefully, I said, calm. If you ever come near me again, my first step will be to have a little chat with your wife. I'm sure she'd be quite interested in what I have to say. My second visit will be to the press. Free publicity for your new voice studio.

I let the words sink in.

Carville blanched.

He quickly fished out a five from his wallet for the coffees and tossed it on the table.

Sure, sure, he said. He stood.

I should have brought a nice wine? he asked. Something fancy instead of coffee? I read somewhere you like tequila. I should bring tequila.

Drop dead, Carville, I said. And walked away.

20

I worked my way through the crowds to the bar and climbed on the foot rail to draw the attention of the bartender.

I slipped, unexpectedly weak at the knees. Someone steadied my back, and I turned to lock eyes with a man in a denim shirt, his straight black hair bound back with a strip of hide secured with a turquoise rock.

Ricky! I flung my arms around the man's neck. Ricky Strongbow, famous local poet and badass rodeo hand, and the only friend from Baker's Dozen I'd stayed in touch with over the years. After the encounter with Carville, running into Ricky was a godsend.

When did you get here? I asked.

Just, he said. He raised a hand to catch the bartender's attention. Get you a drink? I'm ordering a beer.

You smell like saddle leather, I said. My nose wrinkled. How about a couple shots with that, Mister January 2010, I said.

He put a finger to his lips. Hush. You saw that?

Who didn't? I said, and laughed. Suddenly I hadn't a care in the world, safe with Ricky. Carville had been right about one thing, I thought. You're never as alone as you feel.

That calendar, I said. Brilliant fundraiser! For the Tri-State Arts Scholarship Fund, right? They sold the *Bachelors of the Inland Empire* calendar everywhere. You bet I had one on my refrigerator. I elbowed him.

He held his hand up as if to shield his eyes and mock-groaned.

I don't suppose anybody noticed your stellar grade point average printed in those tiny letters next to all that Nez Perce handsomeness though. Imagine, I said. Ricky Strongbow, fur-wrapped in front of a fire. That's one toasty man-wrap.

They don't stop teasing me on the rez, Ricky said. He shook his head. If I'd known the godawful trouble…You know Calvin Klein underwear called me? His expression was genuinely horrified. My grandma about stroked out.

Our drinks arrived and we downed shots in tandem, finishing with Macklin's tap brews.

I gotta be quick, I said, wiping my mouth with the back of my hand. Andi's planned a set.

I hadn't seen Ricky since college graduation, passing through Paulette on my way to Alaska. The last we'd talked he lived downriver, near the town of Lewiston, Idaho. Had a cattle ranch and a bunch of little brothers he was raising, and fortunately, an affinity for hard work. The bachelor calendar suggested perhaps he, too, was unlucky in love.

Still on the ranch? I asked.

Yep, he said. Still got the little—much bigger—brothers. Six footers the lot, he said, and all of 'em married. Except me. He half-winced. No longer got the wife. He went on to explain he'd married a vegan grad student in the microbiology department at the University of Idaho, but the marriage hadn't lasted past a Lewiston winter.

Vegan? I asked, stifling laughter. You ranch for a living and married a vegan?

Ranch life isn't for everyone, he acknowledged. Whole lot of space between fence posts—pardon the sad metaphor.

Speaking of metaphors. Love reading about your poetry, I said. Time to time I'd notice chapbooks of Ricky's poetry reviewed in the papers or on the internet. I only read the reviews, I admitted. One of these days I'll have time for an actual book.

They're poems, Ricky said with a guffaw. You could read the whole damn thing sitting in a drive thru.

Not if one intends to appreciate them, I corrected him. And I do. Appreciate them. To us, I said, lifting a second tequila shot.

Lone warriors, Ricky said, lifting his own.

Still sing? I asked. You were the best in the group, you know. The way you handled the Louis Armstrong stuff. I shook my head in admiration. You totally deserved that U of I scholarship.

His lean face creased in regret. Nope. I don't, he said. Not anymore. I write poems when I get the chance though. Helps me think. Never made it through college, to tell you the truth. Running cattle and rodeo prizes pay the bills. He leaned over. Tell you a secret, he said. Sometimes I do sing to them.

Who, what—the bills? You sing to the bills? I asked. It was hard to hear over the din of the bar.

The cows, nimnuts. You know, cowboy lullabies. Call me Ricky "James Taylor" Strongbow. He chuckled and ordered us a third shot. You were good yourself, Marley, he said. You placed at regionals, a cappella solo. Right?

Yeah, well, you won. And no, I can't sing. Haven't since high school.

Hasn't hurt ya none, Ricky said. I see you and your sister's names everywhere.

I leaned my cheek in my hand. Honestly, I think I need a break, I said.

Ricky laced slender, callused fingers around his beer. Yep, he said. Breaks are good. Take 'em now and then myself. Have a little shack on the Clearwater for when I need to get away.

Tom and Mindy swooped in behind our barstools. Ricky! Ricky! Ricky! Mindy squealed, hugging him tight. Everyone came! Her eyes shone. Even Andi, she said. Can you believe it? And Royal Morton, in like a thousand-dollar cashmere jacket—and not one pocket protector. She glanced around. Lock's here somewhere, she said. Grab your beers, guys. Let's join the gang.

Tom winked. Don't Bogart our Ricky, Marley.

Ricky snorted. No-good-sack-of-horseshit, if you ask my ex. He grinned, showing even white teeth and one missing canine.

Mindy lurched forward for a closer look. Where's your tooth? she said. Tom pulled her up just short of cracking foreheads with Ricky.

Lost, Ricky said. To a bull named Wacky Weed up at Calgary Nationals. He laughed. He got the tooth, I got the ten-thousand-dollar prize.

Get a new tooth then, Mindy demanded. You can afford it, mister.

Naw. I like the little scare it gives the bank tellers.

Mindy giggled. You couldn't scare a fly, Ricky Strongbow. Hell, I don't think you could even shoot one. You're damn near cross-eyed.

Too true, Ricky admitted. Too much rodeo.

I'll grab your drinks, Tom said. You all follow. Using

his broad build to our benefit, he cleared a path from the bar.

I held back. I'll catch up later, I said. My head was swimming from the tequila and Andi's set was coming up fast. I couldn't remember one of our songs, not one. My feet tangled underneath me as I tried to navigate the hallway toward the restrooms.

Easy there, someone said. A hand appeared to steady me and I knew without looking it was Frank.

Frank, I said. Excuse me. I gotta pee.

It's allowed. He smiled. Here you go.

I looked up and realized I was at the door to the ladies' room. Frank let go of my elbow. Once inside, I placed a hand on the wall to steady the room, over-rotated, and fell backward through the bathroom stall door with a crash.

You okay? Frank called from outside the door.

I might need a coffee, I said.

ເຈຈຈ

A single spot lit the stage.

The lead singer for the local Chimney Rock cover band Log Jammer walked into the light and swept off his trucker cap, grinning. Lower the volume, folks, he ordered. Quiet, please! He waited for the room to hush. Ladies and gents, he said. It is my genuine pleasure to introduce Miss Andi Stone, accompanied by sister Marley Stone on guitar! The audience burst into applause. He grinned. Hell, yes. These girls are locals! Let's give 'em a big Macklin's welcome!

The room erupted in a rumble of stomping boots. The last diners from the adjoining restaurant and outside decks straggled in, swelling the crowd. The bar standing room only.

Taking her cue, Andi tipped her hat and swept on

stage. Laughing and waving, she bussed the lead singer on the cheek and twirled under the lights as the cover band's drummer rolled a slow beat. She stomped her heel as she twirled, taking in the room with a sexy wink. Her Stetson glittered under the lights and she swung her hips to set the fringe on her vest in motion.

Are you ready, Lost Prince? she called to the bar crowd. Are ya hot to have some fun? She blew kisses. Let's start off with somethin' off our last album, *Waitin' On You*!

The room shouted approval.

Andi leaned to the drummer and gave him the beat. He adjusted the bandana over his shaved skull and began to bang his sticks enthusiastically. I stood in the shadows, a borrowed guitar slung over my shoulder, pick in hand.

Andi gripped the mic, beaming. Hey, people! Your love means everything to me, she hollered. And don't you forget it! She nodded and waved me into the spotlight, Let's give it up for my baby sister, Marley Stone! And we are…THE ANDI STONE TOUR!

I could hear Ricky's distinctive wolf whistle from somewhere in the back and lifted a hand in acknowledgement, pasting on a show smile. My guts were in turmoil. I wished there had been a keyboard. I was rusty as hell on steel-string—mine was an acoustic guitar with softer, nylon strings. I adjusted the capo to the right pitch for the song and hoped for the best.

Andi snapped her fingers and arched over, bending low, tapping her boot in rhythm with the drumbeat. Shaking loose, she jumped high and launched into the opening of "Everything to Me." I joined on the guitar, tight with the drummer. I'd played for Andi for so long it seemed. I couldn't forget. I melded with the music, invisible in my dark jeans and black lace shirt in the shadow of Andi's glittering gold and fringe. I held the fretted low E in vibrato as Andi sailed away into a higher octave. That's what I did. Cushioned her voice, gave her a musical pocket in which to fall.

Several guys pushed their tables against the wall, grabbed their dates and, beers in hand, began to hoof to The Stone Tour songs they knew so well. Andi swung into the catchy refrain of "Everything to Me" and I swayed in rhythm, guitar at my hip. She tossed her hair and grinned wide, putting her whole heart into even this tiny audience. She was born to this, I thought. She loves the lights. Home in the center of attention.

Andi signaled for the switch into "Bolero Avenue." A song I'd written in San Antonio a decade ago, sitting along River Walk and watching as a sketch artist worked a quick portrait of a young girl. The song was about love, about etching someone on your heart, left with only a drawing when that someone was gone.

Bolero opened on extended solo guitar and I stepped forward into the light, letting my fingers release the song—an arpeggio of intense notes falling to the far corners of the barroom.

My boot tapped the stage as my left hand worked the frets and my right rippled through the complex fingering with a telltale echo of its Texas waltz. The crowd leaned in as I began to sing the backup vocals to Andi's lead. But Andi wasn't singing. She was standing out of the light, keeping rhythm with a toe tap.

I shot her a look of panic. *Get in here!* I mouthed.

She gave me a tiny thumbs-up and I glanced back at the crowd, my vision blurring in the brightness of the spot. You're never alone, you're never alone, I repeated in my head, as I had in every studio session or concert I'd had to join in on since high school. Look up. Remember to look up.

Instead I looked down. At the edge of the dance floor I

spotted a pair of familiar scuffed boots, followed the boots upward, and found Frank's eyes.

He gave me an encouraging smile.

No way I was going to shoulder this alone. Maybe it was the tequila talking but I leaned into the mic, Come on up here, Prom King, 1988, I said. I looked straight at Frank, sustaining the melody with a repeating chord. He frowned. Yes, you, Frank Lockford, I said.

Can an ex-football player dance? I asked the crowd. Someone pushed Frank forward and he climbed up on the stage, pink with embarrassment.

Follow my lead, I whispered. I backed in close to his body and started a rhythm with my hips. He placed one hand on my waist and awkwardly matched my moves.

I began to really sing then. Opened my voice and sang the lyrics the way I'd written them. A love song to the man a girl would never see again, but for his "picture on her wall." Frank knew the lyrics and sang a respectable baritone accompaniment, and I flashed him a happy unselfconscious smile when we hit the last refrain.

The bar burst into applause and Andi stepped back into the lights, waving her hand. Marley Stone, she called out. And Paulette's own, Frank Lockford!

Frank bowed and leapt off the stage as fast as humanly possible. I stepped back and Andi suddenly called out Ricky Strongbow.

The crowd pushed the lanky cowboy forward and I laughed. I could see her brilliant plan—showcase the locals, get the whole place singing. Make the evening something for everyone. Andi, showing love to her hometown crowd. No wonder people adored her.

Ricky jumped in with Andi on the kickass dance tune, "Wrestlin'." Both Faith Hill and Luke Bryan had recorded the song after Andi debuted it, making it a steady moneymaker for us. But to see Ricky belting out the fast lyrics of a man lassoed in love as he do-si-doed Andi about the stage was simply hilarious. Andi hammed it up, waving her Stetson like an extra in *Oklahoma!* The performance more fun than any rendition I could recall.

A half-dozen songs later, Andi announced she had a final treat to wrap up The Andi Stone Tour's special appearance at Macklin's. She stood back, sweeping her hand to one side.

I present once again, my sister, she said. Singing only for Macklin's her newest original song, "Broken By You"!

I froze. Andi, I hissed. What are you doing? It's gone—burned!

She twisted her head and whispered, I found copies with Mom's recipes. She saved it, Marley. It's good! Her eyes shone with love.

She leaned into the mic, looking at me sideways. Don't be shy, she sang out, winking broadly.

Don't be shy! Don't be shy! Chanted the room, taking up Andi's cheer.

I grabbed her arm. I don't remember the words, I said.

Andi clipped a page of music to the mic stand.

Gotcha covered, she said. Tonight, you're the star. Knock 'em dead, sis. She blew me a kiss. She turned to the crowd. We don't mind if she has to read from the class notes, do we?

The room hooted with laughter.

I approached the mic and stared blindly at the sheet music as Andi handed a second copy to the drummer. A guy from the band dragged a stool into the spotlight and then stepped off stage.

I was alone.

Don't be shy! Don't be shy! Elsa and Mindy chanted from the rear, backed by the strong voices of both Tom and Bill.

Give it up, Macklin's! Andi shouted from the side of
the stage. A MARLEY STONE ORIGINAL!

They were waiting. They were all waiting.

21

Play it! Play it! The crowd linked arms and swayed as they chanted, drunk and loud.

I didn't need sheet music. I'd worked on the lyrics the entire summer after Robby Carville, and then hidden the song away the final weeks before Frank left for college. Until yesterday when Andi found the notebook page of penciled lyrics and chords at the cabin, I'd assumed the song was lost—and not sorry. It had haunted me. "Broken By You" felt like a curse, something that would come to be if I'd let it. The way epitaphs become both prologue and summary.

I settled uneasily on the stool provided, one boot catching a rung, my knee bent to cradle the guitar. The heat of the spotlight felt hot on my skin. I did a quick finger-practice through the order of chords, aware of the waiting, expectant faces beyond. I stared at the tip of my boot and laid the guitar across my knees. I couldn't.

Come on, Marley! Lorrie screamed happily from the middle of the crowd. Do it!

The bar began to stomp their boots in unison and sweat tracked slowly between my shoulder blades.

Looking down, I plucked the anchor note of the opening chord and the room hushed. My hand trembled and I dropped the pick. I let it go, staring at it on the floor.

I glanced up and locked eyes with Ricky, standing next to Elsa off to one side. He tapped a finger against his temple, our old choir signal for "Sing it, don't think it."

Here goes, I croaked into the mic. But just so you know—my sister made me.

The room rippled with laughter.

This song is called "Broken By You," I said. There's not much to say about it, except, sometimes, we human folk forget we're stronger than we think. We bury the bad stuff. And then it owns us. But someday you put yourself back together. This song is about that someday.

Girl, that's what makes good country, the bandleader called from the bar, at his elbow a shot glass of rye bourbon. Any damn song that helps with forgettin'.

A woman yelled out, Hell, yes!

Who the fuck cares? demanded someone else beyond the bar. Let's get some music! We're not all Class of Whatever here, ya know!

Mindy threw the anonymous objector a dirty look, handing her drink to Elsa. And then I saw him, saw the man standing in the shadows.

Carville.

I registered the burliness of his build first and then the shaggy hair, the gray beard, the eyes fixed on me behind the tinted lenses.

I stiffened. Trapped on the stage—a sharp white peninsula afloat in an animal dark. All edges and iron and rust.

The drummer slipped me a whiskey shot, his eyes sympathetic. I tossed it back, and in doing so, caught the distant red of an EXIT sign.

I leaned sideways to lift the fallen pick. Play it horse-buggy slow—four/four, I whispered to the drummer. He nodded, and began to beat a single snare, quiet and steady.

All right, y'all, I said, in a voice roughened by whiskey. Listen up. Tonight's performance of "Broken By You" is a shout-out to that man who taught me the difference between the good notes and all the rest.

Mr. Robby Carville, I said, and pointed. Here tonight!

Heads swiveled as people followed the direction of my finger to the far corner of the room. Carville backed two steps into the crowd but found himself boxed in and his expression shifted to one of panic.

A few people clapped then, and he hesitated, smiled weakly, and bowed.

"Broken By You," I said, and rippled the pick down the familiar open A minor.

I became a ghost, a moth wing.

Memories spooled from my fingers, shimmered over the audience, and swirled away in halos of light. They seeped from the guitar and from the notes as I sang them.

Bust me up, break me down, bust my world in two.
I barely knew the world was mine, barely given time.
Then came you.
Forever is forever and forever, broken by you.
Bust me up, break me down, bust my world in two.
I barely knew the world was mine. Barely given time.
Busted, broken, barely grown, forever broken in two.
Forever is forever, broken by you.

I sang to the darkened room.

I sang my secret. I spilled my guts on the floor of Macklin's bar.

I was singing to the past, to innocence. To what I had

confessed to Frank, but could not, did not yet feel. Not until I voiced the notes of that long ago song.

Anybody's heartbreak. Anybody's pain.

But I knew.

And so did the man in the back of the room.

I remembered, my body remembered, even as my voice knew the words to sing.

Early June and the all-state high school choir finals. A van ride across the dry hills to a college town somewhere in central Idaho.

The nerves, the noise.

High school choirs and a cappella groups practiced in the hallways of the campus Music Ed building. There were cans of chilled Coke and hilarious burp-offs. Arley's lucky rabbit foot passed around between us. Stage lights and sing-offs. The solos.

The competitions ended. Stage lights out. Carville, crowing in the bus over the a cappella championship, puffed up on trophies and accolades. Ricky, anxious and proud to show off his individual trophy for Boy's Vocal Solo, did not plan to overnight with the rest of us at the motel. He stood on the music building steps after the competition wrapped and waited for his mother's car. They waved goodbye and headed north to visit family. Carville promised a celebration and left us at the motel. We milled about, chattering and giddy.

Here's to a real party! he announced on his return, holding aloft the case of beer he'd picked up from the 7-11. You kids did it exactly right, he said, beaming. We won! First time in thirty years. We made school history!

Carville carted in beer and chips, packages of cookies and candy. He herded us, just nine now, into his own room at the end of the hall. He shut the drapes and switched the television on low. Dimmed the lights.

Best keep our little party on the down low, he said,

and handed out beer. He held a finger to his lips. Agreed?

We nodded. Most of us had only yesterday sneaked our first cigarettes, stolen kisses at the park.

Humming under his breath, Carville pulled a zippered case out of his travel bag. He lit a joint and inhaled deeply. We looked at each other. We were the townies of Paulette, not Norman. The big city south-side high school was rumored to be full of so-called "pothead kids"—intellectual rebels—the sons and daughters of local state college professors, themselves hippies of the sixties. Norman was notorious for weed. Not Paulette.

Carville's got maryjane! one of the boys whispered, excited. This is just like college! We were as cool as cool could be.

Carville passed the lit joint sideways to Randy Klemper, the mayor's son, and the closest thing our music group had to a jock. Randy stared at the glowing tip and then at us. Carville lit another joint. This is very special dope. Championship dope, he said, and laughed. He smiled, all charm. Talking as though we were his pals, hanging out at a party. You don't want any, he said, and shrugged, you're excused. No worries, man. We won't tell.

He winked at the kid in the corner, a shy boy named Luke.

Get comfortable, he urged, taking a deep toke. The sound of a metallic zipper, the whisper of cloth as Carville's pants fell to the floor and he kicked them aside. He unbuttoned his shirt and sat on a chair in his boxers, his dark chest hair a thing of fascination to us all. He took another toke and held out the joint. Mark, a senior, whipped off his T-shirt and lunged for the dope.

Around the room our eyes collided. It was two hundred miles home to Paulette. Who would know? Who would tell? We were the geeky a cappella choir—chubby, gawky, glasses, braces. But tonight we ruled. We had pot and beer. We had trophies. For once we were the hip kids. The school paper would put our pictures on the front page; give us a whole section in the yearbook. If not now, when? When would we push the limits, hit the accelerator, if not now?

We passed the weed, coughing and gagging. Embracing adult boundaries as we fantasized them to be.

Bust me up, break me down, bust my world in two. I barely knew the world was mine. Barely given time.

I sat on the edge of a double bed in my T-shirt and underpants, holding a beer, the taste of which I discovered I disliked. The knobby-cotton bedcover felt rough against my thighs and I was cold. Across from me, lounging against the motel room desk, was Barbie Wallace, smoking a joint as if she'd done so for years. Barbie had had a crush on Mr. Carville since freshman year, and she was staring at him now.

That man is foxy fine, she wrote in the notes passed between us under our desks. I'd do that. Oh, I'd definitely do that. She mouthed kisses at him from the back of the class.

Barbie claimed to be sleeping with a senior on the basketball team, Clark Elliot. I wasn't sure I believed her, but Barbie was the youngest of six; her brothers and sisters married and gone. Barbie knew things.

She was smiling now at Mr. Carville. Woozy stoned smiles.

The pot passed between us in clouds of old blue, punctuated by the sharp snap of opened beer cans. Re-runs of *Charlie's Angels* played on the television—the blowsy blonde driving her red convertible fast. The skinny boys shivered in their white jockeys and ribbed socks, burping as they drank, telling each other fart jokes, aching to be as chill as the college kids they wanted to be. The girls, in cotton bras and flowered panties, sat cross-legged in front of the television. Giggling. Wishing for bigger breasts.

Carville orchestrated it. I understood this, later. The dark corners. The nakedness. The beer and dope that made everything both secret and okay.

Carville paraded around the trophy, clowning in his underwear, cracking open can after can of cheap beer, telling us how fantastic we were, how ferocious, how marvelous. He passed more joints in each direction.

Barbie was on the floor now with three of the older boys and another girl, Janet, playing reverse strip poker, pulling on a sock when they lost a hand, laughing too loud as they shared each other's beer. The air was unbreathable until finally someone kicked on the air conditioner to filter fresh air. One of the boys had already passed out in the corner against the wall, his head slumped on his slender chest.

I barely knew the world was mine. Barely given time.
Busted, broken, barely grown, forever broke in two.

He moved like a ghost in the shadows. He handed another six-pack to the other boys, who were now laughing at nothing, having hiccup wars. He crossed the room and stood in front of me. He took my beer and set it on the end table and pulled me to my feet. Through his underwear his erection pushed against my thigh.

Let's find someplace more private, he said, gentle, as though he were handing me down a steep and dangerous staircase. He pushed me ahead of him into the room across the hall.

No, I said. No. I'm fine. No. I want to stay with the others.

Had I said this aloud or just thought it? I did not know. There was a knot in my stomach; a queasy sick feeling from the marijuana lodged in my throat and behind my eyes. I could no longer feel my limbs and my head refused to obey. It detached itself again and again and drifted to the ceiling as I frantically grabbed and held on, repeating, You're okay. You're okay. You're going to be okay.

I was going to throw up. I couldn't seem to hear, couldn't get my bearings. I stumbled and I grabbed onto him. Mr. Carville caught me.

What, what did you say? I said.

Carville was talking. His lips moved, close to mine. I made you a star, he whispered. He stroked my back, pulling off my T-shirt.

I stood there, stupid in my underpants. My nothing breasts, barely even a B cup. He lay me backward on the bed, tugging down my underwear, his own.

You're such a fine, fine singer, Marley, he murmured in my ear. Will you sing for me?

And then his hands were on my breasts and he was on top of me. I was drowning in warm stale flesh, pressed beneath the weight of his body. I yelped as his penis entered me. His penetration made me catch and freeze, uncertain if I were whole or cleaved in two. I pushed at his chest with my hands. I could not separate the penis inside from the tumbled, falling, churning turbulence of my body. I concentrated on holding onto my floating head, staying entire, staying me.

I arched backward. I couldn't breathe.

My fine, fine, Marley, Carville whispered in my ear. Sing for me. He rocked inside me, taking his time, until with a groan he pulled out and ejaculated into his palm.

He took a minute to catch his breath. He squinted in the dim light. Shake a Coke up in your...you know, he said. The fizz will clean you out. Stuff's used as a spermicide in the Third World. Bet you didn't know that, did you?

He stroked my knee, stood up, and pulled on his shorts. And then he was gone.

I tugged up my panties in a hurry, hunched on the edge of the bed. Seconds later, I vomited over the floor. I wiped my mouth on the bedspread, dizzy.

I'd just had sex—my first ever sex—with the choir teacher. With Mr. Carville. At least I thought it was sex, and he would be in class on Monday, and so would I, and so would all of us—and oh, God. Would they kick us out of school? Could I go to jail?

Could you tell by looking at me what I'd just done?

I curled up, crying over my vomit, until one of the boys, the quiet one I liked named Luke, came in and wrapped an arm around me.

I'm going to my room, he said to no one in particular, stoned, his voice confused. You should too...go back to your room.

I am in my room, I thought bewildered. There's no other place to go.

The sound of my own voice brought me back to the light, to the stage. To the rapt faces upturned around me. Across Macklin's bar what I saw was an EXIT sign.

Singing, I was singing.

Bust me up, break me down, bust my world in two.
I barely knew the world was mine. Barely given time.

The guitar and the drum carried the melody down, down into the dark.

Forever is forever, what was,
Broken in two.
What belonged to me taken by you.
Some things take a moment,
Some things a long, long time.
Time will take forever.
Forever to forgive you.

I was no longer afraid.

Carville was the one running now, the one afraid.

I took the guitar off my shoulder and leaned it against my leg.

Thank you, I said to the hushed crowd.

I smiled wide, a smile as open as the sky. It's just a song, this smile said. It's just a song.

Now be sure y'all stay, I called out. It's dancing time! Next up—Log Jammer!

Anybody's heartbreak.

Anybody's pain.

I lay the guitar on the floor on its side, stood up, and walked toward the back of the stage, passing the drummer, his drumsticks still suspended in the air.

I jumped off the stage and disappeared from the light.

22

arley! Marley—wait!

Andi caught up with me outside the back entrance of Macklin's. Her eyes were wide. What just happened in there? That song—that was something between you and Robby Carville, wasn't it? She searched my face. What, Marley?

I turned from her, gathering myself. I should have told my sister the truth years ago. I wrapped my hands around my elbows and slowly turned to face her.

Remember that weekend, near the end of junior year, when you went to Nashville with Mom and Uncle Ben? I asked. To record your first single?

Andi nodded. Sure. Before our birthday party. You had a choir thing and stayed home.

I opened my mouth to speak and nothing came out. I looked at Andi in panic. What was happening? Why couldn't I speak? Andi grabbed my hand and drew me to the side, into the shadows behind the kitchen backdoor.

Sit, she said. She ducked inside the kitchen galley and came back out with a glass of water and a borrowed cigarette. She waited as I drank the water, then she lit the cigarette and passed it to me.

It'll steady the wobbles, sugar, she urged.

You know this how? I eyed the cigarette, thinking of Donna.

Lotta rejection in Nashville, Andi answered.

I inhaled and doubled over, coughing. The smoke stung my eyes. Andi took the cigarette back and then stomped it out.

Better, right? Lungs hurt more than everything else? Oh, don't worry, she said, I've never smoked, like for real.

She slipped her arm in mine. Now tell me everything, she said.

The door to the kitchen stood open behind us, releasing heat from the grill and billows of steam, and we huddled close in the slim angle of light. Quietly I told Andi about Baker's Dozen, the trip to state, and winning individual Girl's Vocal Solo. About the motel and Carville.

She listened, her elbow against mine, her head leaning in to touch mine when the words halted, or I choked up.

When I was done, she said, Did you tell Mom?

Yes, I said.

I thought back to that night, and shared what I remembered with Andi. The kitchen table, the coffee ring where Donna set her cup down as she edited radio scripts, the open algebra book in front of me, as distracted, I gnawed on the end of a pencil.

You all right, Marley? Donna asked. She refilled her coffee cup and then sat back down next to me. She placed a hand on my knee. You've been acting strange the last few days, she said.

The gesture, the hand on my knee—the echo of Carville's last touch—unlocked me. Fear and shame rolled in waves through my body and I shoved back my chair, stood before my mother, and in sobs blurted the events of the past week.

Donna rose. She held me as the tears wracked my body.

As tall as I was then, I remember her hug felt huge, an impenetrable wall of safety. A place where there was no fear or danger.

My tears spent, she sat me down at the table and kneeled at my feet. Donna looked up at me.

Are you sure you're all right?

I nodded, wiping my face with the sleeve of my sweatshirt.

You're quite certain? Her expression tightened with some emotion I could not name.

Again I nodded vigorously.

She made a small, almost animal sound, then rose and pressed my head to her chest. I could hear her heart beat and leaned into the muted, steady rhythm as my breathing slowed.

After a minute she let go, but her hands trembled as she fixed us cocoa. We sat quietly together at the table in the halo of the kitchen light, holding our cups of cocoa.

Is this man still teaching the class? Donna finally asked.

No, I said, genuinely puzzled.

We had a substitute all week, I told her. Mr. Carville hasn't come in since the competition.

I pressed the cocoa mug to my cheek, welcoming the comfort of its warmth, the relief to not have to face Carville at school. Most of the a cappella group had skipped class. The end of school was a week away and I wondered if that would be it. Ended. Over. Done.

Ricky heard a rumor from a kid in band, I said. That Mr. Carville took a job in Utah.

Donna digested this. After a time, she took my hand and cradled it in her own, palm up. She traced a line diagonally across my palm with her fingernail.

This is your lifeline, she said, her voice gentle and almost dreamy. And this one here? That's your heart line—your love life. Good and strong, she said, and nodded. And this, this is fate. And this little one here— marriage.

She drew close, her cheek near mine. I swam in the patchouli of her perfume.

Your heart line is deep, she said. That's a good thing. And this lifeline of yours? It's a really, really, long one.

My hand lay open in my mother's. I was uncertain what she was saying to me.

Donna reached out and swept my hair from my face, holding my chin tenderly. I can't undo what happened, Marley. Though I'd give anything— She looked away and then slowly back. I'm sorry I failed you, she said simply. We all failed you. I can't imagine why no one thought to chaperone. There is no excusing what happened to you. To all of you. She shuddered. That— man—is a monster. You're kids! Just kids.

Donna's eyes searched mine.

Baby girl, she said, you are more than what that man made of you. Or made you feel. You are my girl, my star, my heart, Marley. Then she added so softly I could almost not hear her speaking, Please tell me you will remember that. When you...think of this.

I sniffed and nodded.

We can't always control what happens to us in this life, Marley. But we do decide how to live with it. Donna's voice had taken on a thread of steel. We're strongest where our scars grow. Do you know that? No man will ever hurt you in that way again, daughter. Be strong. Be strong because you must be.

She folded her hands on the table.

You have a long life ahead, Marley. Her voice toughened. What you do now is get on with that life. Move on. Don't look back.

Two days later Donna took me to see her own doctor, who was kind and thorough, and we never spoke of it again.

I stopped and Andi stirred beside me on the step. Mom said that? she echoed in wonder. She actually said, We're strongest where the scars grow?

I nodded. She was right, too, I said. I didn't know that until now, until tonight.

What do you mean?

Carville showed up before the set, Andi. He's been looking for me, I said, relieved to admit the truth.

I told her about the emails, the messages.

I shook my head. He's delusional, Andi. He thinks we're supposed to be friends. Like all that in the past was nothing. Like I should have been pleased, or grateful, that he found me—special. But, I said, and squeezed her hand, enough. I've had enough. No more running from things.

What did you say to him? Why was he in the bar tonight? Andi asked, confused.

I don't know why he was there. But I told him I would out him to the world as the bastard he is if he didn't leave me the hell alone.

You must have been so scared, she said.

I stared into the dark trees beyond the parking lot.

Burying the past isn't the same as dealing with it, Andi. I know that now. Mom was right. I'm stronger than I ever realized.

Andi brushed a finger under her lashes, frowning at the mascara that came off. We sat in silence on the step, watching pickups and cars pull in and out of the parking lot.

A drunken fistfight erupted in the dark somewhere and then dispersed outside the bar. A motorcycle roared off into the dark.

When you're ready, let's go back in, Andi suggested. She hugged me. They're all gonna want to tell you how great a song that was—and it is! Maybe the best. Honest to God, girl. You sound just like a girl Hank Williams.

A familiar silhouette walked out of the darkness from the parking lot into the circle of light under the porch, shaking his hand open and shut gingerly.

Andi jumped to her feet.

Lock! she exclaimed. Was that commotion you? Were you fighting in the parking lot just now?

Frank looked beyond Andi at me. He cradled his hand.

Could be, he admitted. Had an impromptu faculty meeting with one Robert Carville.

I stood.

Frank, I said, distressed. His hand was bleeding at the knuckles. You didn't have to do that for me.

I didn't, Marley. He half-smiled. You made your own point sufficiently well in there on your own. He nodded back behind him at the rowdy bar, now rocking and hooting along to Log Jammer. I did it for me.

There you are, Royal said to Frank, strolling out the back door from the bar, in his hands a baggy of crushed ice. He handed Frank the ice. Thought you might need this, Lockford. Good right hook there, he said, nodding. His face creased into a smile.

Frank winced as he applied the ice to his bruised knuckles. The old desert eagle doesn't quite pack the punch it used to, he admitted, flexing the tattoo on his forearm.

You saw them, Royal? Andi brushed off her dress and

fetched her hat from the step. You didn't try to stop it?

It was a race to get there first, to be dead honest, Royal said, looking sideways at me. Carville flew out the side exit before you were even finished, Marley. Frank, Ricky, and me—we lit out after him but Frank got there first.

Royal pulled off his glasses and rubbed the side of his nose, deep in thought. Given what Frank had to say to Carville I get the gist of what happened, Marley, he said. How is it this guy got away with something like that?

I don't know, I said.

I met his gaze straight on.

I think most of us were afraid we'd get in trouble with our parents or the school for smoking pot and drinking. The choir disbanded—none of us stayed friends except Ricky and me. I know I felt nothing but shame. Maybe we all did. Carville must have counted on that.

Did you know he would be here tonight? Frank interrupted, adjusting the ice.

No, I said. But I received these emails out of the blue—Carville trying to contact me about the reunion. I never responded. But he confronted me in the lobby.

Frank and Royal exchanged glances.

He spoke to you? Royal asked. Tonight?

Yes, I said. Just before our set. He said if I gave him five minutes he'd leave me alone.

My God, Frank said.

I looked at Andi, Royal, and Frank, my friends. Overwhelmed by their presence and unexpected support.

I tried to smile and glanced at Frank.

Given that eagle of yours landed somewhere on Carville's face, I said, I feel about as vindicated as I need to. What say we find the others...end this night on a better note?

Royal and Andi nodded. We made our way back

through the bar, threading through the people gathered around the drink well.

Hey, girlie! called a middle-aged man in a Harley shirt seated by the espresso machine. His gray hair was pulled tight in a braid and his handlebar mustache swooped to his chin. That asshole in the song? he said. That guy what broke your heart? He that Carville fella? Needs a fucking pounding. He tugged his mustache. One helluva song though, he said.

Aw gawd, yes, agreed the frowzy blonde beside him, sipping her beer, clad in skimpy cutoffs and an off-the-shoulder sweater. Made me bawl, didn't it, Joe? She punched the Harley guy in the shoulder.

Righteous, he said. He raised his beer.

We reached the back tables and Ricky stood, offering his chair to me as Andi quietly took the only other empty seat. Frank and Royal left to round up more chairs. The assembled group looked at me, but no one spoke.

The bartender walked up and placed a bottle of tequila on the table. From Joe, he said. He nodded over his shoulder at the Harley guy. And me, he added. Paulette grad myself.

Frank and Royal returned with more chairs. This time the ice pack duct-taped around Frank's hand. Aggie asked what happened.

Collided with a post, Frank said.

Still say you might want an X-ray for that, Royal advised.

Royal took one of the chairs and scooted in at Andi's side and Frank pushed in to the other side of Ricky. Ricky leaned on the windowsill, holding a beer.

Bill looked across the table. Damn, Marley, he said. I know you write songs mostly—but wow. You can sing! He shook his head in admiration.

Lorrie elbowed him. They're a duet, idiot. That's what they do.

Fine, Bill said with a wince. I'm just saying Marley hit it out of the park on that last one.

It was something special, Elsa agreed. She glanced down at Mindy, drowsing against her arm. Reminded me of a Tom Waits song. Or maybe even Clapton, the unplugged thing. She looked up and smiled at me. What you need when you really need it.

The others nodded. Someone propped the back door to the deck open and cold air poured in off the lake, easing the pounding that had begun in my head. Tom draped his jacket across Aggie's shoulders. She patted his hand absently.

Ricky opened the tequila and poured each of us a shot. Think maybe we could all use this, he said. He met my eyes and I saw in his silent understanding and acknowledgement.

Andi cleared her throat, pushed back her chair, and stood. The strobe lights behind her from the dance floor bathed her in confetti colors. She glimmered like a gilded firefly. But there was something different in her face now.

I'd like to offer a toast tonight, Andi said. She glanced around the table. As many of you know, I'm divorcing. Yes, again. For the—

Third time! Lorrie interrupted in a rush. From Austrian soccer superstar Stephan Brandt! She broke off, surveying our faces. What? I read the fan magazines, so what?

Yes. Andi half-smiled. The third time. Not something I'm proud of, believe it or not. She looked at the tequila in her hand. After a moment, she continued. Tonight, Marley shared with me something our mom once said.

For those of you who remember, the ever-so-cool Donna
Stone?

Everyone at the table clapped and grinned.

Now none of the jokes, y'all, Andi admonished. Let
me get through this. She took a deep breath. Donna left
us with this. We're—all of us—strongest where the scars
grow. So. She raised her shot glass. To scars, she said. To
my ex-husband, Stephan. To Derek. And Menlo before
him. To Donna, may she rest in peace. She looked at me.
And to my sister, the brilliant Marley Stone.

She downed the shot with a flourish, joined by the rest
of us.

Mindy stirred and shifted upright, rubbing her eyes.
Strong? Oh, I got Aggie's tapes, she said. Look,
everybody! See my arms?

Elsa patted her hand. It's a metaphor, sweet cheeks.

Oh. Mindy covered a hiccup with her sleeve. I never
did get that in biology class.

ควน

Andi remained at Macklin's, dancing away the hours
with Royal and the others, and Frank drove me home.
They'd probably close the place down, I thought.

Frank's pickup navigated the narrow track through the
black pines. His face illuminated by the dashboard dials,
Frank reached over and closed his hand over mine. The
ice pack was gone, but his hand remained red and
swollen, the skin shredded over the knuckles.

You really ought to take care of that, Frank, I said.

Look left, he said. A sliver of white hung in the sky.
See there? A new moon. And there, he let go of my hand
to point. That's Venus.

Not Jupiter? I always thought that was Jupiter.

You're arguing with a science teacher?

I smiled in the dark.

He made the turn toward the bay.

His eyes on the road, Frank said, I really did think you thought I wasn't worth waiting for, Marley. That you broke up with me because I was headed away to college. He glanced over. I'm glad I know the truth.

I felt crushed and bruised and hurt in places I didn't know could hurt—in the sternum, behind the eye sockets, deep in the marrow of my bones.

Too much had happened.

You would have broken up with me once you knew, Frank, I said, my voice low. There could be no us after Carville.

You sure don't put much faith in people, he said. For the record, I would have understood. And stayed. And run the bastard over, he added under his breath.

We were kids, Frank.

What your sister said about scars? Frank said. About moving on? I get it. I know whatever the future holds— for Lynette, for our marriage, for my family—the hurt and the damage will be real. It already is and I've no idea where it's yet to go. There will be scars. I just hope to hell we're strong enough.

He slowed down and took his eyes off the road to look up at the moon. We both knew he had no choice but to move through these challenges. Cross what lay ahead.

Frank made the turn onto the graveled drive and pulled up in front of Dapplewood. He stopped the truck and turned off the ignition. He faced me, his expression somber. I leave in the morning, Marley, he said. It'll take a day and some change to get back to Utah. I'm due back in school on Monday.

I nodded.

His hands rest on the steering wheel. He looked straight ahead.

I'd like to see you again—under different circumstances, he said. He looked at me then, intently. Can I count on that? he asked. Will you keep in touch, Marley? Not disappear again?

Yes, Frank, I said. Yes.

Act Four

Clef & Key

You raised me right but I done you wrong—
Girl in a red Jeep, Montana

23

Frank swung by early the next morning and together we carted boxes from the cabin and packed them into the bed of his pickup. The main room emptied down to the bare walls of knotty pine.

Frank wiped his hands off on his jeans. That it? he asked.

Think anyone will want this sofa? I said, glancing at the ratty orange plaid. Do I haul it to the dump or leave it?

Leave it, Frank said. His cotton crew shirt was damp with sweat and he pulled up the hem to wipe his brow. He shrugged. Hell, mine's brown corduroy.

An odd expression passed over his face then, a look of vulnerability. He turned to the window. Might be packing up myself, soon enough, he said.

I redid the rubber band around my ponytail, looping in stray strands of hair.

Or not, I said. In any event, might depend on who wants all the upkeep and taxes, I said. People negotiate these things, Frank. If it comes to that.

Lynette's sister is a lawyer. He glanced at me. If it comes to that.

246 Glenda Burgess

He looked at the empty shelves. You always loved this place.

This was her, I said softly.

Other than the furniture, everything was gone. The snowshoes remained, minus the mouse nests, still hanging on their nails over the bedroom door. I smiled. The snowshoes had inspired hilarious attempts to tramp the winter woods on what Donna had called our "winter tennis rackets."

The places pictures had once hung were now dark patches against the sun-faded pine.

The memories we would keep.

We're done? Frank asked. Let's go down to the dock.

We walked through the shade across the sandy beach and stood at the end of the dock. The log floats rolled under our feet as wind pushed the waves in.

I would always think of this as a departure point, I realized. The place had Donna made her last.

It was time to go.

There was nothing more to do. Frank had already helped me clear the grounds of storm debris, and the downed branches lay in a heap by the fire pit on the beach, most of which I would burn that night. I breathed deeply, trying to capture the clean green smell of the lake and the sunbaked planks of the wooden dock.

I never thought I would run into you again, you know, I said.

What's that line from "Sundown"? *The promise of another day to come*? Frank shaded his eyes with his hand. He scanned the peaks of the Selkirks, pointing out skiffs of new snow in the upper crevasses. Looks to be an early winter, he said.

I'll be glad when this album wraps, I said, apropos of nothing.

Any idea what you want to do after?

I gazed at the island in the bay.

Still music, I said. But in a different direction, maybe, thinking of the crushed blossom song. I turned to Frank. Are you glad to be headed back to your class?

He nodded.

I love the openness of young minds, he said. So full of enthusiasm and pure unfiltered ambition. You know that moment when something is taken in, processed? That old saw when the light comes on? Nothing like it. It's great when a kid glimpses the bigger world underpinnings behind the ideas I'm bringing in.

He hooked his thumbs in his front pockets, careful of his injured hand, taped and bandaged, I guessed, by Royal.

You're right, you know. I get too absorbed in the classroom, Frank admitted. And track. Mostly to share something with Tallyn. Something that's ours. But everything is a time suck.

And that's wrong? I asked.

Could be, he said, squinting against the sun. Between class and track practice, it's fair to say Lynette doesn't see much of me.

I digested this.

So you're both busy. It takes more than that to break a marriage. You're a great teacher, Frank, I said. Lorrie told us you were nominated as a National Distinguished Teacher. That's a big deal.

Frank dug a quarter out of his pocket and in one fluid motion skipped it across the lake. The coin flashed six times before disappearing with a plunk! below the surface of the water. He counted the ripples expanding outward from the point the coin disappeared.

It's all related, he said. Like that quarter and those ripples. We make things happen by the choices we make.

I thought of something Donna had said about living in

constant evolution. She'd been trying to explain to Andi and me the value of embracing change, which in that instance meant leaving Boise for Paulette, a particular change neither of us was interested in.

You and me, even Grandpa and Grandma. We're always in the process of becoming, Donna said, as she handed us our lunches for school. You don't believe me now, but embrace everything in life! Her smile was bright. You never know what's down the road!

Words that echoed something I remembered hearing as a child from Grandpa Kurt.

Evolution is the secret, Marley, Grandpa Kurt had said to me. Evolution is nature's secret ingredient.

We'd hauled a sled of fresh hay through the snow to the cows and were riding the tractor back to the barn. I remembered his large leather-gloved hands on the wheel of the tractor, guiding the green John Deere through the snow.

Like how cow fur gets thick in winter? I asked.

That's adaptation, honey. What we do when we make do. He smiled. No, I mean the way change becomes a part of what or who we are. Something that lives in us and we pass on, he replied. Like how the mice collect seed at night to hide from hawks in the dark. But now the owl, with his great big eyes, looks for his dinner after the sun goes down. He sees the mice.

Adaptation. Evolution. The refrain of life. Perhaps there comes a time we can't adapt anymore, I thought. We light out for parts unknown, as a melody finds a riff.

I'm beginning to think things change because they must, Frank, I said. Because we must.

Hence the need to make good choices, he said, wry.

We walked back up the dock toward the cabin.

I followed Frank's pickup in my car the thirty miles up

the lake to Branch Creek, the nearest logging town with a full-service post office and grocery. We unloaded the boxes at the freight drop and I posted the music and demo tapes to Ben.

Well, that's done, I said.

To say I was relieved was an understatement.

I wasn't at all sure "Broken By You" was the right choice for the third song, but Andi was adamant. Before I'd left Macklin's she'd told me she loved it. Said the song completed the theme of *Baby Look Away*. A signature lament to the lighter material. Like "Crazy," she said, meaning Willie Nelson's original song for Patsy Cline. Something unforgettable.

She handed me her phone. Got it all right here, sugar. Live from Macklin's!

Before I went to sleep that night, I transferred Andi's recording from her phone to tape. I now had all the week's recordings on both our phones and saved to my laptop. The tapes would give Ben something to work from as soon as the package arrived in Los Angeles.

Frank and I left the post office and crossed the street to the Trestle Café. We took seats in the warm October sun at one of the empty sidewalk tables. Frank bought us coffees.

He patted his pockets for his phone, located it, and opened his contacts. So where can I reach you? he asked, his finger poised to input numbers.

Www.TheAndiStoneTour.com, I laughed, aware of how little we knew of one another's lives beyond the lake.

C'mon, he said. Seriously.

I dug behind a second envelope of tapes in my bag I had yet to deliver to Andi, and pulled out a business card. On the back, I wrote my private cell number and Ben's for good measure.

Keep that, I said. That's my home address, my personal number—and Ben's. If you can't find me, Ben always knows.

He pocketed the card and I realized I was going to miss him. What would it be like when he was gone? A void to be backfilled by more work and bar cowboys? I didn't think so.

Frank stood up and threw our paper cups away. I stood also.

He took my hand lightly. I hope you find your answers, Mar, he said. That you find everything you're looking for. Mystery Fred's letter, the whys of Donna. Your music.

Neither of us mentioned Carville.

I held his glance, noting as always Frank's unusual eyes. The way they changed color with the sky and near water. The man was both elemental and fractured; possessed of a handsomeness of perfection exposed to the accidentals of time. There was so much of the other about him. As perhaps was true of me.

I asked, No reason you can't reach out to your father is there?

If he's even alive, Frank replied.

Only one way to find that out.

You have a point. He sighed, and I could see it was the least of things.

Good luck at home, I said. I scuffed my foot against the curb. You have my number.

He nodded. Keep your eyes on the road, Marley, he said. You never know who might show on your horizon.

Another line for a song? I asked.

He laughed and climbed behind the wheel of his pickup. He closed the door firmly and leaned out over the window. What about that last song for Andi? Did you finish?

Debuted at Macklin's, I said. I grinned. Won't a certain someone just love that tune all over Top 40?

Frank laughed. I'm off to Salt Lake then. Drive safe to Seattle, he said.

He raised two fingers to his brow in a salute as he pulled away.

I walked to my car and unlocked the door, watching Frank's pickup head down the road. Keep your eyes on the horizon, Frank had said. Somehow, I knew I would.

Pulling into the cabin clearing, I parked, thinking how much Dapplewood had changed from the day I'd first pulled in. Or maybe it was only me that had changed.

I shoved open the door and hung the key on the fishhook, seeing Donna's rifle in the corner. I had meant to give it to Frank, but had forgotten. I decided to leave it in the cabin even as the trapper's had. A memento of more than just a bear.

I propped open the back door to the deck, dropping into one of the Adirondack chairs facing the water.

A cloud of late summer gnats funneled under the trees in endless circles through the afternoon sun. I dropped my chin in my hand, staring out at the water.

My phone vibrated from the pocket of my jacket. I answered it.

Marley. It's Ben.

Hey, I said, surprised. What's up?

Besides Charlotte went AWOL in the mall?

His voice boomed across his office on speakerphone.

Had to get security, he said. Found her, the poor dear, in Sears, seated on a riding mower. Thank the Lord for that alert bracelet the boys got her. But say, he said, his tone turning upbeat. Got a call from up there this morning. From Andi. What a surprise! Says you debuted a new song last night and blew the socks off the folks at Macklin's. That true?

He sounded pleased. Absolutely chipper.

That I did. And Ben, you were right about Andi. Seeing the old gang from Paulette was good for her.

Good. Good. Tell me about this song, he prompted.

The title's "Broken By You," I said, and gave him the gist of the lyrics, describing the solo guitar and drum. I said nothing of the origins of the music or the events of the previous night.

I mailed you the tapes and music this morning, Ben. And I've a copy for Andi for the band to play around with—try out a few arrangements before we record.

Title's good, Ben said, pleased. Suits the album. Well done, Marley. Now what? Back to Seattle?

In the morning, I said. I'll drop the keys with the realtor on my way through town.

I absorbed the empty beach, the play of light through the trees. Thanks for handling the sale, Uncle Ben, I said. I don't think Andi or I could. I hesitated. We want Dapplewood to go to someone who will love it as we have.

I hoped you girls would change your mind. But if this is what you want...anything else?

You should know I'm taking some personal time. After the studio sessions.

Sure, sure, he said, all ears now and one-hundred-percent business manager. This have anything to do with last night? Andi said you'd run into someone who—quote unquote—personified the word asshole.

I inhaled. No. I don't think so, I said. It's complicated.

How much time? Ben asked.

Andi's the face of the tour, Ben. And she's already half into this Hollywood shift, right? Maybe book her out a few months as a celebrity spokesperson or judge—

whatever. When the tour hits the road again, I'll be ready. I like what I do.

And it was true. But I was thinking Bart Owens and Amelia Parleur would like it better.

I heard his pencil tapping his desk. What do you know about this Royal Morton fella? he asked.

Royal? Known him since high school. Neurosurgeon. Lives in Portland, I said. Andi had mentioned Royal Morton to Ben? Poor Marco, I thought. The suave playboy from Florida was toast.

Any sign of that letter? He sounded so hopeful I hated to disappoint.

No, I said. Nothing.

We said our goodbyes and hung up.

I left the porch. Inside, I considered the mess of sticky notes arranged on the table. No letter. No note from Donna. Except these, I thought. I shuffled the yellow notes together and tucked them into my workbook.

I grabbed my car keys and headed for the lodge, Andi's phone and her package of tapes on the seat beside me. Come nightfall I'd build one last bonfire on the beach, burn the debris, and say my private goodbye to the lake.

24

I swung by the bar to grab a latte from Macklin's new espresso machine and spotted a familiar couple. Andi! Royal! I said in surprise.

They turned, holding onto their espresso drinks. Marley? Andi said. Her face crinkled in delight. Hey! Join us for brunch.

I nodded at Royal, who was wearing a dark silk shirt and pressed charcoal slacks. I leaned in and hugged Andi, navigating her to-go cup and the white velour jogging suit she had on.

I eyed the pristine suit. Sweat much? I said. She made a face. Can't stay, I said. Just came by to drop some things off. I laid my bag on the counter and fished out her phone.

Miss Stone, I said, handing her the phone with a flourish. All yours.

My phone! she squealed. Oh, I missed it so. She looked at Royal. You know, I'm never without it. It's like part of me.

Try life with a pager, Royal commented dryly. You'll get over it.

I handed Andi the envelope with the demo tapes. Here's the new music, I said.

She looked relieved. Perhaps her threats to replace me were more bluff than muscle, I thought.

I mailed Ben the same from Branch Creek this morning, I added.

All before eleven-thirty? She glanced at her watch. I just got up!

Frank helped me ship the boxes out on his way out of town, I said. All I need from you now is your cabin key to give the realtor. I'm leaving in the morning.

Andi clapped a hand over her mouth. Oh, my God, I completely forgot.

Forgot what? The key?

Mom's ashes, Andi said.

What about them? I asked. Donna spent her days of late in an antique Qing Dynasty urn, thanks to Andi's elevated tastes and expansive budget. As far as I knew, our mother's last known whereabouts was the mantle of Andi's Nashville house, close to the music she loved. Although given Andi had rented her place to Maren Morris, it made sense she'd have taken Donna with her to Florida. No "My Church" vibes for Donna.

I brought her here. To the lake, Andi said, pinking up.

You what? My mouth hung open.

Well...I mean Hollywood? Andi said, her expression conflicted. I gotta do something. Donna won't like LA at all. Not one bit. I thought maybe we could, like, leave her here? She loved the lake.

Andi leaned in against Royal, her head barely reaching the center button of his shirt in her spiked white boots. He glanced down at her. We can drop your mom over in the morning, he said. Do whatever you want to do then.

I looked at Royal. We? I wondered. Had I heard that right?

Given Andi's usual taste for musicians or jocks, Royal Morton was a distinct departure. The man exuded quiet. Calm. Zero flash. Thin and angular with long-fingered narrow hands, his curly black hair was cropped short, and already graying and receded at the temples. Nonetheless something had transpired between the two of them over the last thirty-six hours. Had to be an idiot not to see that.

Leave her urn in the cabin? I gasped. Like, conveys with couch?

No, silly, Andi said, and laughed. Like liberate her! Scatter her ashes in the lake or maybe up the trails. How about that place where we used to pick huckleberries at the top of the bluff? You know, that clearing with the view?

I did know. The clearing was a two-mile hike up along the ridge. Once above the cedar forests, the trail opened to a spectacular view of Dunscott Bay, and in the summer, the clearing flowered, a small meadow of hot sun and dragonflies. One year the three of us had hand-assembled a bench from fallen timbers to have something to sit on and enjoy the view. The last time I'd hiked the trail the bench was still there. I wondered if that remained true or if it had crumbled over the years.

You might be right, Andi, I said slowly. And I like the idea of the meadow. I actually do.

Do you have the time? She looked at me with a strange urgency in her expression. Maybe being keeper of the urn hadn't been such a breezy task after all.

I nodded. I do if you do, I said. But you know that hike—better to get an early start first thing. Meet me at the cabin, say around eight?

Royal interjected himself into the conversation then, handing me the latte I didn't realize he'd ordered for me as we stood there.

How about I bring Andi by? he offered. I'm up early.

Easy enough to make sure your sister is, too. He turned to Andi. Why don't you bring down the box, or urn, or whatever it is. Let me put it in the trunk of the Jag so we don't forget.

Andi and I grinned. Donna in a Jag.

Are you headed home after this? I asked Andi, assuming Florida.

She waved a hand. Not to Florida. That's for sure. Seems Marco straight up found himself a little diversion in Coeur d'Alene. A masseuse named Carla. I talked to him on the phone this morning and it's arranged.

What's arranged? I asked, looking from one to the other.

Marco's going to ship my things to Royal's Malibu beach house, Andi said.

Royal squared his shoulders and smiled at my sister, his arm loose about her waist. Happy to be of help, he said.

I pivoted to Royal. You have a California beach house? I asked. I thought you lived in Portland.

Yes, to both, he confirmed. I do neuro consults down in SoCal and frequently spend weekends in LA, he explained. As a general rule I prefer not to stay in hotels, but as long as your sister wants to she can live at my place.

I'm gonna live in Malibu! Andi squealed, dancing on her toes.

Andi and Marco were no longer a thing, and Andi was moving into Royal's beach house. I shook my head. And I thought I'd been busy before noon. With Royal or without him, I was dying to ask, but kept my mouth shut.

All right. Let's do this, I said, assured that with Royal driving, there was a better than good chance Andi would be on time. See you at eight then. No later. I need to hit the road by one to make it back to Seattle before dark. I smiled at them. Have a nice steak dinner tonight.

But what will you do? Andi demanded. You can't spend the night at the cabin, she objected. Everything's packed.

There are still a few things left to do yet, I said. I brought a sleeping bag, remember? I'll be fine.

I hugged her and whispered in her ear, I'm planning a bonfire.

Her expression softened. Like the old days?

Like the old days, I said.

Carrying my latte and sipping the hot beverage as I walked, I crossed the parking lot toward my car. I felt pleased with all that I'd accomplished that morning, still mulling in some astonishment both the matter of Andi in Malibu and our spontaneous decision to liberate Donna from her urn. I fit the key in the car door lock and casually looked up.

At the top of the boat ramp was a small gas and diesel pump station. A man in a worn biker jacket, motorcycle helmet under one arm, stood with his back to the lodge, filling the tank on a grimy motorcycle.

Carville.

That had to be the motorcycle Andi and I had heard roar away from the back of Macklin's the night before.

I whipped around and faced the other direction. Unable to steady my hand without spilling on myself, I set the latte on the roof of the car.

He's here, I thought, panicked. How would I escape without him seeing me?

I stared at the latte on the roof of my little sports car. Was it always going to be like this? The gut lurch, the fear? The need for escapes and hiding? Had last night mattered not at all?

I closed my eyes.

Don't look back.

Donna.

My eyelids flew open. I turned and faced the gas pumps.

I would not hide.

At that exact moment, Carville looked up. He did a double-take and involuntarily stepped back from the bike. Behind his glasses—bent and held together with duct-tape—the socket under his right eye and across the bridge of his nose was a swollen, purple-black. His nose, taped and splinted.

I stared him down. I took pleasure in the mess Frank had made of Carville's face. Wishing the punch had been mine. More deserved, even, than Frank's—one on principle, the other personal.

Without a word Carville threw a leg over his bike, strapped on his helmet and drew on his leather gloves. The bike thundered to life and spewed gravel at my feet as Carville released the brake and rammed the machine into gear.

He rode up close behind me. His gloved hand squeezed and released the throttle of his bike.

But I wasn't afraid. Not anymore.

Carville goosed the engine, shifted hard and fast, and sped away up the gravel road.

I returned to my car, lifted the cooling latte off the roof, and climbed in and turned down the lane toward Dapplewood.

25

Tucked into the crack between the front door and the doorjamb was a white envelope. Puzzled, I plucked it out of the door and let myself in the cabin, opening the envelope with my thumb. Inside was a handwritten letter, a feather of some kind, and what looked like lines of a poem or a song.

The cabin was cold, the day chillier than the day before. Frank's coat, forgotten, hung on the hook beside the door. I slipped my arms into the enormous sleeves, the cloth thick and warm, infused with smells of wood smoke and pinesap and whiskey. I crossed through the cabin to the back porch and flopped in a chair, resting my boots on the railing. A clamor of distinctive honking crested the hill behind me and a formation of Canadian geese passed overhead.

I unfolded the letter.

Dear Marley,

It was so good to see you. My heart is full now. By the time you read this letter, I will be on my way back to the ranch. I stopped by to say goodbye, and because I wanted to leave you two important things. One, this eagle feather to keep at your side, for our spirts are meant to soar; and two, this poem with its opening eight lines, a reminder to feel your way through the world. Always, back to the light.

The feather is from my ranch, which ironically, is named Broken Song, a name given by my ancestors to the creek that runs through the valley. When you sang "Broken By You" last night, I couldn't help but think of this creek, and what it requires of me to be a good steward of the land. It is not often easy. Let the eagle's feather remind you to be a good steward of your gift— your talent—which must flow free, even over hard rock and difficult going.

The poem, I hope, will be a kind of unbroken chain between you and I, friendship built word by word, the kind I like best. As you will notice, I have sent you eight opening lines. Our poem is yet untitled. When you have something in your mind, send me eight lines more, added after those on this page. We will continue until we feel our poem is finished. I have no doubt it will be epic.

Peace,
Ricky

I set the onyx-and-ivory wing feather to one side and unfolded the paper tucked behind the letter.

Untitled

This still and forgiving snow like sand
Is boundless
And bare
Stretching far to where I cannot see.

Solitary in the dark,

Mercury lamps cast unjudging shadows.
Trees against white.
No colors speak of the sufferings of light.

I read Ricky's lines twice more. I recalled how Hank Williams had long ago said from the humbleness of his heart, "Man doesn't make music. It's a gift from God." How could I add to the power of Ricky's poetry, add to this wonder, this imagery that could be a song, a painting, a photograph?

I folded the papers and held them against my chest, looking out at the trees. The shore pines danced in the light breeze, and their movement rippled across the shadows so that I seemed to be seeing both action and echo, fiction and reflection. The branch bending in the wind the poetic fact. The rest, wonderment.

Quiet, I finished the last of the chores. When I finally set down the broom, the rooms gleamed and smelled of lemon and window cleaner. Within a matter of weeks I knew the porch railing would be littered with squirrel nuts and there would be cobwebs again in the corners—but for now, Dapplewood lived up to its name. The mild October sun cast a fluid mosaic of light across the floor, shifting as the pines dipped in the breezes.

The sun dropped behind the high-most ridge of the Selkirks and ribbons of lavender and fuchsia cloud floated above the peaks, mirrored upon the lake. It was time for the last task of the night.

I layered my sweatshirt under Frank's heavy coat and put a flashlight in my pocket, adding gloves and a knit beanie for good measure. A basket of leftovers from Sam's under one arm, the guitar, and a warm blanket in the other, I hiked to the beach. I dragged the pile of downed wood closer to the stone pit and separated the dead sticks from the wet branches. I laid the driest in the center of the stone ring, adding moss and bark for starter.

I lit the kindling and a fan of sparks rose into the twilight. The expanse of lake, empty of boats, felt tranquil and undisturbed.

The wood began to pop, heat waves rising invisibly to the sky. The cold crept in alongside the darkness and I pulled a stump closer to the pit for warmth, taking my makeshift seat. I rummaged in the basket for the wine and opened it using a corkscrew from Frank's pocket. His coat pockets were helpfully well-provisioned, I soon discovered—finding matches, the corkscrew, a small magnifier, a baggy of AA batteries, a roll of copper wire, and a tire-pressure gauge. I took comfort in the feel of the things he had handled.

I poured a mug of wine as wood crackled and burned. I allowed the flames to diminish before adding more branches. I had nothing but patience for the four or five hours it would take to burn through the fallen debris. The moon shone through thin scarves of cloud, low on the horizon, barely above the tips of the tallest trees on Shelter Island. A beautiful orb, accompanied by a steadfast evening star.

I uncased my guitar and began to play, finding a ramble without any particular word or tune. The notes adrift over the water. I imagined Frank, driving the highway with a thermos of coffee at his feet, looking up at the same majestic moon. *No matter where you are*, I thought, adding words in my mind to Ricky's poem, *the moon shall find you*. We were all of us out there somewhere looking at the same moon.

A fountain of sparks shot upward into the night—a thousand drunken lightning bugs. I watched them dissipate in the darkness. I had crossed such distances, and hardly traveled anywhere at all. Whoever I had been, the time had come to let go. Whoever I might be I was ready to discover.

Lake mist clung to the dark surface of the water. The lake now warmer than the night air. I laid down the guitar, crossed the sand, knelt, and trailed my fingers across the surface. The impulse to slip in for a swim— one last skinny dip—seized me. I raced back and shucked my clothes by the fire, wrapped the blanket around my body, and returned to the edge of the lake.

The moon had climbed higher. Above the island now. Spooling a path of fractured starstones to the brim of sand at my feet. I tossed the blanket behind me and waded in to my knees, feeling the way with my toes along the sandy bottom. The water closed about my body like silk, slipping between my thighs. My skin rippled in goose bumps.

I waded out further, to my hips in shining water.

I made my hands into a V as Donna had taught us and plunged headfirst. Down and down I went, parting the darkness with my hands. I arched upward and broke back to the surface, rivulets of water funneling down the curve of my back and arms. The dark waters weren't to be blamed or feared. I dove under again, stroking out to deeper water and rose into an unexpected pocket of warmer water.

I rolled over onto my back and floated, resting. I studied the stars above my head, wishing I knew the constellations. Frank would know. There must be a million points of light. My heart raced with the radiant enormity of the universe. Perhaps Donna had said goodbye like this, I thought. Eyes to the velvet sky.

I flipped back onto my stomach then and swam toward the dock. I hauled myself onto the boards and perched on the edge. I shivered as lake water dripped from my hair.

I hope you find what you're looking for, I whispered to my mother.

I jumped up and ran down the dock, back to the beach. I dried off quickly and wriggled into my discarded clothes. I threw the biggest branches on the fire and huddled near the blazing heat, dazzled by the red-gold light thrown high against the shadows of the trees.

I was singing. Singing the songs of our childhood. The old-timey late-night country on Grandpa Kurt's radio—Dolly, Merle, Johnny, and Loretta. Hank crooning "I Saw the Light." I sang Donna's folk blues, Lyle Lovett, the west coast rebels, Neil Young and Jerry Garcia.

I balanced on my bare feet on the heated rocks and let my voice open into the long-ago church songs.

"Amazing Grace," the song Grandma Laila had sung as she hung the wash, floated upward to the stars, twirling away on sparks and ash.

And then I sang my songs—the songs Andi made famous. The songs I knew were Donna's favorites.

I stood in the firelight, head thrown back, face to the glittering night.

See you. See you. See you under a different sky.

26

Sunday dawned overcast and cool. True to his word, Royal pulled up at exactly eight o'clock with a groggy-eyed Andi, barefaced, and attired in the closest thing to hiking clothes she possessed.

I surveyed her getup.

Everyone wears capris, Andi said defensively, glancing at her tight aquamarine pants and rhinestone belt, the white blouse knotted at her middle. On her feet white court shoes, minus socks. She clutched a pink canvas backpack. In it, Donna's urn.

The entire effect was almost too much for me.

In Palm Beach maybe, I said. I caught a glimpse of her diamond chandelier earrings—little country music guitars - and broke out laughing. For God's sake, Andi. What is this? Rodeo Babes of Miami?

She wrinkled her nose. I may have to hike, she said. But I don't have to look awful doing it.

I handed Andi my last pair of clean jeans and MSU sweatshirt.

Here. Put these on, I said. You'll freeze to death otherwise. I glanced at her feet. The shoes you'll have to wear.

I'd already made sandwiches, filled two water bottles, and tucked rain slickers in my backpack. I hoped the weather would hold, but I wasn't taking any chances up the mountain.

The place looks sad, Andi said when she returned. She twisted her hair into a ponytail and pulled on a baseball cap. Her earring snagged and I leaned in to free it.

Yeah, I said. It's weird. I slept in the sleeping bag, and all I could think of was fifth grade summer camp. Remember the cabin bats?

I remember the spiders. Andi made a face.

You were the star of the talent show, I grinned, easing the wire hook of the earring out of the cloth of the ball cap. That Dolly Parton "Nine to Five" number. Remember? You had your hair all teased and tied up with a washcloth—and stuffed those rolled socks down your swimsuit. They bounced out halfway through your dance!

I was openly laughing now.

Rolled right off the stage into the laps of Bobby Deacon's and Susan Simon's dads, Andi finished on a giggle. The camp cook's hiking boots were too big. I tripped. She clapped her hands. But Dolly! So much fabulousness.

More than Reba? I asked.

One cannot choose between true loves, Andi said.

Our eyes met, and together we chorused "Heart to Heart," Reba McEntire's signature hit from our childhood.

The snag released, the earring dropped back in place. There, I said. Your earring's free, but you might want to leave those here. Hate to lose a diamond guitar in the woods.

Andi grumbled but pulled the earrings off. She slipped her shoulders into the straps of her pink daypack after peeking in to check the urn. All good, she pronounced.

Thinking of Donna's rules, I asked, Do we leave a note?

No worries. Royal knows we're headed up the mountain, Andi said.

We locked the cabin behind us and headed on foot to the trailhead off the shore road. We located the opening through the trees and zigzagged briskly up the bluff three-quarters of a mile before Andi signaled for a stop.

Hands on her hips, she frowned, breathing hard.

Holy cow, I am not in shape for this, she said. She leaned over, hands on her knees. Worst part? I pay that personal trainer of Marco's one major fat bundle! You're so fired, Heather, she muttered under her breath.

Standing dead-center in the trail, I uncapped my water bottle and took a long swallow. It was eerily quiet. The birds and insects of summer were gone, the woodlands faded to a brown and dusty gray. From the tree tops a solitary crow paced us. Straight above, in what patch of sky we could see, clouds veiled a hidden sun.

Want me to carry the urn? I offered.

I've had her this long, Andi said, I might as well lug her the rest of the way.

Nice sentiment, I said.

Oh, Mom and I have an understanding, Andi said. I buy her this expensive Chinese urn and she doesn't complain about what I spend on shoes. Andi adjusted the pink daypack and pulled the hood of her sweatshirt up and over her cap. Turns out, she continued, she doesn't care for Florida much. Or Marco.

You know this how? I asked, with an arched brow.

She talks in my head like all the time, Andi said, quite serious. You try living with her!

I shook my head. No thanks, I said. Too many voices in there as it is.

We resumed the climb, walking single file up the trail. I took the lead, helping Andi over the trunk of a fallen tree. The loose dirt underfoot shifted to stretches of exposed rock and unexpected pockets of mud where the trail crossed a hillside spring. Andi stopped again, this time to work a clod of wet earth free from the sole of her shoe with a stick.

She glanced up, troubled. Are we doing the right thing? she asked.

The *Free Willy* thing?

Yeah. She straightened and tossed away the stick. Don't you feel strange? she asked. Dumping Donna here and leaving? I mean, really leaving?

Without answering, I opened my backpack and handed Andi a banana, taking one for myself as well. We ate in silence. Above us a dense tree canopy blocked the sunlight, casting the trail in shadow. I scanned the trees. I'd once told everyone in school the flying monkeys from *The Wizard of Oz* lived in this forest. Black bears, the occasional mountain lion, yes. But flying monkeys, no.

Andi tossed her banana peel into the woods.

I looked at her sharply, tucking mine in my pack.

Biodegradable, she said.

To answer your question, I said. Yes. I think this is the right decision. Donna loved these woods, Andi. As to the cabin…we should do what's right for us now. Mom would understand.

The day Donna pulled us out of Boise she'd said nearly the same thing. A trucker with a wife and three kids had purchased the cottage, and before we were even out the door, had hauled their things in on the back of his flatbed and stacked the load in the driveway.

Boise's done, Donna said with finality, loading the station wagon with bags and kitchen boxes. Paulette is what's right now. She stood up and tightened the

spangled Moroccan scarf holding back her tangles of
blonde hair. Cheer up, girls, she said. Paulette will be fun.
You grumpy pusses will love the mountains. There's an
ice cream parlor on Main with seventeen homemade
flavors—including huckleberry!

Andi and I rode in silence in the back seat of the
Pontiac the entire drive north to our "new" hometown.
We counted the hours in miles between pin dots on the
map, watching the buff-colored hills, the color of stones,
fold into black mountains and dense forests of pine and
cedar that towered over our heads.

Now this, too, was done.

I miss her, Andi said, her voice faltering.

C'mon, I said, and grabbed her hand.

We followed the trail into a vale of downed trees,
weathered and splintered, lying like broken sentinels on
the forest floor, their enormous root structures upended
like grasping claws. Andi halted and looked around. I
don't remember any of this, she said, nervous.

I shifted the pack. We're fine, I said.

My feet hurt. She frowned at her court shoes, stained
and muddy.

We're nearly there. You can make another mile, I said,
hoping she could. She rolled her eyes as I pushed her to
the front, but I was certain she'd fall behind otherwise.

At the split in the trail we followed the weathered sign
pointing up the mountainside to the right. It was rough
going, steep and narrow.

Between gasps, Andi asked, You really over that
whole Carville disaster-and-a-half?

It helps to imagine him dead or miserable, I said.

Why not both? Dead and miserable.

Works for me, I said. But yes. It's in the past now.

We moved along single file, switch-backing up the
shoulder of the mountain. Every now and then a flash of

blue from the lake below sparkled through the trees.

You really going to date Royal? I asked. Or is this just—convenient?

I felt protective of them both. Royal was, to all appearances, the epitome of a successful surgeon, steady and responsible. And I liked the guy, although to me he'd always be the goofball with a handful of blue and green leaky pens stuffed in his shirt pocket. But Andi...her interest in Royal seemed sudden and off-the-cuff, even for her.

What about you and Frank? Andi parried. She threw back the sweatshirt hood and removed her cap. She raised the hair off the back of her neck, fanning herself. I'm sweaty, she complained.

Frank? Just friends, I said flatly.

Frank Lockford was back in my life. That was true. And I had made a promise after the events at Macklin's to stay in touch, to give our friendship a chance.

Having a male friend is a good start for someone like me, I admitted to Andi. I've just discovered you don't always have to sleep with them. Or move in with them.

Andi broke into a grin. I knew it! she crowed. She blocked the path, poking a finger into my chest. You gotta have faith, Marley, she said, earnest. You and Lock? The real deal. Any dumb cluck can see that.

Andi, that's not what I meant.

Oh, I think—She broke off. What did you mean?

Just that it's been a long time since I trusted someone enough to let them close, I said. Having Frank around was good for me.

And hopefully, I thought privately, I had done some good for him.

Oh, Andi said, visibly deflated. Male friends. Blech, she said. Who needs that? As to Royal, I do like him.

Isn't that odd? Doctors usually bore me. All that medical gibberish, the crazy hours. Five in the morning? Not for me.

She dropped back on the trail and linked her arm in mine.

He isn't married. Never has been, she said. There is that, she added speculatively. God knows I've enough baggage for the both of us. She glanced sideways. He says he wants kids. That part kind of threw me.

We walked in silence, and then she said, I mean I like kids. I think. I won't be on tour forever. I could maybe adopt? Do you think?

Kids? I said, nearly stumbling. Sure. I mean why not. Your own eggs might not be entirely expired, for all that.

She winked. Fun trying at least.

Honestly, you'd make a great mother, Andi. You're sweet—and fun.

Just like Donna, I thought.

Andi, happy to leave the dead forest and be back in the dappled light of a cedar grove, launched into a Scottish round Donna had taught us years ago on these same trails. Her voice sailed out, light and joyous, affecting a rich Scottish burr. *I'll take the high road*, she sang sweetly, *and you'll take the low road. And I'll get to Scotland afore ye!*

The "Bonnie Banks o' Loch Lomond"? I demanded. Seriously?

I laughed. Andi was full of surprises today.

As girls, we'd sung the tune as a round, holding hands as we marched along, separating only to circle trees or jump over rocks or tiptoe across the mired logs that spanned the soggy springs. We had matching voices then, children's voices—high and clear. But it was the voice of Donna I heard in Andi now, full of undertones and hopefulness. The voice of someone lovely.

I picked up the thread of the round, joining Andi on harmony, swept up in an odd joy. Here we were—in the woods on a spontaneous mission to the meadow. The kind of adventure we might have had with Donna. That we were having with Donna.

A quarter mile later we summited at the viewpoint, a natural clearing that opened to a vista of Lost Prince Lake below. Dry grasses bent in the light winds. The abundance of butterflies remembered from hikes before, gone with the summer. Below, the lake was flecked with white.

Look! I said and pointed. The rustic bench we'd cobbled together of fallen logs still stood, decomposing gracefully into the earth. I brushed bits of bark and dirt off the top of the logs and plunked down, opening the backpack. I pulled out both windbreakers and handed Andi one.

Andi zipped the windbreaker over her sweatshirt and sat down next to me, taking a sandwich from the backpack. Umm, she said, taking a large bite. Salami and cheese.

All that was left, I said.

Not complaining. Love the stuff, she grinned. Macaroni and cheese, baloney and mayo, meatloaf sandwiches…All those cheapo meals we used to have, you know, before the checks came in.

Peanut butter and honey sandwiches, I added.

And creamed tuna on toast! Remember how Kurt and Joey called it Shit on a Shingle? Andi's eyes twinkled.

We ate the sandwiches looking out over the lake, watching the red-tail hawks circle lazily above the trees.

Finally, I stood up and opened Andi's pink daypack. The sun stood directly above us, the morning cloud-cover burned away. I handed her the urn.

It's time, I said.

We walked to the far side of the meadow and faced west, toward the continuation of the trail. From where we stood the ridge trail followed the crest of the mountains another half mile to an intersection with a trail into Canada.

It had always been Donna's plan to hike onward someday, make a true backcountry expedition north into the wilderness.

It was not to be.

It was here we agreed to spread Donna's ashes. Above the lake and the western sunsets she loved. Facing onward around the bend.

We stood shoulder to shoulder, listening to the rustle of the trees. Andi rotated the urn in her hands, her expression mournful, crushed. I snugged my arm around her waist. Andi was the one to bring home the wounded rabbits, the stunned birds, the flea-bitten skinny cats, and Donna had made the unfortunates nests in old boxes, put milk out for them, held the sad little funerals in the backyard.

If you wish, keep the ashes, I said softly. But this is where she was happy.

I just don't understand, Andi said, her voice low and strained. Were we horrible daughters?

No, Andi, I said.

But why? she asked, voice breaking. What was she looking for? What did she need?

I gazed unseeing down the trail. I wish I knew, I said.

I'd had a sensation all week at Dapplewood of weightlessness and drift. Floating, like a drowned leaf rolled along the bottom of a pebbled river. Aware of Donna as never before, aware of peace in the waters lapping against the dock, the endless peace in endlessness itself. Whatever Donna had carried to the dock's edge had weighed more on her soul than the bricks in her pocket.

Let's do this, I said, swallowing hard. Let's set Donna free.

Andi hugged the urn, her eyes solemn and large. Do you believe in God?

I shrugged. God simply is, I said.

That's what Mom would say.

Andi pried off the top of the urn, and together, she and I sifted ashes into the light wind. Donna slipped through our fingers easily. Silky and powdery, light. I thought I saw an outline in the fine white cloud as it caught the wind. And then the shape was gone.

Bye, Mom, Andi whispered.

Should we sing something? I asked.

Andi shook her head. We stood in the silence, our arms wrapped around each other.

After a moment, Andi brushed her eyes and placed the empty urn back in her pack. We retraced our steps and hiked rapidly down the trail, anxious to be off the mountain. We had gone two miles before either of us said a word, and then it was Andi as she stopped and shrugged out of the windbreaker, overheating in the extra layers of clothing.

You know I envied you this, she said, plucking at the borrowed MSU sweatshirt.

Montana? I asked, surprised.

College, Andi said, and blushed. I barely finished high school—and with a tutor! But you, you made something of yourself. Improved your mind.

I pulled off my windbreaker then, and stuffed both jackets in my pack.

That's funny, I said. I envied you, knowing what you wanted to do in life and having the balls to go do it. I dug out a chocolate bar and broke it in two, handing Andi half. You make people happy, Andi, I said. I hear them in elevators, bank lines—everywhere—humming along with you on their earbuds. That beats a paper diploma for sure.

Songs you wrote, Andi said with emphasis. She nibbled her chocolate as we started down the trail again. I'm just Honky-Tonk Glitter Barbie, she said ruefully, with a shake of her ponytail. All pretty face and attitude.

Not at all, I protested. But even as I said it, I was aware of the jealousy and competitiveness with which I'd often dismissed my sister. I've always envied you your glamour and enthusiasm, Andi, I admitted slowly. There's not a room you walk into and don't own. That takes real confidence.

I said this with genuine admiration.

Not the same as smarts though, Andi said. Why else do you think Stephan divorced me?

I stopped in my tracks. I'd thought Andi had been the one to walk.

But he's a jock, I said. The man uses his head to hit black-and-white balls!

I know, right? Andi moaned. How bad can I be?

Our eyes met and we burst out laughing.

Isn't it strange, I said. Us envying one another. Damn, we're two of a kind.

Literally. Andi laughed. She folded her empty chocolate wrapper into her pocket. This, right now? Her expression was shy. It's nice, she said. I always thought twins would automatically be best friends. I mean, how can you not like someone exactly like yourself? But you and me— A mix of emotions played over her face mirrored in a shift of light through the trees.

I wasn't that nice, was I? I said. I wish I could take it back. I worked so hard for things that came easily to you. I was jealous.

And you're bossy, Andi said.

You're flighty, I replied.

Well, you're picky.

You're not.

No shit. Three marriages!

I laughed and pushed Andi down the path ahead of me.

She tossed over her shoulder, Oh, let me count the ways. Number one. Menlo Garland, the heel. Stole all the profits from the first platinum and cost me a gazillion to divorce him—and we still never got our money back! Number two, Derek Cauley. Now Derek, poor dude, was just dumb. Never got the idea of managing anything past his pot stash. But number three, Stephan? A jerk. A mean one, as it turns out.

What about Marco? I asked.

A diversion, Andi replied. I'm smartening up, see? I didn't even want to marry him.

She hopped over a small log. Do you ever think of Fred?

My breath caught. Was now the time to tell Andi about Ben's conversation with Donna? About the letter from Fred? But was there a letter? I wondered. I had nothing to prove there was.

The sperm donor? No, I hedged. Do you?

Sometimes, she confessed. Sometimes I wonder if Donna told him about us but he just wasn't interested. She squinted. Like maybe she lied about his not knowing to spare our feelings. I mean, walking off on your own babies would make you a bonafide asshat, right? And who wants a dad that's an asshat?

She wrinkled her nose, embarrassed. When I won the first Grammy, I fantasized some middle-aged guy would walk up to the stage and say, Hi, I'm your dad, Fred. Well done, you.

And ask for money, I said, dour.

And ask for money, Andi agreed.

We squished through a small stream.

Maybe he's dead, she said. He'd have to have heard Donna on the radio. Who hasn't? Wouldn't that make you curious? Unless you're dead?

I snorted. Sure, and maybe he's an undersea geographer, I said. Mapping the floor of the sea the last forty years. Tried to call, but, hey, no reception.

No, I know, Andi said. He studies polar bears on the Arctic Circle. Can't call. Frozen radios. She suppressed a giggle.

He lost his hearing in a tragic astronaut training accident and sits alone in a room now, reading Chaucer, I said.

Chaucer? What's Chaucer? Andi asked. Her eyes lit up. He went back to Ireland! And has lots of little Freds who wear teensy cable sweaters and bog boots.

Manned mission to Mars? I offered. Super-secret CIA?

San Quentin, Andi deadpanned. He brainwashed Patty Hearst.

Sidewalk vendor. Hot dogs and wurst.

Ripley's Invisible Man!

We burst onto the road back at the trailhead and into the bright sun, laughing.

27

I let Andi take the first shower as I emptied our packs. I set the empty urn on the mantle and vigorously stirred the embers in the fireplace, throwing on a few splits to warm the cabin.

Andi came out of the bathroom, once more in her turquoise capris and white blouse, her muddy tennis shoes dangling from one hand. She dropped them unceremoniously into a box of trash at the door.

Ruined, she said. And, I've got blisters.

Wear these, I said, and tossed her a pair of beach thongs. She caught them, and after inspecting the faded and dinged rubber, slipped them on her feet.

I called Royal, she said, applying fresh lipstick as she peered into her pocket mirror. He'll be here whenever.

She sighed. Seems he rented a boat and took Lorrie, Bill, and a few of the others sightseeing around the lake.

They're still here? I said, surprised.

Making a weekend of it, Andi said.

And Royal? I asked. When does he leave?

I don't know, Andi said, and shrugged. He told me he's got a bunch of brain rewires—or whatever it is—

lined up for next week. She paused and slid her eyes my direction. He offered to drive me home.

Home? Home as in—

LA, silly, Andi said. She put away her lipstick. Oh, and I talked to Ben. He said it was okay, so I rented Royal's Malibu place for the year. She fluffed her hair. Ben's sending a moving crew for the stuff in Florida. Done and done, she said, pleased with herself.

I couldn't have heard her right. Royal wants to drive you fifteen hundred miles to Los Angeles? I asked.

Andi batted her eyes.

Wow, when you slay them, they are yours forever, I said. I'm impressed.

Don't look so worried. She laughed. I told him no, Marley. Relax. Ben booked me a flight tomorrow out of—out of somewhere. I'll have to check. I told you, I'm not marrying anybody. She winked. At least not anytime soon.

Thank God for that, I said. I stripped off my muddy jeans. Balling them up, I shoved them in the plastic bag of laundry by the door, along with Andi's bundle, and pulled a somewhat cleaner pair from my duffle and tucked them under my arm. I'm going to get cleaned up, I said.

Andi rubbed her hands together. It's cold in here, she complained. I'm gonna make us some coffee.

Suit yourself, I said. There's fresh ground from Seattle.

I shut the bathroom door and turned on the shower. Hot water shot down over my head and layers of trail dirt swirled away at my feet. I dressed quickly, returning to stand by the fire grate. I backed near the heat and began to untangle my hair.

Marley? Andi called.

She came out of the kitchen. She clutched the cabin

coffee tin in her hands—a plain white-painted tin with a red lid that usually sat on a shelf by the stove.

Not that, I said, shaking my head. The coffee bag's in the fridge. Can's empty. I was planning to leave it here with the dishware. Cute, it's so vintage.

Andi said nothing.

What's got into you? I asked. Dead mouse?

No. This.

She reached inside the tin and pulled out an envelope. She thrust it at me. I found this, she said.

She poked her hand back in. And there's more, she said.

My breath caught. I took the envelope from her hand. It was addressed to Donna, the cancellation blurred and unreadable. The return was a street address in Beacon Hill, Massachusetts.

Who do we know in Beacon Hill? I asked. Too far north to be Fred, I thought, simultaneously disappointed and relieved. Fred was from Baltimore.

Nobody, Andi said. It's been opened, Marley.

Don't look so worried, Andi, I said. It's just mail.

People don't keep mail in coffee tins, Marley.

Unless you're Donna, I said, shrugging. You should have seen the sticky notes in the kitchen. What else is in there?

Andi pulled out a few sheets of blue-lined notebook paper, folded in thirds, and a clipping from a newspaper from the looks of it. She laid the items on the table, drawing her hands back quickly as if the papers might singe her fingers.

Shall we see what this is? I asked.

Andi nodded.

I opened the Boston envelope first and drew out a folded two-page letter. I smoothed the pages and glanced at Andi. Should I read it aloud? I asked.

Yes, Andi said, sinking into a chair at the table. She set the coffee tin down, one hand still gripping the red lid.

I pulled out the chair beside her. This is dated January 15, 2012, I said.

Two winters before Donna died. I felt a strange wave of emotion sweep through me. The timing was about right. But this could be anything, I reminded myself, anything at all. I closed my eyes for a moment, trying not to get my hopes up.

Andi twisted the lid in her hands. Read it, she said.

I pressed the letter against my heart. Andi, I've got to tell you something first, I said. I've wanted to tell you this since you arrived…

What? Andi demanded. Tell me what?

I took a deep breath.

Donna called Uncle Ben a few months—or maybe it was more like a year, I can't remember what he told me—but anyway, sometime before she died.

I steadied my voice.

It was totally out of the blue, he told me. She'd received a letter from Fred, our Fred.

As if there were another, I thought, grimacing slightly.

She wanted his advice, I continued. She wouldn't go into details about what Fred had to say, but without knowing what the letter was about, he advised her to ignore it.

Andi was sitting quite still, her gaze fixed.

Andi, I said, Ben only just told me this. Donna made him promise not to tell us. But now he is wondering if— And here I hesitated —if perhaps that had been a mistake.

Andi laced her fingers together, her head tilted. You knew the entire time you were here there might be a letter? From our dad? she asked in wonderment. You've been looking for this?

No. I haven't, I admitted. I didn't believe there ever was a letter, to be honest. Donna never said a word about it to you or me. It seemed strange she would say something to Ben, but not to us. I assumed maybe she was talking about an old college postcard or something and Ben misunderstood. I paused. If there had been a letter, she wouldn't leave something like that lying around. Not after all these years.

Andi glared at me. You guys never tell me anything! she burst out. I'm tired of you and Ben treating me like a baby idiot. It's got to stop! I mean, my God—

I wanted to tell you, I said. Things just— I broke off. I don't get any of it, Andi. But before we read this, you realize this could be that letter. The one Ben warned me about.

Warned? Andi asked, alarmed.

In case I ran across something clearing out the cabin. And given the timing around Mom's death. I met her gaze squarely. Andi, Ben is looking out for us. He hardly knows any more than we do at this point.

I watched my sister struggle to process what I was telling her and the implications of this discovery in the coffee tin.

I guess we better read it then, she said.

January 15, 2012
My Dear Donna,
How many times I have started this letter, uncertain how to even begin. Dear Friend? My Dearest? So, I begin like this. Simply. My Dear Donna.
You will wonder how I came to find you, and why. The story is straightforward. One day in the middle of fall semester I showed up at your dorm to invite you to a play and they told me you were no longer at school. I searched for you. But without your written consent the registrar

wouldn't reveal your whereabouts. You were just gone.

Yes, it was 1970—people dropped out, traveled on. In my heart, I hoped you were following the dream you'd shared about backpacking Greece. Seeing Socrates's tomb, the Oracle at Delphi, The Parthenon. Quite despondent, I did wish you had left me a note, or asked me to go with you. I would have. But maybe you didn't know that. We hadn't known each other but a summer.

Long story short, I graduated, went to law school at Penn, and joined the family firm in Boston, where I practice trust law. Would you have liked me as much if you knew I was going to become a lawyer? I like to hope so.

Imagine my surprise when twelve years later, I traveled to Seattle for a deposition and heard none other than your voice on the car radio—The Donna Stone Show. I was impressed as I listened to your show—you sounded happy and accomplished. I imagined your blonde braid and that flowy shirt you wore as we danced to the Dead. Remember?

Back in Boston, I couldn't forget your voice. At last I had clue, something more than just your name. I did some investigating and found out where you lived. And then I learned about your girls and realized there might be reasons in your life (a husband(s)?) that might mean you wouldn't necessarily be pleased to see or hear from me. I am myself married, with four children—two each, boy and girl. You'd like them. Smart. Handsome like their mother.

I digress. Weighing the pros and cons, I decided not to contact you. But a few months after that trip to Seattle I happened to see a music program on television, featuring "The Stone Girls." The last name caught my attention. And when I saw the twin girls on stage—that straight hair the color of good oak as my father always said, and green eyes like my mother Estelle's—well, I just knew. The girls are mine, aren't they, Donna?

Is this why you left school in the middle of the semester? Why, dearest? Why didn't you find me and tell me? You could have if you'd wanted to enough. I found you. I would have done the honorable thing by you three. Gladly.

After the initial shock passed, I realized you'd made a choice. I reluctantly decided to respect that choice, much as it troubled me to know I had two little girls out there who would never know me. I followed your lives from a distance. They take after you—impressively talented. You've done a superb job raising them, Donna. They would not have cared about me, despite my fantasies otherwise. They had you. I often wondered what my Boston kin would think of two country music stars in the family. How very un-Aaron Copland!

Again, I digress. Forgive me. I am writing this letter to you now because it has become unfortunately necessary to do so. Donna, dear Donna, I have been diagnosed with a form of aggressive early-onset dementia that will soon rob me of your name, my very memories, and thereafter, my life. If ever there was a time to address a question to me, to inquire about family history—even dare I say, speak?—it would be now. If I do not hear from you, I will assume our chapter, after all these years, is to remain closed.

Yours respectfully, and with great affection,
Frederick Allen Barry
37 Prospect Street
Beacon Hill, Massachusetts

For a space of heartbeats neither Andi nor I said one word.

Fred! Andi blurted. It really is Fred!

In Boston! I said in the same breath.

We stared at each other.

Mom did know his last name, Andi breathed. Barry. Frederick Barry.

I set the letter between us on the table. Mystery Fred was no mystery at all.

I picked up the clipping.

Andi, I said, this clipping is an obituary. Dated August 27, 2012. That's about—I glanced again at Fred's letter to do the math—around eight or nine months after this letter. Oh, God, I said. It's his. It's Fred's obituary.

She leaned on my shoulder, and together we absorbed the small black and white photograph of our father, taken in his middle to late fifties. A distinguished looking man in a finely tailored suit, Frederick Barry gazed steadily into the camera. We recognized our own smiles, the chubby ear lobes, and the fine blond-brown hair.

He's dead? Andi demanded. I can't believe it. How goddamned unfair! Dead Fred is worse than Mystery Fred! She crumpled, about to burst into tears.

I scanned the small print. It says here he didn't die of any illness mentioned in the letter though. This says a heart attack.

Poor Fred. Fred died of a broken heart. Andi sniffed. You know he did.

We don't know that at all, I said.

I glanced again at the letter on the table, noting the fine handwriting, the expensive linen stationary. If Donna hadn't wanted Ben to tell us about Fred's letter, or ever intended to tell us herself, why keep his letter? His obituary?

I wonder how she got this, I said.

What difference does it make now? Andi said, her voice breaking.

She had taken the clipping from me and was staring at Fred's kindly face, her own a mixture of grief and longing.

Do you think she wrote him back? I asked. Ever called him?

Andi leaned her cheek on the back of her hand, elbows on the table.

That must be all there is, she said. She'd have kept them if there were more, right?

It just didn't add up, I thought. I refolded the letter and slipped it back in the envelope.

She could have destroyed this, I said, holding the letter in my hand and looking at Andi. But she didn't.

So we would find it some day? Andi asked.

But, Andi, I never would have. I never opened that tin. You did. By accident.

What's that? That notepaper? Andi asked, pointing.

I laid Fred's letter down, resisting the inclination to place it back in the tin as we'd found it, and picked up the pages of what seemed to be college-ruled notebook paper, shredded out of a spiral binder and creased in thirds.

I gave a quiet gasp. Andi, I said.

What? she demanded, leaning forward.

It's Mom's handwriting.

I met my sister's eyes.

I—I think she wrote Fred back. Or started to, I said, overwhelmed to the point I stuttered.

Read it! Andi said with a stifled cry.

Pacing back and forth in front of Andi I began to read aloud from the scribbles and cross-outs on the handwritten page.

August 22, 2012

Dear Fred,

You have no idea how many times—thousands!—I have started this letter to you. I must say, I was shocked to hear from you. A lifetime and a continent lay between us, not to mention two separate families, yours and mine. Yet. I've always felt connected with you somehow, and not just because of the girls. Did you know? They call you Mystery Fred. I've always rather liked that. It kept you in our lives even though you were not.

Forgive me for taking this long to finally reply. I've spent months trying to sort out what it is I feel, and how best to give you some of the answers your letter asks of me. Your words are gracious and respectful. I would expect nothing less having known you. But that you only reached out under these terrible circumstances, and knew about the girls all this time, has forced me to evaluate my own choices. I see now that not all were good.

However brief our summer together, I loved you, Fred. I say that unequivocally. I might even have married you, had the pregnancy not occurred when it did. But we were young, you were my first love, and I knew you would marry me straight away if you so much as suspected I was pregnant.

That I could never allow. You see, I would need to know you chose me out of love, not duty. And how could I, if you married me because it was the proper thing to do?

Yes, there's a story here. My story. I grew up a legacy of duty. I was ten when I learned my parents married very young because my brother Ben arrived unannounced early in their courtship. They made the best of it—a working partnership—but ours was never a family built on love. My parents were raised to "do the right thing" and so they did, as they understood it. By the time I came along, the distance between them was vast and permanent. I grew up feeling a chill between them I never understood. I could not want this for our girls. Can you understand?

I am sorry for pretending to the girls we did not know each other's last names, and for telling them that you were a brief romance when we were so much more. This was wrong. Everyone needs to feel they belong and I kept them from knowing they also belonged to you, not just me. I was selfish.

By telling them I never knew your last name, I thought to spare them ever feeling rejected their father wasn't in their lives. I know. Only because of my decision to raise them on my own. I robbed them of knowing the greatest man I have ever known. And I robbed you from experiencing how wonderful and special they both are. I hope one day you all three will forgive me. Perhaps, if time permits, this is one wrong I can atone for—

I broke off, choking on a sob.

Please, Marley, Andi said so softly I almost couldn't hear. Finish it.

I continued,

Don't feel sorry for us, Freddie. I wanted the girls very much. They have always known that—even if we were different in many respects than other families. In retrospect, I should have reached out to you as they grew up and began to make choices for themselves. But as time passed, they accepted the story of Mystery Fred and we made a life for ourselves. And even if it lacked some or all that you might have been willing or able to give us, it was happy. For this I have no regrets.

I am sorry time is no longer that luxury we believe it

*to be when we are young. I am saddened to hear about
your illness. And yet here you are, penning me a letter,
still looking for ways to be of service. I knew you had the
makings of a fine man. I see I was not wrong.*

*After reflecting on your situation, I think your letter
should be shared with our girls, and if they want to meet
you, they have my blessing. So yes. Let's get together if
you still wish to and your family is agreeable. If I have
learned one thing in this life, it is never the no's that
matter. No's are dead-ends. It's the yeses we must find.
The yeses lead us to the places we need to go—*

There's nothing more, Andi, I said. It's not even
signed.

Andi pressed her fingers to her temples. Mom's is
dated when? she asked. The week before Fred died? You
think she wrote this and then found out Fred had died and
just never sent it?

I wasn't listening. I was heart struck with notes,
daggers of them, minor and major. I stared upward at the
ceiling of the cabin.

She sounds so lonely in her letter, Andi, I said finally.
You really suppose she left Fred because of Grandma and
Grandpa?

I thought back to the farm, the warm memories that
made up everything I knew family to be. Grandpa Kurt
had never cared about a Fred or no Fred. He had folded
us into his arms like the springtime bummer lambs he
allowed us to nurse on the big bottles of special milk.
Making family when family was needed; knowing a
motherless lamb born in the cold late winter months
possessed no other hope.

But there had always been a subtle tension between
Donna and Grandma Leila I'd never understood.

Arguments over men. Worry in our grandmother's eyes when our shoes showed holes, when we couldn't do our basic maths.

Andi picked up the obituary and reexamined the print date on the clipping.

This was in the Boston paper the end of the summer before Mom died, she said and looked up. Really, just months.

She pushed the obituary away.

It's all there in her letter, Marley. Mom loved him. She wanted to make amends. To get us all together. And then—then she finds out she's too late?

She collapsed into tears and wept openly into her hands.

I came close and stroked her hair.

When her tears subsided, we looked down at the letters on the table. This, the narrative of our lives. The no's and the yeses. Everything beyond the ordinary and ordinary in the humblest way.

I tucked Donna's unsent response, along with the obituary in with Fred's folded letter. And all three inside the envelope from Boston.

Andi reached for a paper towel and blew her nose. Don't you think it's sweet—that for all those years he watched over us?

He seems to have cared about Mom, I said. I'm glad of that.

He did, didn't he? Andi said. It's kind of romantic.

Heartbreaking, you mean.

Two hearts, one secret.

In the short years following Frederick Barry's death, no personal memento had been set aside and mailed on to Donna. Nothing forwarded on to me, or Andi. Not the smallest bequest. No ripple across the silence of the years. Frederick Barry had died with their secret intact.

Was it possible our grandparents had known more than they let on, keeping their daughter's secret? I was certain Ben had known less, even, than we did. It occurred to me then there was a remote possibility Donna had tracked Frederick Barry down earlier, on her own. Perhaps through the alumni office, given he'd graduated. If that were the case, why not act on the information?

Perhaps Donna had always believed that one day Fred would find her. And then when he finally did, been devastated to learn of his other family.

Why hadn't Donna written Frederick Barry back sooner?

Andi seemed to be thinking the exact thing.

Do you think we should contact his family and tell them who we are? I asked.

Andi stilled.

A visible celebrity, she'd had more than her share of phantom relatives fishing for handouts. Not to mention stalkers and crank calls. The fact of our existence was not on the face of it to be welcomed by Fred's relatives— especially his adult children, our half-siblings—who were in truth, strangers. While we had always known about Fred and Donna's love affair, it was a good bet the Barry kids had not heard one word about Donna. And neither Donna nor Fred were now present to decide for themselves how things should go in the aftermath of their "great reveal."

I guessed Ben would advise us against contacting the Barrys. Just as he had similarly advised Donna regarding Fred.

I always wanted to know Mystery Fred, Andi said. She met my eyes, troubled. But to be honest, she said, I have no desire, none, to adopt a stepfamily. It's always been just the three of us. I think…Mar, I think I want to keep it that way. I vote we say nothing.

I picked the envelope off the table and stroked the stationary with my thumb, willing Donna to tell us what to do.

And then I knew.

We were the Stone girls. Whether Donna had hoped for a different future with Fred or believed the past its own keeper, their letters to one another were between them. One to the other and no one else.

Andi was right.

I agree with you, I said. And I believe Donna wanted us to know the truth. That must be why she kept all this. But after learning Fred died, maybe she worried knowing somehow made both too much and too little difference. Does that make sense?

I looked down at the envelope in my hand. In any case, I said, she left it to us to decide.

Andi rubbed at a stain on the table with her fingertip. Fred's dead, she said. There's nothing more to be learned there.

This really is the last chapter in their love affair, I said. After a moment's quiet, I said, What do you say we leave the secret with them?

You mean forget we found this?

I nodded. Yes. Exactly. Leave our lives as they are. You and me and our amazing mom—and somewhere out there the mysterious Fred.

Andi sat up straight.

And maybe now they're together, she said. I like that thought.

We tell no one, ever. Pinkie-swear?

Pinkie-swear.

We twined little fingers, pulling tight.

I handed Andi the letters and before either of us could change our minds, she tossed them in the fire.

Who could carry the weight of such a broken heart?

There's nothing to forgive, Mom, Andi whispered.

We held hands as the envelope from Frederick Barry caught fire and in mere moments burned to ash. Delicate petals of gray that floated away on the updraft.

Ashes that reminded me of cherry blossoms.

28

Out here! Andi called from the porch. Her feet were up on the deck railing, a mug of coffee in her hand.

I glanced enviously at the coffee. Made a pot after all?

Yep. It's on the Black Bomb, she said, adjusting a blanket over her knees. Grab a cup and join me.

I filled a mug for myself in the kitchen and shrugged back into Frank's jacket, returning to the deck and slipping into the chair at Andi's side.

She sipped her coffee contentedly. Look, she said, pointing. It's a tequila sunset. Or maybe that's a Greyhound or a Cosmo. Possibly a Mai Tai.

I grinned. Coffee not cutting it?

It was indeed a citrus sky. Streaks of tangerine and lemon cirrus cloud fanned wide across the Selkirks.

Ya like this country geisha look? Andi asked. She was making toe splits in each of her thick socks for the thong of her flip-flops. Hot, right? She giggled and then the grin faded. Damnedest thing, she said. But Dolly's cover of "Night Train to Memphis" has been on repeat in my head.

That cowboy gospel thing? I asked. The old Roy Acuff song?

A venerable country gospel song, "Night Train to Memphis" had its roots in the old spirituals.

I've been thinking about the car rides with Mom back when we were little, for some reason. The way she'd say, Time for the Night Train, girls. Remember?

I do, I said.

Donna's late-night whispers had not meant time for gospel jubilee or the blues. The words were not a reference to redemption, or to the faces of strangers on trains or landscapes glimpsed through passing windows.

Night Train, to Andi and me, was the essence of trust. What it was to be carried away. Sometimes without warning or cause, it was true. But always wrapped in the magic of our mother's love. Always to wherever it was we needed to be.

I'd forever feel the rumble of the Pontiac in my bones. What it was to be half in a dream and tucked deep in warm blankets. Waking to midnight pit stops for gas, Donna humming to the radio.

Night Train with Donna was a yes when the world said no.

Mom loved driving under the stars, said Andi.

She did, I agreed. I reached out and squeezed her hand. You okay? With Stephan, and LA, and Donna and everything?

She hitched her shoulder to a more comfortable angle against the hard back of the chair.

I'm good, she said. Maybe better than good. She set her mug on the deck at her feet. Might be a song there, Marley. How about you write us our very own "Night Train"? Something for Donna?

I stared into the distance. I'd never be able to capture what those nights meant, I thought. Not ever.

I have a favor to ask, Andi.

Sure, Andi answered with an easy smile. Anything you want.

Fire me.

What? She swiveled sideways in her chair, her eyes wide. Fire you? Like, as my songwriter?

Yes. I nodded. Fire me.

Why on earth—

Because it's time, I said. There's this different kind of melody in my head— I broke off and whistled a few rising bars, encouraged when she didn't immediately look away with one of her well-known sighs.

I leaned forward.

I was at this busted old bar piano and it just came to me, Andi! I've been calling it the crushed blossom song because it reminds me of petal blossoms in the street. How fragile they are. How easily flattened in an early rain.

Flowers? Rain? You want to quit country for a nature song? Andi asked, her tone puzzled.

I searched for better words.

No, not nature, I said. More like blossoms on a barroom floor.

I caught my breath, struck by the truth.

Blossoms on a barroom floor.

A packed music house. That swirling frenzy. Float. The bittersweet dissolution of a heat-hungry night. The emptiness of daybreak and its stark loss. The single moments notes of almost calligraphic beauty. Brushstrokes of desire against the night's inevitable end.

This, this was the music of my life.

I folded my legs up under me in the chair.

I can't get it out of my head, I said. It keeps getting in the way. Even when I'm writing songs for the new album, I confessed.

Andi listened, hearing me out.

I think…I think my music is changing.

Meaning what? Andi asked.

Notes are not what they used to be, I said. Chords, beats…It's all different somehow. Mean different things. The melodies are becoming wordless. Or less about words, I amended, confused by my own uncertainty. Like they're songs, but without words, and then when there are words, in my head they're so spare.

I shrugged, frustrated. How could anyone understand what I was trying to say? Even I didn't understand me.

I don't think I can write a good Stone Tour song anymore, I said. I'm sorry, Andi.

My sister plucked the blanket from her knees and tossed it aside, and then picked it back up again, toying with the frayed edge.

Her glance sideways was confused.

What will I do? she asked. The band will collapse without you, Mar.

No, it won't, I protested passionately. The Tour is you, Andi, not me. Hire that songwriting duo, I said. Those kids from Catalina.

Owens and Parleur? She seemed nonplussed I would suggest my own replacements.

Yes! Shake up your sound a little. LA should mean a new look, new tunes. It could work. Right? I'll work with them to get things rolling. Promise.

Well…We wrap this one first? Her brow furrowed. You'll transition things?

Absolutely.

What if it doesn't work out?

I won't leave you in the lurch, Andi.

I held her gaze straight on. Giving my word. Making a promise about the band and everything more than the band. About family.

Andi rose and pulled me to my feet, drawing me close in a fierce hug. She released me and looked me direct in the eye.

Marley Stone. You're fired.

She laughed suddenly. Don't let me down, she said. I expect greatness!

Just watch me, I whispered.

She dug in the pocket of her pants and handed her cabin key to me. Before I forget, she said. And Royal has my suitcase. We turned the rental car in yesterday in Branch Creek. He's my ride to the airport.

I placed the key in my bag, collecting my cell phone from the counter.

I'll drop everything at the realtor's office on my way through Coeur d'Alene, I said.

We rinsed our cups and placed them back in the cupboard and I doused the coals in the potbelly and fireplace one last time.

Andi pushed the deck chairs against the side of the cabin and gave the deck a final sweep. She called out, Hey, is the shed locked?

Ready to go, I answered, giving the kitchen a final wipe down.

I pushed the lid back on the coffee tin and set it back in its place by the stove. I stared at the red lid, abruptly emotional. I reached out, and for some reason, patted it.

Together we hauled the music equipment, guitar, my duffle and sleeping bag, and various things I was taking back to Seattle out to the roadster. Andi returned to the cabin then for one last look around and to collect her backpack.

Leaning into the trunk, I opened my music bag and pulled out the picture from the cabin of the three of us on the beach with marshmallow sticks. I climbed the front steps and handed the photograph to Andi.

Here, I said. Donna kept this on the mantle. You keep it.

Andi gazed down at the framed photograph. She sniffed then and wrapped the picture in her scarf before placing it inside the pink canvas pack with the empty urn. She set her backpack on the top step.

As she did so I caught her arm with my hand and raised her wrist. What's this? I asked, examining a row of numbers in neatly etched ink.

Royal's phone number, said Andi and rolled her eyes. He wrote it in effing Sharpie this morning so I wouldn't forget.

Area code included? I laughed. How high school.

Exactly high school, said Andi. Her cheeks were pink. She tucked her hands in the pockets of her capris and straightened. Don't ask me why, little sister, she said with sudden conviction, but I believe the Stone girls' luck has changed. Did I tell you, Ben got me that gig as a judge on *So You Think You Can Tap?*

Tap? As in dancing? I said. What on earth do you know about tap?

Absolutely nothing! Andi's chandelier earrings bobbled. Not one damn thing—not left from right. But I don't care if it's double-dutch jump rope. I'm headed to LA and things are gonna be different. They're going to be fabulous!

But tap dancing?

We looked at each other and burst into gales of laughter.

Andi rubbed me lightly on the shoulder.

What will you do now, Marley? Beside noodle on flattened leaves or whatever. You want to do some shows in LA with me? Guest judge?

I shook my head and linked arms with my sister.

We stood together in the doorway of the cabin haloed

in soft October twilight. No one waited inside. Gone were the wonderful summers, the familiar objects of the years of our childhood.

Three tapestries, three skeins of known things. Threaded colors spun around us in the silence.

Time to catch the Night Train, girls.

Andi laid a hand against the splintered wood beam that supported the porch overhang. She touched the cabin name plaque, tacked on a nail beneath the porch light. She ran a finger along the engraved grooves burnt into the wood. Dapplewood.

She tilted her head. Can I keep this? she asked.

You should, I said. Hang it at your beach house.

Andi lifted the sign off the nail and placed the weathered board on the bottom step alongside her backpack. The sky above us the color of coals.

Acknowledgments

There are three remarkable people who supported this book to publication that I'd like to acknowledge. First, my thanks to Michael Magras, book critic, writer, and friend, who consistently asked, Does it sing? My deepest affection and appreciation to Pamela Milam, book whisperer, theater lover, lamplighter—who read, brainstormed, and loved this novel into being. And finally, heartfelt thanks indeed to Julie Buckles for the gift of her stunning photograph of Lake Superior and the canoe she crafted by hand that graces the novel's cover.

To my literary agent Kimberley Cameron, thank you for believing in me these many years, for loving this story, and for a million little things, not least of which, the chicest book parties. My thanks as well to my book editor Lauri Wellington, her staff, and to David Ivester for his marketing and publicity wisdom.

My thanks also to Blake Leyers, my talented developmental editor, who peppered my life with questions throughout the early drafts and mailed sustenance in the form of the best Tennessee peanut brittle ever. And a very special thank you to Benjamin Dreyer, who reminded me it's truly okay to begin a sentence with "and."

To the amazing voices and songwriters who lent their authenticity and gritty gorgeous originality to this story, thank you. And my thanks to the ever-so-cool Jenifer Smith, for sharing the phrase that became the novel's greatest lyric of all time, "Dinner's in the Dog"— courtesy of those anonymous, chronically late home, country-music-loving colleagues of hers from "way back when" at the FBI.

My gratitude to David Grunzweig. To say I surfed the hours writing in my study on the force of your musical genius is to understate the power of your gift, not to mention leaning on your expertise in music composition, recording, and live performance. And to Kate Grunzweig Fellowes, You always had the right advice or needed bit of encouragement. And finally, to Gregory Miller, who made dinners, opened the wine, and tiptoed past the burning light at night— it's finally done.